Titles by Laura Griffin

Standalone Novels
FAR GONE

LAST SEEN ALONE

VANISHING HOUR

The Texas Murder Files Series

HIDDEN	MIDNIGHT DUNES
FLIGHT	DEEP TIDE

The Tracers Series

UNTRACEABLE	EXPOSED
UNSPEAKABLE	BEYOND LIMITS
UNSTOPPABLE	SHADOW FALL
UNFORGIVABLE	DEEP DARK
SNAPPED	AT CLOSE RANGE
TWISTED	TOUCH OF RED
SCORCHED	STONE COLD HEART

The Wolfe Security Series
DESPERATE GIRLS

HER DEADLY SECRETS

The Alpha Crew Series

AT THE EDGE	TOTAL CONTROL
EDGE OF SURRENDER	ALPHA CREW:
COVER OF NIGHT	THE MISSION BEGINS

The Glass Sisters Series
THREAD OF FEAR

WHISPER OF WARNING

The Borderline Series
ONE LAST BREATH

ONE WRONG STEP

The Moreno & Hart Mysteries, with Allison Brennan

CRASH AND BURN	FROSTED
HIT AND RUN	LOST AND FOUND

LAURA GRIFFIN

DEEP TIDE

BERKLEY
New York

BERKLEY
An imprint of Penguin Random House LLC
penguinrandomhouse.com

ISBN: 9780593546710

First Edition: April 2023

Printed in the United States of America
1   3   5   7   9   10   8   6   4   2

Book design by George Towne

CHAPTER

ONE

A CELL PHONE WENT off during the vows.

Leyla Breda kept her attention on the bride and groom, trying not to react as her aunt leaned forward and glared down the pew. Two seats over, Leyla's cousin rooted around at her feet and looked dismayed as she picked up a stylish silver clutch.

Leyla's stylish silver clutch.

Her heart skipped a beat as the phone chimed again. Leyla grabbed the purse and quickly silenced the ringtone—but not before noticing the number on the screen.

Which could only mean one thing.

Leyla stood up and quietly slipped out of the pew. Reaching the door to the chapel, she darted a glance toward her brother, who was so enamored with his beautiful bride that he didn't notice the disruption.

Yeah, right. Her brother noticed *everything*. Joel was a police detective. But he had wisely chosen to gaze into Miranda's eyes and not destroy the moment.

Leyla hurried into the foyer, trying to imagine what level of catastrophe would prompt her assistant to call her right now. She opened the chapel's outer door and stepped into the late-day sun.

"What's wrong?" Leyla asked Siena, the second-in-command at her fledgling catering business.

"They haven't started yet, have they?"

"They started at six."

Siena gasped. "I thought six thirty!"

"It's okay, I stepped out. What's wrong?"

"I'm *so* sorry! I didn't mean to—"

"Siena, *what's wrong*?"

"It's the cake."

Her heart skipped another beat as she envisioned the glorious four-tier tower of buttercream smashed to the ground.

"What about it?" Leyla asked.

"Well . . . I can't find it."

"What do you mean? Rachel was supposed to deliver it to the venue at four." She checked her watch. "It's six twenty-five."

"Rachel called in sick."

"What?"

"And Wade, too. Rachel said she asked Amelia to fill in for her, but I haven't seen her yet, and the wedding coordinator said—"

"Did you call Amelia?" Leyla was already striding toward her car.

"Yes, but she's not answering. Neither is Rachel or Wade and—"

"I'll get it myself."

"Are you sure?"

"Yes, I'm on my way now."

"I'd go get it, but we're shorthanded and I'm still finishing the canapé trays. If you want, I can—"

"No, finish the canapés. I'll be there in ten minutes."

Leyla slid behind the wheel of her SUV and glanced at the little white chapel. Any moment the doors would open, and the happy couple would emerge, and Leyla didn't want them to see her speeding out of the parking lot.

Shorthanded was an understatement. If Wade and Rachel were out sick, that meant only four servers for a reception of an estimated ninety people. But it was going to be more than that. Leyla had counted every last body in that chapel, twice, and she'd come up with a firm one hundred. Why didn't people RSVP anymore? It was so infuriating.

Four servers wasn't going to cut it, not by a long shot. Siena would have to help replenish food at the buffet table, and Leyla would have to cut the cake.

Leyla raced down the highway toward her beachfront business. The Island Beanery was known far and wide for scenic views, creative beverages, and mouthwatering pastries that had been written up in magazine features. Leyla had recently expanded into catering. Her brother's wedding was only her fourth gig, and that was *if* you counted the bridal shower she had thrown for Miranda. But Leyla didn't count that because the menu had consisted of finger sandwiches and petits fours—*yawn*—and anyway, the whole thing had been a gift.

Leyla eyed the clock on her dashboard as she neared the coffee shop. She had probably fifteen minutes to get her cake to the reception venue, unbox it, and decorate the table with rose petals, all before the newlyweds arrived for their big entrance. The endless task of posing for wedding photos had taken place already. As a photographer herself, Miranda had insisted on having the pictures completed beforehand, so the wedding party wouldn't be held hostage by a fussy photographer when everyone was ready to hit the bar. Once the ceremony was over, it was time to celebrate!

Leyla had wholeheartedly agreed with this approach, but now she wished she had more time to get her act together.

She whipped into the Beanery parking lot and used the key fob to pop open her SUV's cargo space. Lifting the skirt of her long dress, she dashed up the sidewalk, taking care not to trip. Her sky-blue satin dress and strappy sandals were perfect for a springtime wedding at the beach, but not so perfect for cake deliveries.

A lone pelican perched on the deck rail, looking on as Leyla unlocked the door and let herself in. The café closed at six, and the interior was dim and quiet now, with dust motes floating in the air. Propping the door open with a rubber wedge, she glanced behind the counter to the refrigerated display case and immediately spied the wedding cake with its cascade of sugar-icing roses. Everything looked intact.

"Thank God," she murmured.

Pride surged through her, quickly followed by panic.

She glanced at the clock on the wall and looked around, wishing she had someone here to help her move the damn thing. The cake was surrounded by a custom-made box with a sturdy base and cellophane sides. Leyla opened the refrigerator, and chilled air wafted over her. She stuffed her key chain into her strapless bra, slid her hands beneath the box, and eased the cake from the fridge. It was heavy. Peering around the box, she maneuvered around the counter and crossed the dining area to the front door. Scooting sideways through the opening, she gripped the corners of the box as a breeze gusted over the sand dunes.

She prayed that she wasn't about to trip on her hem as she crossed the parking lot to her SUV. Sliding the box into the cargo space, she released a breath of relief. But her relief was short-lived as she rushed to lock the shop, then jumped behind the wheel and checked the clock. Speeding toward the reception venue, her mind toggled between the twin horrors of slamming on the brakes and making the cake topple over and—literally—bumping into the bride and groom with their wedding cake at the moment they made their grand entrance.

Leyla turned onto the palm-lined drive of The Breakers and sucked in a breath. Guests were arriving, and the first few rows of cars had already filled in. She pulled right up to the front and parked, leaving just enough room for Joel and Miranda's limo, in case they showed up before she had a chance to move. Springing from her SUV, she glanced around for someone to help her.

A man in a black tuxedo leaned against the building, scrolling through his cell phone. He was one of the groomsmen, someone who had been through the police academy with Joel. Leyla had met him at the rehearsal dinner last night, but damned if she could remember his name. Was it Eric? Ethan?

"Evan, hey!"

He looked up, startled, and Leyla flashed him a smile.

"I need some help."

"Me?"

"Yes! Can you give me a hand with this?" She looked around and spied a tall, dark-haired man sauntering down the sidewalk. Leyla had no idea who he was, but he wore a suit and was obviously a wedding guest. "And you!" She waved him over. "I need your help!"

He glanced over his shoulder.

"Yes, *you*. Can you give me a hand here, please?"

The groomsman was standing beside her car now, eyeing the giant cake box with a look of abject terror.

"You want me to carry that?"

"No. *I'll* carry it," she told him. "I need you to open the doors."

"I'll carry it."

She glanced up to see the man in the suit gazing down at her with the most amazing ocean green eyes she'd ever seen.

"It's heavy."

He raised a brow.

"And kind of wobbly," she added. "*I* can carry it, if you'll just hold the doors as I go in and clear any obstacles."

"You're liable to trip in that dress." He eased past her and smoothly lifted the cake from the cargo space.

"Careful," she said, her throat tightening as she watched him casually holding more than a dozen hours of painstaking work—the very future of her business—in his hands.

"Where to?" he asked.

She glanced at the door, which was now being held open by the groomsman—who looked immensely relieved not to be tasked with walking a towering wedding cake across a banquet hall.

"The main room, just past the buffet table," she answered. "There should be a special table set up and—" She looked past the man's shoulders as a black limousine turned onto the palm-lined driveway. "Crap, they're here! We need to hurry!" She clapped her hands at him. "Go go go!"

S EAN MORAN SLIPPED away from the party. The bride and groom had left under a shower of rice, but people were still milling around beneath swags of white lights, drinking the couple's booze and enjoying the breeze off the water. Sean would have liked another drink, but he needed to get back to his condo. As he crossed the wooden bridge spanning the sand dunes, he spied a woman on the beach with a champagne flute in hand.

Leyla Breda.

Her formfitting dress looked silver in the moonlight, and it shimmered against her body as she strolled toward the surf. Nearing a piece of driftwood, she dropped her shoes to the sand and sat down. She nestled the flute at her feet, then lifted her arms and twisted her dark hair into a knot at the top of her head.

Sean stopped at the end of the bridge. He had about a hundred things left to do tonight, including contacting his boss.

Instead, he walked over to Leyla.

"How's the champagne?"

She jumped and turned around. Recognition flickered across her face, and her shoulders relaxed.

"It's good." She held up her glass. "You didn't have any?"

"Nope. Can I get you a refill?"

She smiled. "What, are you a waiter now, too?"

He stepped closer. "I'm Sean Moran, by the way." He held out his hand. "We never actually met."

"Leyla Breda." Her handshake was brisk and business-like, but the warm look in her eyes gave him hope.

"Joel's little sister," he said.

"That's me."

He turned toward the water so he wouldn't be tempted to stare down the front of her dress.

"I didn't get a chance to thank you earlier," she said. "Things got really hectic."

"Looked like you had your hands full."

"So, are you here for Joel or Miranda?"

He looked at her. "Joel."

She tipped her head to the side as she gazed up at him. "And you know him from . . . ?"

"Work."

She frowned. "Here?"

"No. We go way back. We were in the same academy class in Houston, spent some time at HPD together."

"Oh. That was a while ago."

"Yeah."

"So . . . the vice squad, then?"

"Yeah. Mind if I sit down?"

"Not at all."

Sean lowered himself onto the other end of the sandy log. He didn't like the direction the conversation had taken so he steered it back to her.

"So, how long have you been a caterer?" he asked.

"Hmm . . . let's see. I guess it's been about three weeks now." She turned and smiled at him, and he felt a hot jolt of attraction. "Why? Can you tell?"

"Not at all."

"Right."

"Well, the timing seemed a little bumpy."

"Just a little." She rolled her eyes. "We had several staffers no-show. It happens a lot in this business. People are flaky. Despite all my planning, you could say we were a bit rushed."

Rushed was right. No woman had ever *clapped* at him before. He'd discovered it was a turn-on.

"Well, you pulled it off," he said.

"Barely." She closed her eyes and tipped her head back. "God, what a relief."

A breeze wafted up, and her scent drifted over him— something spicy and sexy. She pulled her knees up and rested her bare arms on them.

"Okay, I want a straight answer." She looked at him. "What did you think of the food?"

"It was amazing," he said honestly. "I liked those ham things with the toothpicks."

"Prosciutto-wrapped figs with balsamic."

"Yeah."

"Those were Miranda's pick. Glad you liked them."

Really, he'd liked all of it. The highlight had been the

meat-carving station at the end of the buffet. The juicy beef brisket had melted in his mouth.

But Leyla seemed to have moved on from the topic of food. She smiled as she gazed out at the water.

"The waves are up tonight," she said. "I'm surprised no one's surfing."

"At night?"

"Sure, why not? The moon's perfect."

He looked at the silvery foam rushing over the sand. He couldn't think of the last time he'd swum in the ocean. It had been way too long.

"Must be nice waking up to this view all the time," he said. "I bet it never gets old."

"I wouldn't know. I live over a bike shop. There's a spectacular view of a parking lot."

"Sounds loud."

"Not Harleys or anything. Those bikes the tourists rent with the little bells on the handlebars. Still really annoying, though."

She stretched her legs out and stared at the water wistfully, and he wondered what she was thinking. He'd been watching her all night as she glided from place to place, directing people and food. And when she wasn't directing, she was smiling and laughing with wedding guests. Every person in the room seemed to be a long-lost friend. Except for him. He was the odd man out here.

She drained the last of her champagne and sighed. "Well. I should go."

"Can I buy you a drink?"

She gave him an amused look. "It's an open bar." She glanced behind her. "And anyway, I think they're closing down now."

"That place isn't." Sean nodded down the beach, where colored strobe lights and music emanated from a thatched-roof building. Several of the tourists walking in that direction seemed to be headed there.

Leyla followed his gaze. "That's Buck's Beach Club. I think we're a tad overdressed." She turned to him with another smile—this one polite. "Anyway, it's midnight."

"Bedtime?"

"Yes."

He stood and offered her a hand getting up.

"Nice talking to you, Sean." She leaned over to scoop up her sandals and—by some miracle of fashion—managed not to spill out of her dress.

He retrieved the champagne glass and handed it to her. "Sure you wouldn't like to have a drink with me?"

She gazed up at him. "Anyone ever tell you you're very persistent?"

"Yes."

She looked down the beach, and he could see there was some kind of debate going on in her head. Leyla Breda was smart, and she probably knew exactly what he'd been thinking about when he walked over here. And he was still thinking it, but he'd also enjoyed talking to her.

A lock of hair blew against her cheek and she peeled it away. "Do you like coffee?" She turned to face him.

"Sure."

"I can meet you for a latte tomorrow."

He kept his expression blank, even though she was clearly putting him in the friend zone. He couldn't remember the last time that had happened, but it had definitely been a while.

She watched his reaction, and he knew this was a test.

"Sounds great. Where?"

Surprise flickered across her face, but then it was gone.

"You're new in town. Have you been to the Island Beanery? It's—"

"The place on the beach with the flower boxes."

Her eyebrows arched. "You've tried it?"

"I saw it on my drive in. It's just down from the condo I'm renting."

She nodded. "I'll meet you there at noon." She started to walk away.

"Wait. You want to trade numbers in case you need to change the plan?"

She smiled over her shoulder. "I won't."

CHAPTER

TWO

THE STARS WERE still out as Leyla drove to work. Because it was Sunday, she'd rolled out of bed at five instead of four, but the extra hour of sleep had done little to energize her. Between all the relatives in town and the wedding and her first big catering job, the past few weeks had been an emotional roller coaster.

And then there was Sean Moran.

Leyla had gone to sleep buzzed from champagne and wondering whether she'd made the right decision turning him down for that drink.

Of course she had.

She didn't date tourists. Ever. It was her most important rule. Growing up in a resort town, she'd learned quickly where those encounters would lead. She had no illusions about what men wanted when they sidled up to her at a bar with their charter-boat tans and designer shades and offered to buy her a beer.

So, why had she asked Sean to meet her for coffee? She didn't know.

Well, she did know. She'd wanted to mess with him a little. She'd wanted to see the look on his handsome face when she'd basically called his bluff. She'd been curious how he'd wiggle out of it when he realized he wasn't getting lucky last night, but now he had a platonic coffee date to contend with. Chances were, he wouldn't show up. Him being her brother's friend helped the odds a little, but even if he *did* show, he was almost certain to walk in with a handy excuse about how something came up with work and he had to be getting on the road soon.

And then there was the other thing, the second reason her mean streak was showing.

He'd lied to her.

She didn't know why, but he had. His story about working vice with Joel in Houston was pure bullshit. Joel had worked property crimes in Houston, full stop. Leyla had thrown that out there because she sensed Sean didn't want to talk about his connection to her brother. Maybe he knew Joel from some context he didn't want to discuss with her. But what? Her brothers weren't saints, for sure, and Owen in particular had been pretty wild in his twenties, but Leyla would have been surprised if Joel had any kind of checkered past he wanted to keep hidden.

But who knew? Her three brothers no doubt had secrets they didn't tell their little sister, just like she had secrets from them.

She pulled into the lot and parked in her favorite spot beneath an old oak tree that had been bent and twisted by decades of wind off the Gulf. After cracking her windows so her car wouldn't get too hot, she crossed the parking lot and was surprised to see lights on in the surf shop next door. The mannequin in the window was naked, so maybe they were putting out new inventory today.

Leyla let herself into the café and turned on the lights. The chairs were up, the floor was clean, and the air smelled faintly of the vinegar they used to clean the coffee machines—all good signs. But several of the syrup bottles needed filling and a dirty shot glass sat beside the espresso machine. Also, the steam wand was sticky—her major pet peeve—and the countertop needed a wipe-down.

But first, coffee. And then she had to get her muffins going so they'd be ready by seven.

She switched on the espresso machine to warm and checked her phone as she headed into the kitchen. It was 6:05, so Siena would be awake.

"Hey, it's me," Leyla said. "You up?"

"Absolutely."

"Liar."

"I'm just getting up," Siena said. "Are you at the shop?"

"Yes, and the pastries aren't here yet. Is Rogelio sick, too?"

"I don't think so."

The Island Beanery had a sister location at the Windjammer Hotel. Besides giving them some steady foot traffic, the location gave them access to the hotel's kitchen, which had three big ovens to Leyla's one. Most of their pastries were made there and delivered each morning.

"He should be bringing the croissants and doughnuts, plus cherry kolaches," Siena said. "You're doing the muffins, right?"

"Chocolate-chip coconut." Leyla grabbed a bag of Ghirardelli chips from the baker's rack. "And lemon poppyseed. Our lunch special is tomato basil soup."

"Okay."

"How are we on coffee beans?"

"I honestly don't know." Siena yawned. "We got a delivery yesterday morning, but I didn't get a chance to open it yet. I can do it when I get in."

"Thanks. See you in a few."

Leyla glanced at the clock above the baker's rack before heading down the hall to the stockroom. A full trash bag sat by the back door, and she felt a dart of annoyance. She grabbed the bag and hurried out back, where she heaved it into the dumpster behind the café. The sky was brightening but the moon was still out, and she remembered Sean Moran standing in the moonlight on the beach last night.

Anyone ever tell you you're very persistent?

Yes.

She pictured his sexy half smile as he'd waited for her to succumb to his charm and go have a drink with him, which would have turned into an invitation back to his place. He didn't get turned down a lot—of that, she felt sure.

Leyla reached for the door, and a movement in the alley caught her eye. She stepped toward it, then jumped back as a large black bird flapped toward her.

She caught her breath and stepped forward, peering into the shadowy alley beside the surf shop. The breeze kicked up, and a stench hit her. There was something dead there. An animal or . . .

She lurched back, gasping.

Not an animal but a *person*.

Leyla's heart seized. She recognized the hair, the shirt, the chunky silver rings on the outstretched hand.

"No. *No no no no.*"

Leyla's breath came in short, shallow gasps as she fumbled with her phone and switched on the flashlight feature. She shined the light into the alley, hoping hoping *hoping* she was just asleep or passed out.

Leyla's chest squeezed as the beam of light fell over the woman's face. A line of ants marched into her lifeless mouth.

NICOLE LAWSON GAZED down at the woman seated on the curb in front of Surf's Up. She had black nail polish and a cigarette between her fingers—which were shaking, either from nerves or nicotine or a combination of both.

"Okay, and do you *typically* park your bike at the rack in front?" Nicole asked, giving her a variation of the question she'd asked twice already.

"It depends," the young store manager said. "I parked in front today because I rode here from my boyfriend's. He lives south."

"And are you sure you didn't see any people or vehicles in the alley when you arrived?"

"Yes. But it was, like, five thirty when I got here. Still pretty dark."

Nicole tamped down her frustration. This woman kept shifting her timeline. A few minutes ago it had been *like, five fifteen* when she arrived early at the shop to unpack the load of new inventory that had just come in. Luckily, she mentioned she had clocked in with a time card, so Nicole would probably be able to pin it down with more certainty.

She jotted a reminder in her spiral notebook to follow up with the woman's time card.

"Okay, and, Olivia, you said the coffee shop was *dark* when you arrived?"

"That's right."

"No lights on at all?"

"No."

"Outdoor lights?"

She glanced up, clearly exasperated to be asked about

this yet again. "No. None." She blew out a stream of smoke and flicked her ash onto the pavement.

"All right." Nicole made a few final notes and tugged out one of the business cards she kept clipped to the back of her notepad. "Please don't hesitate to reach out if you remember anything else that might help us."

Her eyebrows shot up. "I can go?"

"For now, yes. We'll definitely be in touch, probably later today. You said you guys close at six?"

"Yeah." She jumped to her feet.

"In the meantime, don't hesitate to call."

The woman slid Nicole's card into the pocket of her cut-off shorts and nodded. "Got it."

Nicole turned her attention to the police SUV pulling into the lot. Emmet parked beside the ME's van and climbed out, looking around. He stopped in his tracks when he saw Leyla Breda leaning against the back bumper of her white Toyota.

Emmet nodded in Leyla's direction and then approached Nicole. He wore what they referred to as their field uniform—a blue Lost Beach PD golf shirt, sand-colored tactical pants, and all-terrain boots, which were good for tromping around the island's beaches and marshes. Today he also wore his darkest wraparound sunglasses. As he neared her, she saw that he hadn't shaved and his hair was messy. Like Nicole, he was clearly hungover from the wedding—not to mention the after-party that had lasted till two. But at least Nicole had had the sense to pop some aspirin and down a glass of water before crawling into bed.

Emmet stopped and gazed down at her.

"How're you feeling?" she asked.

"Shitty. How 'bout you?"

"Same."

"We have an ID yet?"

"Amelia Albright, twenty-five."

He glanced at the alley where a pair of the ME's guys in white Tyvek suits knelt beside the body, doing their thing. "She have a wallet on her?"

"This is according to Leyla, who found her."

He winced. "Shit."

"Yeah."

He turned toward the sister of two of their detectives, one whose wedding they had all been partying at merely hours before.

"The victim is a barista here," Nicole said. "Leyla tells me she's worked here almost a year."

Emmet rested his hands on his lean hips. "Anyone talk to Joel yet?"

"No. And don't, by the way. Brady wants to wait until noon."

"What happens at noon?"

"He gets off his flight to Costa Rica, supposedly. The chief doesn't want him canceling his honeymoon if he hasn't already left yet."

"You think he would?" Emmet asked.

Nicole lifted a shoulder. "Who knows? I mean, it's Joel we're talking about."

In addition to being their senior detective, Joel was also a workaholic. Not to mention a bit of a control freak. If a homicide occurred at his sister's business, he'd definitely want to be involved, whether he'd *allowed* to be or not.

Emmet turned to look at Leyla again. "How's she doing?"

"No idea."

Leyla—like her brothers—didn't wear her emotions on her sleeve. Nicole had known the Bredas most of her life but knew very little about Leyla personally. Whenever Nicole stopped by the coffee shop, Leyla came across as brisk and efficient. She gave friendly smiles to her customers and bossed her staffers around, clearly running a tight ship. Her employees seemed to like her, though. Nicole had once seen Leyla politely tell a customer to leave after he'd cursed at a barista for getting his coffee wrong.

A big black turkey vulture flapped over from a neighboring rooftop and settled on the fence to watch the ME's guys work. The birds had been hovering around all morning.

"I freaking hate those things," Emmet muttered.

"Me, too."

"Who's the woman by the deck there, looking at her phone? The tall one?"

"That's Siena, one of the managers," Nicole said. "We need to get her statement, too. She talked to the victim yesterday afternoon before leaving here to go help with the catering."

"I'll handle it," Emmet said, as Nicole had expected.

He walked off to talk to the pretty manager, leaving Nicole to deal with the much thornier issue of Leyla Breda.

Nicole wiped the sweat from her brow and crossed the parking lot. Leyla spotted her coming and squared her shoulders.

"Thanks for your patience," Nicole said because she'd been out here more than an hour already, and the day's heat was already setting in. "Can I get you some water?"

"No, thanks."

"We'd like you to come to the police station to give an official statement," Nicole said.

"All right. But I need to get inside first."

"Why?"

"I need my purse." She cast a look at the door, which was blocked by yellow crime scene tape. "It has my car keys in it. And also, I need that employment application you wanted. It has contact numbers and some of the biographical information you were asking about for Amelia. It should be in the file cabinet in the office."

"Let me go check with the crime scene techs, and I should be able to escort you in there."

Nicole walked over and ducked under the yellow tape. The café's interior was dim and cool compared to outside. The CSIs had put a piece of butcher paper on the floor by the door, and Nicole stopped to pull on disposable shoe covers before walking through the dining room and kitchen. In the hallway, she found a CSI crouched near the back exit, dusting the doorframe for prints. His name was Justin, and they'd borrowed him from the county crime lab on the mainland. Lost Beach PD had a full-time CSI/forensic photographer on staff, but as of this morning, she was on her honeymoon.

"How's it going, Justin?"

He glanced up. "Fine."

"Has the photographer finished the office yet?" Nicole nodded toward the windowless room that was about the size of a broom closet.

"She hasn't even started. She's still photographing the victim's car in the back parking lot."

"Any idea how long that might take?"

Justin looked annoyed. "We just got here ten minutes ago."

"Not trying to rush you. I just need an ETA on when the owner can get into the office and grab something from the file cabinet."

"Talk to Katie. But go around back, okay? I can't let you through here yet."

Nicole walked out the way she'd come. As she removed her paper shoe covers, she spied a familiar pickup truck in the parking lot.

"Crap," she murmured.

Owen Breda stood beside his sister, leaning close and talking to her in what looked to be a tense exchange. He set his hand on Leyla's shoulder, and she shrugged it off.

People had different reactions to violent crime scenes. Some wailed and became hysterical. Some threw up. Leyla Breda got prickly, apparently.

Nicole crossed the parking lot.

"Owen?"

He glanced up.

"Can I talk to you a sec?"

He gave his sister a long look and then walked over.

"Yeah?" he asked, not bothering to take off his sunglasses.

"What are you doing?" she asked, keeping her voice low.

"Talking to Leyla. What's it look like?"

"You can't be here."

He tipped his head to the side. "Get real, Nicole."

"You can't. This is exactly the reason Brady didn't call you."

Right now the police chief was rushing back from San Antonio, where his daughter had just given birth to his first grandchild. He'd specifically sent Nicole and Emmet to this crime scene, and he'd specifically *not* sent Owen.

But Owen didn't like people telling him what to do, especially Nicole. As the department's newest detective, she ranked dead last in the detective pecking order.

"You shouldn't talk to her, Owen. You shouldn't even be here."

He peeled off his sunglasses. "Are you serious right now? She's my *sister*."

"Yeah. Your *sister*. Who's now a witness in a homicide case. Whose business is now a *crime scene*."

Owen gave her an icy stare with those Breda blue eyes. Leyla and Joel had them, too. Owen's looked tired and bloodshot because he'd been out late drinking after the wedding. But he wasn't just tired. Owen was worried sick— she could see it in his face.

"Owen, come on. Leyla's got enough to deal with today without you making this even more complicated. Do the right thing here."

He gave Nicole a long, hard look.

"Fine." He slid his shades back on. "I'll see you at the station."

He turned and looked at his sister, who was watching them closely. Some unspoken communication passed between them. Then Owen glanced at Nicole and stalked back to his truck.

As he pulled out, Nicole returned to Leyla. She looked pale and tense, and beads of sweat had popped up along her brow. But Nicole didn't bother offering her water again.

"What's next?" Leyla asked. "I'd like to understand the timeline here."

Nicole nodded. "When the CSIs give me the go-ahead, I can take you to retrieve those items from the crime scene."

She blanched at the words *crime scene*.

Nicole cleared her throat. "From the café," she amended. "Then you'll be done here, and I'll take you to the police station, where we'll go over all your information. I'm sorry to make you do it again, but we'd like to get it on video."

She gave a tight nod, and Nicole felt a wave of sympathy for her. She'd been through all this twice already, going into minute detail about how she'd discovered her young employee's brutalized body in the alley beside her shop and called 911. Then she'd had to send home her employees as they arrived for work and turn customers away, all while fielding a barrage of questions from police. She was in for a marathon day, and it was just getting started.

Leyla looked at the alley again as another vulture landed

on the fence. There were four now, watching the action. One of the ME's guys unzipped a body bag, and what little color was left in Leyla's face drained away.

Nicole stepped closer. "Leyla . . . I'm sorry you have to go through this."

Her gaze snapped to Nicole. She pushed off the car and squared her shoulders. "I'm fine. Let's get this done."

THREE

Nicole returned from a hot and hectic afternoon and spotted Emmet in Chief Brady's office, probably debriefing him on the evidence they had been gathering all day. With Owen sidelined, Emmet would no doubt be taking the lead role.

She stopped in the doorway. "Congratulations on the baby, Chief."

He smiled and ran a hand over his white buzz cut. "Thank you."

"How's Lindsey doing?"

"Tired. They had a long night." He waved her in. "Come in. Close the door."

Nicole stepped into the office and pulled the door shut behind her. Emmet occupied the only chair. He still looked hungover, but the supersize Mountain Dew in his hand was probably helping.

"I talked to that witness again," Nicole said, following up on the conversation she'd had with Brady over the phone.

"The surf shop manager clocked in at five twenty-two. Didn't see any activity in the alley at that time."

"She'd probably been there awhile by that point," Emmet said. "I talked to one of the ME's people, and he estimated the body had been there about twelve hours, give or take."

"How's the evidence looking?" Brady asked Nicole.

"Well—" She darted a glance at Emmet because she didn't want to step on whatever he'd already reported. "We found the victim's purse in the dumpster behind the café. The keys were there, along with a wallet that had her ID in it, but no cash and no credit cards. No cell phone either, just some makeup. So at this point—and it's preliminary—it's looking like maybe a robbery that got out of hand."

"And the murder weapon?"

According to the ME's people, the victim had been stabbed in the back—a fact Brady had probably already learned.

"We're still searching for the knife." She glanced at Emmet. "Last I heard, we hadn't found it."

"We combed a four-block radius," Emmet said. "Dumpsters, trash bins, everything. Nothing turned up, so we think he took it with him."

Brady leaned back in his chair and frowned. "So, you're thinking she was killed over cash and credit cards? How much money would a twenty-five-year-old barista likely have on her?"

It was a good point, one that had been bugging Nicole all morning.

"Probably not a lot," she said.

"What about the café?" He looked at Emmet. "You said the register was full?"

"That's what Siena told me," Emmet replied. "She's one of the shift managers. They were short-staffed yesterday because of the wedding. Then a couple of people called in sick—Wade Tallow and Rachel somebody or other—"

"Davies," Nicole put in. "I interviewed her at her apartment several hours ago."

Emmet nodded. "This girl Rachel was supposed to take the wedding cake to the reception venue and then work the party, but she came down with a stomach bug and asked Amelia to do it."

"And she never made it over there," Brady stated.

"That's right," Nicole confirmed. "According to Rachel, Amelia was working by herself yesterday afternoon because everyone else was either out sick or helping with the wedding. So, Rachel told her to close up a few minutes early and take the cake over there around six."

Brady frowned as he listened to all this.

"From the looks of it, the victim was surprised in the alley behind the building as she was closing up shop," Emmet said.

"In broad daylight," Brady said, still sounding skeptical.

"Apparently."

"Any drugs on her? Drug paraphernalia?" the chief asked.

Nicole shook her head. "No."

"And no obvious sign of sexual assault," Emmet added.

Of course, they wouldn't know for sure until they heard from the medical examiner.

Nicole looked at Brady. "When is the autopsy?"

He leaned forward and rested his elbows on his desk. "I just got off the phone with the ME. It's scheduled for oh seven hundred."

Emmet's eyebrows shot up. "He couldn't do it today?"

"He's got his hands full with a pair of traffic fatalities."

"I'd like to go," Nicole said.

Well, *like* was an exaggeration. But she wanted to be there.

"If it's okay with you," she added, looking at Emmet.

"Have at it."

"Ask him about track marks on the body and any signs of drug use," Brady told her. "I want to know more about her lifestyle. We'll get a tox screen, too, but those always take a while."

Nicole nodded. "All right."

"Also, we need whatever he can tell us about the weapon we're looking for, based on the stab wound."

"I'll ask him."

Brady looked from Nicole to Emmet. "Any other questions?"

"Yeah," Emmet said. "What's going on with Owen?"

The chief seemed to be expecting this question. "I told him to sit this one out because his sister is involved. He understands."

Nicole traded skeptical looks with Emmet. She had passed Owen on her way in here and he didn't look "understanding" of anything. He looked extremely pissed off.

"And, Nicole, you're the lead on this one."

She glanced at Brady. "You want me to—"

"Yes."

She wouldn't have been more shocked if he'd asked her to step in for him as chief of police. She was the youngest detective on staff. And she'd only worked a handful of homicide cases since earning her detective's shield.

Emmet looked as shocked as she was.

"I want you to brief the team when we convene in a few minutes," Brady told her. "Go through everything we just covered, and I'll delegate jobs. We clear?"

"Yes, sir."

"Good. Be in the conference room in ten."

Emmet got up and didn't even look at her as he left the room. Great. Now she had two colleagues pissed at her.

She darted one last look at Brady, in case he suddenly changed his mind, but he was already on his phone.

You're the lead on this one.
She tried not to show her panic as she walked out.

LEYLA TRUDGED UP the creaky wooden stairs to her apartment. She was utterly tapped and even her arms felt heavy as she fumbled with her keys and unlocked the door. Stepping inside, she closed her eyes and leaned against the wall.

Quiet. Finally. The sudden lack of sound and motion made her feel dizzy, the way she used to feel as a girl after spending all day playing in the waves.

She dropped her keys and purse on the armchair just as her phone chimed. Sighing, she checked the screen. Owen. She'd ducked two calls from him already, so she picked up.

"Hey," she said.

"Hi. How's it going?"

The casual question was loaded with worry.

"Fine," she told him.

"Where are you? I went by your place earlier and—"

"I just got home."

"Where were you before?"

"I went by the Windjammer shop to talk to the staff."

"Is everyone okay?"

"No. But I guess I expected that." Many of Leyla's staffers worked shifts at both coffee shops, and they were a tight-knit group. "A couple of Amelia's friends were pretty emotional, so I told them to take some time off."

"I'm sorry, Ley."

"Me, too."

She turned and locked the door, then slipped off her shoes.

"I can swing by there," Owen said.

"Don't do that. I'm fine."

"I want to."

"No. Really. My back is in knots, and all I want to do is take a shower and go to bed."

"You sure?"

"Yeah."

"Okay, well—"

"Thanks for the thought, though. I'll call you tomorrow, all right?"

"Lock your door."

"I did."

She hung up with her brother and silenced her phone before tossing it on the chair. No more people. She glanced around her cramped apartment, taking comfort in the familiar surroundings. What it lacked in square footage it made up for with a location just minutes from work. The main downside was the tiny galley kitchen, but she maximized the hell out of it. Every stockpot and sauté pan had a place, and she kept everything rigorously organized.

Tugging the elastic band from her hair, she stepped into the kitchen and opened the refrigerator. She hadn't eaten all day, and she wasn't hungry, but a glass of chardonnay sounded really, really good.

Of course, she didn't have any.

"Crap," she said, staring at the shelves. Her weekly grocery run, like everything else she'd planned to do today, had fallen off the table. She checked the pantry.

No red wine, either. She had a dusty bottle of Tito's, but just the thought of vodka turned her stomach, and she opened the fridge again.

So, no wine tonight.

What she *did* have was wilted arugula and expired yogurt.

She dragged the trash can out from beneath the sink. With a sudden burst of energy, she combed through every corner of the fridge, checking expiration dates and pitching items in the trash. Slimy mushrooms—gone. Moldy ginger root—gone. Crusty anchovy paste—gone. By the time she was finished, the entire produce drawer was empty except for some sticky gunk and a handful of petrified blueberries. She moved the drawer to the sink and scrubbed it down.

When she finished, the refrigerator was clean, organized, and nearly empty except for condiments. She tossed her sponge into the sink and gazed out the window. Like her bedroom, the kitchen had a view of the parking lot behind the bike shop. Through a gap in the buildings, Leyla could see tourists streaming back and forth on Main Street, which was lined with bars and restaurants. As dusk fell over the island, the Sunday family crowd was heading in for the night and the pub crawlers would soon take their place. Beautiful young people would come out in droves in search of loud music and cheap drinks. They'd do Jell-O shots and shoot pool and sing karaoke as they partied their way down the strip. And most of them would make it home fine, but some of them wouldn't.

Leyla glanced around her home, anxious for something to do. She'd been rushing around all day, but whenever she stopped, even for a moment, her thoughts returned to that dark alley and Amelia's pale face in the glare of the phone flashlight.

Leyla's chest constricted. Her heart started racing. She squeezed her eyes shut to block the images, but they wouldn't go away. All she could think about was that outstretched hand and those half-closed eyes.

Leyla had missed her by minutes. The thought was agonizing.

If she had left the church just a few minutes sooner, Amelia wouldn't have been alone closing up. And what if no one had called in sick? Or what if Leyla had listened to her brothers and installed better lighting around the store?

What if a cop, or even just a tourist, had walked past the alley during the attack and intervened? *What if what if what if...*

A hot lump lodged in her throat. She felt like she was choking on it. She forced herself to take a few deep breaths and then splashed some water on her face. She grabbed a dish towel and patted her cheeks dry.

A sharp rap on the door had her whirling around. Through the window shade she saw a man's silhouette on her front porch.

"Damn it, Owen."

Looking closer, she realized it wasn't Owen. This was someone shorter and stockier. She crept over to check the peephole.

Sean Moran.

He stood there in the yellow porch light, looking down at the street below, as if he hadn't heard her creaky floorboards and didn't know she was right there on the other side of the door.

"Crap," she whispered, glancing down at herself. She looked like hell, and whatever makeup she'd had left from this morning was now smeared under her eyes. He was the very last person she wanted to see right now, but she somehow knew he wasn't going to simply shrug his shoulders and walk away.

She tossed the towel on the chair and opened the door.

"Hi," she said, blocking the opening.

"Hey." His gazed swept over her, taking in every detail. "I heard what happened and came by to check on you."

She waited for the predictable *Are you all right?* but it didn't come.

"Sorry about coffee," she said. "I didn't have a way to reach you." Not to mention the entire thing had flown out of her mind. She hadn't remembered it until midafternoon when she'd been sitting at the police station and a uniformed officer had put a cup of stale coffee in front of her.

"Don't worry about it." He continued to look her over with concern. Last time she'd seen him, he'd been in a suit and tie. He was dressed casually tonight in jeans and a plain gray T-shirt that stretched taut across his muscular chest.

"Have you eaten?" He rested his palm on the doorframe. "I thought maybe you'd want to go grab something."

She stared at him.

"You know, get out of the house instead of being alone."

"How'd you know where I live?" she blurted.

"You told me."

She arched her eyebrows.

"The bike shop. There's only two in town, so I had a fifty-fifty chance." He smiled slightly, as though testing her mood.

She wasn't hungry at all. But getting out of her apartment suddenly sounded extremely appealing and spending the evening alone with her thoughts—not so much.

"Where?" she asked.

"I was thinking the food court."

"Food court?"

"On the corner there." He nodded toward the street, and she realized he was talking about the vacant lot where a building had recently been torn down to make room for a high-rise. In the meantime, some local food trucks were using the space.

"Come out with me," he said. "You don't want to sit here all by yourself, do you?"

She gazed into those sea-green eyes, annoyed that he seemed to know exactly what she was thinking. She wasn't ashamed to spend an evening home alone, but not tonight. Tonight she needed lights. Noise. Anything to distract her from her thoughts, which were on some kind of torturous loop that she couldn't turn off.

"One sec."

She closed the door on him, even though that was rude, and hurried into her bedroom to slip on some sandals. She didn't want to take time to change, but she cleaned up her makeup as best she could. Then she grabbed her purse and keys and stepped out.

He was leaning against the railing of her porch, which was little more than a landing with a row of flowerpots on it.

"All set?" he asked.

"Yeah."

She locked up, and he gestured for her to precede him down the stairs.

The moment her feet hit the sidewalk she second-guessed her decision. The bar crowd was out already, and she was hit by a wave of body heat, accompanied by the usual smells— sweat, perfume, marijuana smoke, all mixed with the typical sidewalk aromas of French fries and funnel cakes.

Sean guided her out of the traffic flow, positioning himself between her and the throng. "So, what do you recommend?" His hand was light on her waist as he skillfully steered her around clumps of people. "Barbecue? Burgers? I think I saw a sign for chicken and waffles?"

"Fish tacos."

He glanced at her. "Really? From a food truck?"

"Tiki Tacos is the best thing down there. Trust me."

"Tiki's it is."

Reggae music emanated from a T-shirt shop as they strolled down the sidewalk. She glanced up at him.

"I'm surprised you're still here," she said.

"Why?"

"I figured you'd be back home by now."

"Since I was coming down for the wedding, I thought I'd tack on some vacation time. I hear the fishing's good here."

"It is. Are you planning to do a charter?"

"Maybe."

They reached the corner food court, which consisted of half a dozen food trucks arranged around picnic tables. She led him toward the silver Airstream beneath a strand of rainbow lights, and they stepped into line behind a pair of girls in cutoff shorts and bikini tops. One of the girl's tops was see-through macrame, and Leyla was impressed that Sean didn't even give her a second look.

"So, do these places have a beer license?" he asked.

"Some do, some don't. Tiki's sells beer and hard seltzer."

"We're in luck."

They got to the window and ordered tacos and Coronas. Leyla took out her wallet, but Sean was quick to hand over his credit card.

"Thank you," she said, grabbing the beers as Sean paid.

"Of course."

She spotted a group of college boys getting up from a table and rushed over.

"Y'all done here?" she asked with a smile.

They relinquished the spot, and she set down the beers. Grabbing some napkins from the dispenser, she wiped down the table and tossed the trash into a nearby bin.

Sean took the seat across from her. "Two-thirds of the people here are eating Tiki's, which is probably a good sign."

"I told you. Did you think I'd steer you wrong?"

"No."

The banter faded as they settled in to wait for their number to be called. Sean looked around, and Leyla watched him. In his T-shirt and jeans with his two-day beard, he almost looked like a tourist.

Almost.

She'd noticed the bulge above his boot where he had an ankle holster. Like her brothers, he probably never went anywhere unarmed. Cops were cops, twenty-four seven.

She sipped her Corona. It was cool and bitter, and she realized she was parched. She took another sip and set the bottle down, tracing the condensation on the glass with her glittery silver fingernail. Her nails were usually a lost cause because of her work, but she'd splurged on a manicure for the wedding.

A thought hit her like a gut punch.

Twenty-four hours ago, she'd been at the wedding, laughing and mingling and toasting her brother's future. All that time, Amelia lay dead in an alley.

"Leyla?"

She glanced up. Sean was watching her closely. Again, he had the sense not to ask whether she was okay.

"Have you had a chance to crash yet?" he asked.

She shook her head. "I was gone all day. I just got home when you showed up."

He watched her eyes, as if gauging her reaction. He had probably been to countless crime scenes and dealt with some awful untold number of victims—the ones who had lived and the ones who hadn't. He seemed to understand that her emotions were bouncing around like pinballs, and she felt intensely grateful not to have to explain everything.

She cleared her throat. "I was just realizing how this time last night—this exact time—I was walking around chitchatting and mentally calculating the ratio of hors d'oeuvres to people."

He didn't say anything.

"Seems surreal now."

He nodded.

"I wish . . ." Her stomach knotted as she tried to put her thoughts into words.

He leaned closer. "What?"

"Forget it," she said.

"What?"

She shook her head.

Their number was called, and he stood. "Want another?" He glanced at her beer, and she was startled to see she'd managed to drink most of it. Her cheeks warmed. How had that happened?

"I'm good," she said.

He went to get the food, and she looked around, suddenly uneasy sitting alone at the table. Which was ridiculous. She was surrounded by people. Nothing bad would happen here.

She took a tiny sip of beer. She was all over the map today, and she needed to snap out of it. Soon. Before she did something impulsive like unravel in front of this man she barely knew. Or invite him home with her.

He returned to the table with a pair of red plastic baskets. He'd ordered his fish fried with ranch sauce, while Leyla had ordered grilled with mango salsa. She popped a tortilla chip into her mouth.

Sean shook Tabasco onto his tacos before chomping down. She could tell from the look on his face that he liked it.

Leyla ate another chip, not sure how her stomach would do with fish tonight.

"So, I take it you spent your afternoon at the police station?" he asked.

"Some of it." She nibbled her taco. "I spent the rest at our sister location in the Windjammer Hotel."

"Java Place?"

"You know it?"

"I was there yesterday. Good kolaches."

She felt a twinge of pride. "If you were there yesterday,

you would have had the blackberry. They're a customer favorite. It's my grandmother's recipe—on my mother's side. She's Czech."

Leyla was babbling, but he seemed too preoccupied with his food to notice.

"How's your staff taking the news?" he asked.

She sighed and looked away. "Amelia's friends were pretty distraught. Most of them went home early."

Rogelio had stayed. She pictured him in the kitchen, wiping tears on his shoulder as he dipped biscotti in chocolate and stoically finished his shift.

"Did you know her well?" Sean asked.

"No. Not really."

"Was she from around here?"

"Port O'Connor. I think she grew up there."

He sipped his beer. "Did it seem like she ran with a rough crowd?"

"I have no idea," she said, feeling defensive on Amelia's behalf.

"Did she have a boyfriend?"

"I don't know. Why?"

"Just curious."

He was probably thinking about the case like a cop. Female homicide victims were often killed by an intimate partner. The circumstances didn't really fit in this case, but she didn't want to talk about it.

"I know she was a part-time student," Leyla said. "She took classes at the community college on the mainland."

"Oh yeah?"

"She was interested in graphic design. She did amazing chalkboards."

His eyebrows arched.

"In the shop," she explained. "We make them every day with the specials."

When Leyla first heard about Amelia's interest in art, she'd asked her if she wanted to try her hand at the boards. Her entire face had brightened.

Tears stung Leyla's eyes, and she looked away. Sean handed her a napkin, and she dabbed her nose.

"Any chance you can take the week off?" he asked.

"God, no. I can't afford to close the shop. And my people need the work. I'm hoping they'll release the scene soon so I can clean up and reopen."

"Did they say when they'd release it?"

"Tomorrow. That's what they told me, anyway. They said they need to go back tonight after dark. Something about an alternative light source."

She dipped her taco in salsa and tried another nibble. Sean was watching her closely.

"Any idea what that's about?" she asked.

"Probably the parking lot. Or the alley."

"What about it?"

"I'm guessing they're looking for blood trails," he said. "If the victim struggled with her attacker, maybe he left some DNA at the scene."

A shudder moved through her, and she closed her eyes.

"Sorry," he said.

"No. I asked."

She picked at her food for another minute or two, then wiped her fingers on a napkin and dropped it in her basket.

"You finished?" Sean asked.

"Yes. Thank you for dinner."

He'd eaten every morsel, so at least one of them had enjoyed the food. They gave up their table to a group of tourists who looked to be fueling up for a big night.

The walk back was quiet, but not tense. They reached the bike shop, and Leyla stopped beside the stairs.

"Thank you again," she said.

He lifted an eyebrow, obviously picking up on her body language. She wanted to say good-bye down here. If he walked her upstairs, she didn't trust herself not to invite him inside.

"Let me give you my number," he said.

"Why?"

"In case you need anything."

"Like what?"

He smiled. "I don't know. Like a drink some night. Or a walk on the beach."

He gazed down at her, and a warm tingle rippled through her. The phone number thing had become a game between them, and she still hadn't decided how she wanted it to turn out.

"When did you say you're leaving town?" she asked.

He hadn't.

"I'm not sure." He looked away. "It depends."

"On?"

"The weather. The fishing." He shrugged. "I'm on vacation. My plans are loose."

She was getting that vibe again, like he was being evasive for some reason.

"Send me a text, and then I'll have your info," she said.

"Okay. What's your number?"

"I'll put it into your contacts."

He pulled his phone from his pocket and tapped in his passcode as she eyed the screen, looking for a woman's picture or any hint of a significant other. But his background photo was the tip of a kayak splashing through whitewater.

He handed the phone over, and she entered her name and number into his contacts.

"Thank you," he said as she handed it back.

"You're welcome."

The moment stretched out as he gazed down at her, and

she though he might kiss her right there on the crowded sidewalk. Her stomach fluttered at the thought.

"Good night, Leyla."

"Good night."

He stepped back. But the heated look in his eyes told her she'd be hearing from him again.

CHAPTER

FOUR

"WE GOT BUMPED," Nicole said, stepping out of the busy hallway.

"What's that?"

"*Bumped*," she repeated over the phone. "Postponed. Something came up, and the ME didn't get started until nine, so we just wrapped up. Can you tell Brady for me?"

"Why don't you tell him?" Emmet asked. "You're the lead detective."

Nicole gritted her teeth. She really didn't want to get into a pissing war with him right now. Or ever. But obviously, he still had his back up about her being tapped to lead the investigation.

She stepped deeper into an alcove beside the water fountains and restrooms. The county headquarters was unusually busy today.

"I tried calling," she said, "but he didn't pick up. So, would you mind letting him know I won't be back for another hour? I figured if you're at the station—"

"Fine, I'll tell him."

"Thank you."

"What did you learn?"

"A lot."

"Such as?"

"Well, it sounds like we're looking for a big knife. Something with at least a six-inch blade and a serrated edge on one side."

Emmet whistled. "Damn. A hunting knife."

"Sounds like."

"Okay, what else?"

"And he found no signs of sexual assault," she said. "They're going to send off the swabs and all, but there were no indications of anything."

"We hadn't really expected any."

Nicole wasn't sure *what* to expect with this case anymore. Different elements of it had seemed odd from the beginning.

"The other thing the ME took note of is the hands," she said.

"What about them?"

A man in blue scrubs emerged from the restroom and stopped short when he saw Nicole. He nodded and walked away.

"Hey, let me call you back," she told Emmet.

"Why?"

"I'll call you from the car on my way home."

She hung up and hurried down the hallway. "Dr. Bauhaus?"

He turned around, a wary expression on his face as he looked her over. He obviously thought she'd been staking out the men's room, waiting to ambush him.

"Glad I bumped into you," she said with what she hoped was a charming smile. "Any chance you have a minute? I just had a question or two about the autopsy."

He stared at her for a long moment, then checked his watch. "Walk with me."

"Thanks. This shouldn't take long."

Nicole tried to keep up with his long strides. The medical examiner was tall and had the lean build of a distance runner.

"I wanted to follow up about one of your observations during the exam," she said.

"All of my observations will be in my report."

"I know, but I don't want to wait on that. Those things always take a while."

He shot her a look, and she knew she was quickly rising to the top of his shit list. The first time she'd met him, she'd thrown up on his shoes. And now here she was stalking him to the men's room—or so he thought—and taking potshots at his work.

"So, during the procedure you said something to your assistant about a scratch on the victim's hand?"

"That's right."

The autopsy assistant had written down everything the doctor said, presumably so that he could reference it later without having to go back through the voice recording of the procedure.

"Do you think that's a defensive wound?" Nicole asked. "You didn't specify when you were talking to your assistant."

"It's undetermined."

"It was her right hand, though, correct? So if we find out she's right-handed—"

"It could be a defensive wound."

"Okay. Thanks. And then the abrasions on her wrists? Could you tell me more about those?"

He stopped and looked down at her. "What about them?"

"You mentioned *both* wrists. So, I was wondering, is that another possible defensive wound, or something else? I'm wondering if it's possible she may have been bound at some point."

"Yes."

Nicole's breath caught. "Yes, she was bound?"

"I said yes, it's possible. In my opinion, it appears that she *was* bound shortly before her death."

Her stomach clenched. "Just her hands or—"

"Yes." He folded his arms over his chest. "All of this will be in my report, Detective Lawson."

"I know, I just—" She combed her hand through her hair. The victim being bound changed things. A lot. "I just want to understand what we're dealing with *now*, you know? Are you saying she was—"

"I'm saying her hands—and that's hands only, not feet—appear to have been bound at the wrists with some sort of textured cordage. What kind of cordage, you'll have to wait on the lab. Based on the response evident in the soft tissue, she was kept this way for at least a few minutes—"

"How long? Can you be more specific?"

His jaw tightened. Clearly, he didn't like being cornered in the hallway and asked to give his scientific conclusions, but Nicole really didn't care. She need this ASAP.

"I would say ten minutes, at a minimum. Probably more like twenty."

Her breath whooshed out.

"All of this will be in my preliminary report, which—by the way—I had planned to finish by tonight, because I understand the urgency of your investigation."

"Thank you."

He held her gaze for a long moment. "I get it, you know. I've been doing this awhile. I don't like delays any more than you do, but we're stretched thin here, as I'm sure you've noticed."

"I have. I understand."

"Good." He checked his watch again. "Now, my next procedure starts in five minutes."

"Just one more thing." She smiled. "Sorry—then I promise to let you go. You mentioned some 'grit' on the front of the victim's shirt?"

"All the clothing is on its way to the lab."

"I know. But now with this information that she was possibly *bound*, I'm wondering if you think it looked like grit that came from an outside location, such as the alley where she was found, or maybe inside?"

"I couldn't say. The grit was dark. Maybe dirt, soil, something like that."

"Could it possibly be coffee grounds?"

"Possibly? Yes. Can I say that with certainty? No. For that, you'll need to talk to the lab."

S EAN SCANNED THE busy sidewalks as he drove.

"I thought you said this was a sleepy beach town," Moore said over the phone.

"It is, usually," Sean told his boss.

"Isn't that why they picked it?"

"That's the theory."

A theory Sean was beginning to question.

"Well, how's it looking? I assume you talked to the investigators?"

Sean hadn't yet, so he dodged the question.

"I spoke with a contact in the ME's office," Sean said. "Cause of death is sharp force trauma."

"She was stabbed."

"Correct. No sexual assault."

"Okay."

"Also, her hands were bound."

Sean pulled into the Surf's Up parking lot. A pair of

orange traffic cones blocked the entrance to the Island Beanery parking lot. There were three vehicles there now: a small silver car, an unmarked police unit, and Leyla Breda's white SUV.

"Bound," Moore repeated.

"That's right."

"Doesn't sound like a random street crime."

"I don't think it was."

Sean pulled into a space facing the coffee shop. A **Closed** sign hung in the window, and a plainclothes detective stood just inside the glass door, talking to a tall woman with dark hair. Sean recognized both women from the wedding. The detective was one of Joel's co-workers, and the other woman was with Leyla's catering staff.

"So, what is it then?" Moore asked.

"I'm trying to find out. Let me work my sources and get back to you."

Sean's "sources" at this point were hypothetical. He knew which people he needed to talk to, but he hadn't managed to track them down yet, and he still hadn't decided the best way to approach them when he did.

"When?" Moore asked.

"Soon. I need to do a little more digging."

"Don't dig too long. You're down there for Virgil, not whatever other shit they're dealing with."

"I just want to make sure they're not connected."

Moore sighed on the other end of the phone. "Fine. But don't get distracted."

Too late for that.

He thought of Leyla standing in her doorway last night. She'd looked drained and shell-shocked, stripped of all that sparkly self-assurance she'd had the night before. One look at her had activated all of Sean's protective instincts, even though he suspected she would bristle at the idea of someone protecting her. Their dinner together had helped, but it had been over much too soon. He'd wanted to take her upstairs and make her forget about her shit day. But he hadn't even tried. Instead, he'd watched her go upstairs alone, knowing full well that if she needed something, he was probably the last person she'd call.

At least he'd managed to finally get her number so now he could call *her*. And he would. Soon. As soon as he could pull it off without her thinking he was some weird stalker.

"You got me? We need to focus," Moore was saying. "This is about Virgil."

"I know."

"Let's keep our eye on the ball."

CHAPTER

FIVE

LEYLA WATCHED WITH frustration as the crime scene photographer traipsed into the kitchen.

"I don't understand." She turned to Emmet. "You said they were finished."

"They were. But then something came up."

She arched her eyebrows, waiting for him to explain. But of course he didn't. She'd been cleaning the store with Siena when Nicole had shown up and told her to stop what she was doing. Then a crime scene van had arrived, and now Emmet was here.

Something had happened with the investigation, obviously, but no one was telling her anything. She could call Owen and ask him. But he might not know either. Yesterday, he'd told her that Chief Brady was keeping him off the case.

"Again, I'm sorry." Emmet pulled a pair of paper booties over his shoes. "We'll try to be quick."

"I don't need you to *rush*. Do whatever you have to do. I just—I wish someone had let me know you were coming back again. I told my staffers we'd be ready to open tomorrow."

Emmet cast a look over his shoulder toward the back of the shop. No fewer than four people were back there now—two CSIs and a forensic photographer, plus Nicole, who seemed to be running things.

Leyla peered through the kitchen to the hallway beyond. She couldn't see what they were up to, but they were talking in hushed, tense voices. The sound of a camera clicking away put a ball of dread in Leyla's stomach.

She looked at her brother's friend. She'd known him for years. "Emmet, *what* is going on?"

"Let me go see."

He headed back there, and she could tell from the guilty look on his face that he knew exactly what was going on, but he didn't want to tell her.

"Leyla."

She turned to Siena, who stood beside the condiment bar, spray bottle in hand. She had spent the past hour cleaning fingerprint powder off doorframes throughout the shop. The stuff seemed to be everywhere, and it was difficult to get rid of.

"What do you want me to do?" Siena asked.

"I guess . . . nothing." Leyla checked her watch. It was almost noon. They still had the afternoon to work but given that the CSIs were just getting started again, Leyla had no idea when they would finish.

"Let's call it a day," she said, making a snap decision. Siena's eyes looked puffy and tired, and being here at all today was obviously a struggle. Leyla didn't want to make her wait around. Who knew how long the investigators would be busy back there? She didn't even know what the hell they were doing.

"So . . . do you think we'll be reopening tomorrow?" Siena asked. "Or is that off now?"

"I'll let you know." She checked her watch again. "I'll make a call by three o'clock. In the meantime go home and get some rest."

"I can wait with you."

"No need. I'll handle it."

A rapid *click-click-click* in back made Leyla's stomach turn. The photographer was snapping pictures of something. Siena cast a worried look toward the kitchen.

"Are you sure?" Siena asked.

"Absolutely. Here, I'll put all this away." Leyla stepped forward to take the spray bottle and rag from her hands. "You go on."

"Let me know what happens."

"I will."

Siena darted one last glance at the kitchen and dug a set of keys from the pocket of her black apron. "All right. Call me if you need anything."

"Thanks."

Leyla watched out the window as Siena walked to her car, taking her cell phone out as she went. Leyla hoped she was calling her boyfriend. She needed emotional support right now.

The typically crowded parking lot was nearly empty today, and a pair of orange traffic cones blocked the entrance. Siena maneuvered around them, bumping over the curb as she drove out of the lot.

Leyla turned back to survey the shop. She set the cleaning supplies on the nearest table and strained to listen. The voices were hushed again, and she got a sick, slimy feeling in her stomach. Something was very wrong.

Of course it was—everything was wrong about this situation—but even more wrong than yesterday.

Nicole emerged from the kitchen. "Leyla, could you come back here a sec? The CSI has a question."

"Sure."

"You'll need to put on some shoe covers."

Leyla was already slipping the paper booties over her Converse sneakers.

"What are they doing back there?" Leyla asked as she followed Nicole into the kitchen.

"Just covering some bases. We think it's possible we might have missed something."

They'd missed something *inside*. Leyla's heart thudded as she followed Nicole down the narrow hallway. A man in a white Tyvek suit was crouched in the doorway of the storage room near the back door. Emmet stood behind him, arms crossed, looking over the man's head as another CSI looked on.

Leyla's feet felt like cinder blocks as she made her way down the hallway. The door to the restroom stood open, as though they'd spent some time in there. But right now everyone was focused on the room across the hall.

"This storeroom is used for paper goods and cleaning supplies, that sort of thing?" Nicole asked.

"Yes."

Emmet glanced up and stepped out of the way.

Leyla stopped beside the door. The photographer stood opposite a metal shelf filled with paper towels and jugs of cleaning solution. A mop and bucket sat in the corner, and black aprons with the Island Beanery logo hung from hooks along the wall.

"There are some interesting markings on the floor in this room," Nicole told her. "Can you tell us whether this shelving unit is usually located here? Or does it look like it's been moved recently?"

Leyla surveyed the tiny space, head spinning as she tried to process what they were asking. Her gaze fell on two dark streaks on the dusty tile floor.

"Yes. I think."

"Yes, the shelf has been moved?" Nicole asked.

"It's usually up against that corner there," Leyla said. "It looks like someone slid it over a few feet."

Nicole shot a glance at Emmet. Leyla turned to look at him. "What—"

"Thank you," Nicole said, cutting her off. "That's all we need for now. Let's clear out, so they have space to maneuver."

Leyla stepped aside as the photographer moved into the hallway, leaving only the CSI with his evidence kit in the room. He closed the door with a *click*.

She looked at Emmet. "What is he—"

"Luminol."

Leyla stared at him, absorbing the words. They were looking for blood. On the floor. Where the shelf had been moved.

"So . . . you think Amelia was attacked *in here*? Not outside, in the alley?"

"We don't know," he said.

"It's something we're checking into," Nicole added. "Some new evidence has come to light."

"What new evidence?"

No response. Nicole just watched her, stone-faced. Leyla looked at Emmet, but his expression was blank, too. Same for the photographer.

The door swung open, and the CSI stepped out. "Guys, we got it."

"It lit up?" the photographer asked.

He nodded. "Like a neon sign."

I T WAS AFTER four by the time Nicole and Emmet made it back to the police station. The door to Brady's office was closed and the bullpen was nearly empty. Looked like most of their uniformed officers were out on patrol.

"Who's in with the chief?" Emmet asked Adam McDeere, who sat alone in the sea of cubicles.

"No idea." The officer glanced up from his computer. "I just got here. I was clearing the accident on the causeway."

McDeere looked as tired and irritable as Nicole felt. The back of his neck was sunburned, and his khaki uniform was soaked with sweat. He had a Dairy Queen bag on his desk, and just the sight of it made Nicole's stomach growl. She'd strategically skipped breakfast before this morning's autopsy and planned to eat lunch afterward. But the day had gotten away from her and now she felt light-headed.

Emmet tossed his keys on his desk and dropped into a chair.

"Hey, you want to grab some food?" she asked him. "We've got an hour before the team meeting."

"I'm good," Emmet said, not looking up.

And there went another effort to get things back to normal. Since yesterday, he'd been keeping his distance, and their usual good-natured ribbing was nonexistent.

"Lawson."

She turned around to see Brady standing in his doorway.

"Got a minute?" he asked.

"Sure."

Despite the chief's low-key tone, she could tell something was up as she crossed the bullpen. When she stepped into his office, a man got up from the visitor's chair. Muscular build, thick brown hair. He wore jeans and a black leather jacket that was too warm for their eighty-degree weather.

Brady closed the door behind her. "I'd like you to meet Agent Moran."

He offered his hand, and Nicole gave it a firm shake, noting the holster beneath his jacket. Was that *agent* as in DEA? ICE? Being near the border, they dealt frequently with both.

"So . . . is that DEA?" she asked.

"FBI."

The sense of dread that she'd been feeling all afternoon intensified. She glanced at Brady, who stood with his arms folded, watching their exchange.

"Detective Lawson is leading up our case." Brady turned to Nicole. "How'd it go at the coffee shop?"

"Good," she replied, looking at the agent again. What did the FBI want with her homicide case?

"They finished processing the storeroom?" Brady asked.

"That's right."

Nicole had filled him in on the details over the phone, and clearly he was comfortable sharing them in front of this agent.

"Someone cleaned up blood in there with a mop or sponge," she told Brady. "But with Luminol, they found streaks on the floor and traces in the tile grout. They got pictures and took some swabs."

"So, they think she was attacked there?" Brady asked.

"Looks like. We'll see what the lab results say."

"Agent Moran has some questions about the case. He thinks it might be linked to something he's working on."

"It's possible," the agent said. "Right now, we're just trying to learn more."

"And what is it you're working on?" she asked.

"It's a multiagency investigation. That's all I can really say at this point."

She glanced at Brady, wondering if he knew, but his expression gave nothing away. She looked at the agent again.

"What is it you'd like to know?" she asked.

"I assume you've been to Amelia Albright's apartment?"

The fact that he knew she lived in an apartment was a bit disconcerting.

"We were there yesterday but didn't find a whole lot." She glanced at Brady. "In light of today's new evidence, I'm planning to go back and take another look around."

"Mind if I come? I'd like to see it," the agent said.

She looked at Brady, who gave her a slight nod.

"Sure. When?"

"The sooner the better."

"Go now," Brady told her.

"Don't we have that meeting at five?"

"I'll move it out. You two go ahead."

She glanced at the agent, who stood there casually watching, as though he was used to getting what he wanted, when he wanted it. Must be nice.

Nicole pointed at the evidence box sitting on Brady's file cabinet. "Mind if I . . . ?"

The chief stepped aside, and she scooted past him. The box contained the murder book—a two-inch binder she had started Sunday that didn't have much in it yet—along with an envelope containing a key that had been provided to police by the victim's landlord. Amelia's key chain, which had been recovered from a dumpster, had been sent to the lab for testing, along with a bunch of other evidence that would probably take forever to analyze.

Nicole signed out the envelope and turned to Brady. "Want me to tell the team we're bumping the meeting?"

"I'll do it."

"Thanks."

Brady opened the door. "Let's aim for six thirty. Call me if you get sidetracked."

"Got it."

Nicole was aware of Emmet and McDeere watching her as she left the station with some guy nobody knew, which was sure to fuel speculation.

As they stepped into the late-day sun, she put on her sunglasses. "I'll drive," she said, striding toward her unmarked police unit. He didn't object.

She popped the locks on the car and slid behind the wheel. It was hot, and she immediately got the AC going.

"She lives on Palmetto," she said as she crossed the parking lot. "But I guess you know that already."

He nodded.

Annoyed now, she pulled onto the highway headed south.

"Thanks for letting me tag along," he said.

"I didn't think I had a choice." She looked at him. Up close, she noticed that his eyes were a striking shade of green and he had thick eyelashes that he probably didn't appreciate at all.

He glanced at her, and she focused her attention on the road.

"So, you're with the Brownsville office?" she asked. "You look familiar."

"I was at the wedding Saturday."

She glanced at him, startled. She'd known she recognized him from someplace, but she'd assumed it was work-related.

"You know Joel, then?" she asked.

"We go way back."

"I see."

But she didn't see at all. Joel had grown up on the island, and this guy wasn't from here. Maybe they knew each other from Houston, where Joel had started his career.

Interesting that he'd been at Joel's wedding *and* he happened to be working a case down here in south Texas. Coincidence? Somehow, she doubted it. Maybe they had worked together on the task force Joel was on, which was going after drug and sex trafficking in the region. The team included deputies from the sheriff's office, as well people from an alphabet soup of federal agencies.

She passed a pickup truck with a trio of teens in the front and a pair of surfboards in back. The waves were up today, and lots of people were hitting the beach.

She glanced at Sean Moran. It wasn't lost on her that he still hadn't answered her question.

"So, you *are* with Brownsville or—"

"I'm down from D.C. But I'm coordinating with several agents in Brownsville."

Washington, D.C. Of course. Because everything about this case wasn't already giving her an ulcer. She'd dealt with the FBI on a case last summer, and it had been a major pain. They were territorial, pushy, and they hoarded information. It wasn't an experience she wanted to repeat.

She turned the AC down and glanced at the man beside her. He didn't look quite as uptight as the feds she'd met last summer. And he was younger, too, probably mid-thirties.

"What exactly are you looking for at the apartment?" she asked.

"Honestly?" He sighed. "I'm not sure. I'm hoping I'll know it when I see it."

She appreciated the glimmer of honesty, however faint.

"Well, what exactly put this case on your radar?"

He glanced at her, and she wondered if he was going to give her something, anything, that might be useful. The agents from last summer had considered information "sharing" to be a one-way street.

"You don't get a lot of homicides here," he said.

"Thankfully, no. Although, that seems to be changing with our recent population boom."

"This one isn't your garden-variety street crime."

"No."

Although, what was *garden-variety* in a place like Lost Beach? Until a few years ago, they'd had very little crime at all. They mostly dealt with drunks, property crime, and a fair number of assaults. But the population growth had brought all sorts of problems to the island. And their homicide rate, as low as it was, had spiked over the last three years.

She glanced at him, wondering how much he knew about her case. "What in particular caught your attention?"

"Well, her hands were bound, which is somewhat unusual. No sexual assault. And it seems the stabbing occurred inside the store, but the cash register wasn't hit."

Nicole's shoulders tensed as he rattled off all the elements of the case that she found most disturbing.

"We recovered her purse from a dumpster near the body," she said. "No cash or credit cards. And no cell phone."

He shot her a look. "You don't really think this was a robbery, do you?"

She fixed her gaze on the highway. No, she didn't. She had been having trouble with that theory even *before* they knew the victim had had her hands bound and that she'd likely died inside the building, and not in the alley where her body was left.

"The outdoor crime scene seems staged, don't you think?"

She glanced at him. "Yes, but why?"

"I don't know."

"So . . . you're thinking the victim might have been involved with drugs? Or maybe a local crime syndicate?"

"I don't know."

What else would it be? What other sort of case would attract the attention of a federal agent down here from Washington?

Nicole tamped down her frustration as they pulled up to

a stoplight. He knew way more than he was telling her, and his vague answers only underscored how behind she felt with this whole investigation—an investigation she was supposed to be leading.

For what had to be the hundredth time, she wondered why Brady had put her in charge when he could have tapped Emmet, who had more experience.

Nicole glanced left, toward the beach. They had passed the last of the high-rise hotels and condominiums. Soon they'd reach the southern part of the island, where the topography was low and marshy, prone to frequent flooding. Like many other year-round residents who worked in the tourism sector, Amelia Albright had lived in an apartment on the bay side. No canal access or beach views—just cramped quarters and cheap rent.

The traffic thinned out as they passed the causeway linking Lost Beach to the mainland.

"You have an issue with FBI agents?"

She glanced at her passenger, surprised by the question. "Why do you ask?"

"You seem reluctant to tell me about your case."

He wasn't wrong. And she realized she was being just as petty and territorial as the agents who'd pissed her off last summer.

"No *issue*, really. But it's been my experience that you guys are possessive. And stingy with information."

He smiled. "That's been my experience, too."

The sign for Palmetto Drive came into view, and Nicole put on her turn signal. Despite the name, there wasn't a palmetto or any other kind of tree in sight—only a rusted water tank and a twenty-four-hour gas station. She turned into the neighborhood.

"Well, let me just say I'm not here to steal your case or take credit for your work," he said.

"Okay. What are you here for?" she asked, hoping to elicit at least some scrap of useful information from him.

"Really, just covering my bases. It's an unusual homicide, and I want to make sure it's not connected to my case."

"What kind of case is it?"

"I can't get into it."

She rolled her eyes.

"Sorry."

He actually looked like he meant it. But still, she felt a spurt of annoyance.

"Well, is it some kind of undercover thing?" she asked. "Because we'd appreciate a heads-up if the feds are sending undercover agents in here while we're working a homicide."

"I wasn't sent here undercover."

"No?"

"No. But I *am* trying to keep a low profile."

"In other words, don't talk about who you are and the fact that you're down here working on something."

"I'd appreciate it."

"Even though I have no idea what that something is, based on what you've told me."

He just looked at her.

Amelia's apartment building came into view, a two-story walk-up with weathered wooden siding. The parking lot was empty, except for a few beat-up cars. Most of the residents were at work. Nicole swung into the lot and drove to the end, where Amelia had rented a one-bedroom unit. Nicole and Emmet and a pair of CSIs on loan from the county had spent three hours here yesterday combing through the entire unit. They'd collected a day planner and an iPad, and lifted some fingerprints here and there, but nothing jumped out that might shed light on what, at that time, had seemed like robbery-turned-homicide behind Amelia's workplace.

But it was becoming clearer by the minute that there was more to this case than a simple robbery gone awry. And now the feds were swooping in.

Nicole cut the engine and turned in her seat. "Can I be straight with you, Special Agent?"

He smiled. "It's Sean. And yes, please be straight."

"All right, Sean, here's the thing. Ever since this case hit, we've been working round the clock. Everyone. Not just the detectives, but everyone else who's had to pick up the slack. And we're short-staffed, as you well know, because our top detective and our CSI are on their honeymoon. The last thing I want to do is see everyone bust their asses on this, at the expense of everything else we're dealing with, only to find out that our victim was a confidential informant, or some other such shit that you guys knew all along and didn't tell us."

"That won't happen."

"Really? Because you don't seem to be very forthcoming with information, and I get this funny feeling that you have some that could be relevant. For example, you just dodged my question about whether Amelia Albright was a confidential informant."

"She wasn't."

"Are you sure about that?"

"I'm sure." He pushed open his door. "Trust me."

LEYLA JOGGED DOWN the beach, keeping her gaze focused on the distant horizon. Her usual turnaround was the kayak stand in front of the Oasis Hotel. As she neared it, she poured on the speed until her quads burned. Pumping her arms and pushing herself to the limit, she passed the first rack of boats.

Leyla staggered to a halt and bent over, panting.

She was out of shape. Or at least, more out of shape than she liked to be. Between the wedding and getting her catering business off the ground, she'd been immersed in work, and she hadn't exercised in more than a month.

She straightened and stretched her arms over her head. The evening sun cast long shadows, and the tide was out. She walked toward the water and plopped down on the ground beside someone's abandoned sandcastle. This one had two tall turrets and was decorated with cockle shells. It was a drip castle like the ones she used to make with her brothers when they were little kids.

She and her older brothers had been close growing up, with Leyla always clamoring to tag along with whatever they were doing, whether it was fishing or skateboarding or taking out their dad's boat. Now, Joel was married. Alex practiced law in Houston. And Owen was busy with his job and a serious relationship. Everyone was consumed with their adult lives, and all that carefree time they used to spend together as kids was long gone.

She rested her arms on her knees and looked out at the surf, where a couple was paddling a tandem kayak. Sean's question about Amelia came back to her.

Did she have a boyfriend?

Leyla didn't know. Amelia had worked at the coffee shop for nearly a year, but Leyla knew next to nothing about her personal life. She'd had no idea until yesterday that Amelia had had a twin brother, and that she'd loved surfing, and that she'd done some modeling after high school before moving to the island and enrolling in community college. Amelia had made a lot of friends while working at the Beanery, and for the past two days, flowers and cards and teddy bears had been piling up on the sidewalk in front of the shop. Not wanting anything to get damaged by the elements, Leyla had gathered the mementos into a box to take to Amelia's parents. She couldn't even imagine what they were going through, losing their daughter in such a horrific way. Leyla couldn't stop thinking about what Amelia's last moments— or possibly last *minutes*—must have been like, how utterly terrified she must have felt.

Leyla stared at the surf. Tears burned her eyes and she squeezed them shut. She had gotten through the entire day without crying, but something about watching the waves always stirred up her emotions. She wiped her cheeks and focused on a pair of sailboats just past the second sandbar.

"Leyla?"

She turned to see Sean jogging over and felt a flutter of panic. He wore shorts and running shoes and a Muse T-shirt that was soaked with sweat. He stopped beside her, breathing hard, and took out his earbuds.

"Thought that was you." His brow furrowed as he looked her over. "You all right?"

"Yeah." She turned toward the water. "Just, you know, watching the boats."

He didn't say anything, and she could hear his breathing returning to normal. He sank down on the sand beside her and stretched out his legs.

Had he followed her here? He'd been running for a while, from the looks of it.

"How far did you go?" she asked, brushing her cheeks.

"To the park and back. What is that? Three miles?"

"Probably. You're staying at the Windjammer Hotel?"

"Sea Isle," he said, nodding down the beach.

"Oh, that's right. You said you had a condo. How is it?"

"Fine, if you don't mind drinking games at two a.m." He rolled his eyes. "The people above me were having a rager last night."

"That's a Sunday thing. Sundays and Fridays."

"Oh yeah?"

"They'll probably quiet down by tomorrow."

He smiled slightly. "How do you know?"

"Most people rent for the week or the weekend. People generally like to party the first night."

He had three days' worth of beard now, and it looked good on him. She turned to the surf again. He smelled like sunblock and male sweat, and she had no idea why the combination put butterflies in her stomach.

"Sounds like you're an expert," he said.

"I am, unfortunately. The apartment beside mine is a short-term rental."

He was watching her closely, obviously picking up on the fact that she'd been crying just now. He turned to look at the water.

"Nice cat out there."

She followed his gaze to the catamaran farthest away. "That's the *Eclipse*."

"It's big. Looks about sixty feet."

"Bigger, I think. It belongs to the hotel. They do sunset cruises every night during the season."

"Is it the season already? Late April?"

"The season runs pretty much Easter to Labor Day. But Memorial Day is when we really get going. That's why Joel and Miranda wanted to get married now, before the real rush starts and the police get swamped."

And just like that, her thoughts boomeranged right back to the topic she'd been trying get out of her mind by going out for a run.

She looked at Sean. "So, how's the fishing going?"

"Don't know. I haven't gone yet."

"No?"

"I slept in."

She watched his eyes closely. "Oh yeah? And what did you do today?"

"Not much. Hung around the condo, mostly."

She shook her head and looked away.

"What?"

She sighed. "Sean."

"What?"

"I grew up in a tourist town. I can spot guys' bullshit a mile away. What are you really doing here on this open-ended trip? And don't say fishing."

He just looked at her.

"Are you here drying out? Did your wife give you the boot? What?"

"I'm not married."

She rolled her eyes. "Okay, your girlfriend, then?"

"I told you, I'm here on vacation."

She sighed and pushed herself to her feet. "Forget it. I don't want to know." She dusted the sand off her hands as he stood, too.

He gazed down at her with those ocean green eyes. "You really think I would ask you out if I was married?"

"I don't know you well enough to answer that."

"Well, I wouldn't. I'm not like that."

But what he *would* do was lie to her and evade all her questions. She shook her head and looked away. He'd caught her crying twice—and she wasn't even a crier! Meanwhile, he wouldn't give her a straight answer to even the most basic question.

She checked her watch. "Well, I'm off. See you around."

He rested his hands on his hips as he watched her walk away. "Leyla—"

"Enjoy your run."

CHAPTER

SIX

THE LIGHTHOUSE CAME into view as Nicole crossed the causeway over the sparkling water of Laguna Madre. *Finally.* Just the sight of the landmark helped loosen the knot in her shoulders that came from driving all morning. Her trip to the county crime lab had taken longer than expected, and then she'd hit a half-hour traffic snarl on the on-ramp to the bridge.

She dug her phone from her pocket and called Emmet.

"Hey, where are you?" he asked.

"About to exit the causeway," she told him. "Are you at the station?"

"On my way. I just picked up a burger for lunch."

She eyed the wrapper in her cup holder. Her lunch had consisted of a smashed protein bar from the bottom of her bag.

"So, did that phone dump finally come in?" she asked. They'd been waiting on Amelia Albright's phone records for days.

"Yeah. I spent some time on it this morning," Emmet said.

She felt a rush of relief. "Anything interesting?"

"I'm still going through it and running down numbers. The day of the murder, it looks like the last incoming call that connected was at three fifty-five, and it's from Rachel Davies."

"We knew about that one."

It was Amelia's sick co-worker calling to ask Amelia to fill in for her and deliver the cake to the wedding reception.

"That call lasted seven minutes," Emmet said. "Rachel called again at five fifteen, but it went to voicemail. After that, nothing."

"The perp probably took the battery out after he grabbed the phone so no one could ping it and locate it."

"Yeah, probably."

Nicole turned onto the highway leading into downtown and hit another patch of traffic.

"I've been focused on the last two weeks," Emmet continued. "There were some calls to her parents in Port O'Connor. Also, some local calls. So far, it's all her friends' numbers. But nothing that really jumped out at me."

"Damn."

Nicole had been hopeful about the phone records. She'd thought maybe the victim's phone was stolen to hide communications with someone.

"Also, I checked back with the bank on her credit card and debit card," Emmet said. "No hits since the day before her death."

Nicole sighed. They had expected that, but still it was disappointing.

"I set up an alert, so they'll notify us if anyone tries to use it," he said.

Now that they had concluded the robbery was likely

staged, they weren't really expecting any hits on the cards. But it was a base they had to cover, nevertheless.

"How'd it go at the lab?" Emmet asked.

Brady had sent her to the county crime lab to try to get a preview of any results they had and also to impress upon them the urgency of their case. *Go up there and be a squeaky wheel*, he'd told her.

"I didn't really get much," she said. "I tried to rattle a few cages, but you know how that goes. They're backlogged, running behind, yada yada yada. They don't have the DNA results yet. I thought maybe we'd get lucky, and they might have found something from the perp, maybe if he nicked himself with the knife or something."

She pulled up to a stoplight and sighed. She was hungry, cranky, and irritated with Brady for sending her on an errand that killed half her day.

"You sound pissed," Emmet said.

"I'm frustrated. All that driving just to wait around in a lobby to have a ten-minute conversation with the lab supervisor."

"I knew that was going to happen when Brady sent you," he said. "So, you completely wasted your morning."

"Maybe not completely. I did get one new lead. Did any of those numbers in Amelia's phone records have a three-six-two area code?"

"I don't know. I don't have the records in front of me. Why?"

"Well, the lab tech who examined her work apron found a matchbook tucked inside the pocket. It's from Playa del Rey."

"Like, our Playa del Rey? The golf resort?"

"Yeah. It's their logo on the front, and then there's a phone number written in pencil on the inside flap."

"You try calling it?" he asked.

"No answer. And I googled it, but nothing comes up. I'm

wondering if the number is for someone she met at the resort."

"That would make sense," he said. "But that place is pretty rich for a barista."

"Yeah, I know. I'm wondering if she maybe spent the night there with someone. Or met someone for dinner."

"You're still going down the boyfriend route," he said, and she heard the skepticism in his voice.

But they didn't have a lot of options. All evidence suggested the alley crime scene was staged to cover a different motive, and that Amelia had been stabbed *inside* the building after being bound and held in a storage room. Yet the cash register was full, and no computers or valuables had been taken from the restaurant.

"I thought her best friend said Amelia wasn't seeing anyone lately," Emmet said.

"Yeah, *lately*."

"I don't think it's a boyfriend. I mean, why would he do it at her workplace? Why not get her to meet him somewhere private?"

"Maybe he's an ex and they had a hostile breakup."

"Still, a coffee shop? Much too risky."

She sighed. "That leaves what, though, in terms of motive?"

"I don't know. Nothing good," Emmet said. "What does the fed think?"

She felt a dart of annoyance. He knew about Sean Moran somehow, even though she hadn't told anyone about his involvement.

But of course Emmet knew. After seeing him in Brady's office, Emmet would have made it his mission to find out who the guy was and what he was doing there. He'd probably sweet-talked their receptionist into telling him. Or maybe he'd just come right out and asked the chief.

"Nicole?"

"I don't know. He was pretty tight-lipped when we went by the apartment yesterday. He didn't tell me what he's working on."

"Big surprise. Did he collect any evidence?"

"No. So listen," she said, eager to change the subject. "Brady wants a meeting at two. The whole team. Could you do me a favor and tell McDeere for me when you see him?"

With Owen sidelined and Joel out, they were using McDeere for some legwork, even though he wasn't officially a detective.

Emmet didn't respond, and Nicole wondered if he was being prickly again because she was relaying the chief's orders, which was part of her job as the team leader. Was this because she was a woman? She'd never picked up any sexism from him before, but she was beginning to wonder.

"Emmet?"

"If I see him, I'll tell him."

"Good."

"What's the meeting for, anyway?"

"He wants an update on what each of us is working on. Bring your notes on the phone records."

"Yes, ma'am."

SIENA LEANED AGAINST Leyla's kitchen counter, watching her peel shrimp for a batch of gumbo.

"Are you planning to go to the service?" she asked Leyla. "It's Thursday afternoon in Port O'Connor."

"Yes. Do you need a ride?"

"I don't know. I may not be going." She folded her arms and looked out the window above the sink. "I haven't decided yet."

Leyla lifted an eyebrow but didn't say anything. She'd thought Siena and Amelia were close and had assumed she planned to attend the funeral.

Leyla grabbed another shrimp and peeled off the shell. She used the efficient, two-pinch method that her uncle had taught her on his boat dock when she was five.

"Dana plans to cover the shop," Leyla said. The newest manager didn't know Amelia, so she'd offered to work a double shift so Amelia's friends could go to the service. "And I've got Wade covering the Java Place."

"That's not the issue," Siena said. "I'm just not comfortable at funerals."

"No one is."

"I know, I'm just not sure if I want to go." She uncrossed her arms. Then crossed them again.

"Here." Leyla handed her a cutting board and a bowl of peeled shrimp. Clearly, Siena was antsy and needed something to do with her hands. "Devein these for me, would you?"

Sighing, Siena selected a paring knife from the wooden block on the counter.

"Are you worried about talking to her parents?" Leyla asked.

"No, it's not that. I already talked to them."

"You did?"

"They asked me to read a scripture during the service. I'm not sure I should, though."

"Is that why you don't want to go?"

"Maybe." She shrugged. "Probably."

Leyla kept working, waiting for an explanation.

"The thing is, I'm not really religious," Siena said. "I don't know why they asked me to do it."

"Do they have a scripture in mind for you to read, or do they want you to pick something?"

"It's something from Corinthians." Siena sighed. "But I don't know. I haven't been to church since my grandfather's funeral. That was years ago."

Leyla peeled the last shrimp and dropped it into the bowl.

"What would you do?" Siena darted a glance at her.

"You want my honest opinion? I think you should do it."

Siena looked pained.

"I think you'll regret it if you don't."

"Even if I haven't set foot inside a church in forever?"

"That doesn't matter. What matters is that it will bring comfort to Amelia's family."

Tears welled in Siena's eyes.

"What if I get up there and lose it? I'll ruin the whole thing."

"You won't lose it. And even if you did, that wouldn't ruin anything. You'll be surrounded by people who loved Amelia, and everyone understands."

Siena nodded stiffly. "You're right. I know." She took a deep breath. "Amelia would want me to. It means a lot to her mom. I know I should feel honored that they asked me, and I do and all, I'm just being selfish."

"You aren't selfish." Leyla reached over and squeezed her hand. "And you'll do fine. I know you will."

Siena finished the last shrimp and looked around. "Well. I guess I'd better get going."

"Don't you want to stay till it's ready? I've got way more than I need here."

She was making the gumbo for Miranda's sister and her fiancé, who had stayed on the island to house sit and take care of Miranda and Joel's dog while they were on their honeymoon.

"Thanks, but I've been gone all day. I need to get home." Siena washed her hands. "Thanks for talking."

"Of course." Leyla handed her a dish towel.

"Sorry to just show up and crash your evening."

"You didn't," Leyla said, walking her to the door.

"I'll handle the special tomorrow. What is it again?"

"Pesto pasta salad."

"Got it." Siena grabbed her duffel off the chair and slung it over her shoulder. She'd come from the gym, saying she just wanted to drop by and say hi, but Leyla had known there was something weighing on her mind.

"See you in the morning." Leyla opened the door.

"Bye."

Siena tromped down the stairs.

And nearly bumped into Sean Moran on the sidewalk.

He looked up at Leyla, and her heart did a little dance. He kept his gaze locked on hers as he ascended the steps. She hadn't seen him since yesterday on the beach. After the way they'd left things, she hadn't expected him to come by again.

He reached the landing and gazed down at her. "Hi."

"Hi."

"You got a minute?"

She looked at him, debating. She had no idea why she would want to let him in after he'd practically admitted lying to her. She didn't trust him.

And yet . . .

He gazed down at her with those eyes, and she felt a warm tingle rush through her. And damn it, this was the problem with this man. He was much too attractive. And he had this intense way of looking at her, as though he could read her thoughts and *knew* she was attracted to him, even though she didn't want to be.

"Sure." She moved back to let him inside, chiding herself for being a pushover.

As he stepped over her threshold for the first time, she

took a quick look around, gauging the messiness of both herself and her apartment. The apartment was passable, but Leyla was wearing a stained white apron and had her hair in a damn scrunchie. And why she should care, she had no idea. It wasn't like she'd invited him over for dinner. Or invited him at all.

"Smells amazing," he said, peering into the kitchen. "What is that?"

"Gumbo." She swung the door shut.

He stood in the cramped bit of space between the armchair and her drop-leaf table. It was the only place to stand unless he moved into the kitchen itself. Her place was tiny, especially with him in it.

But she wasn't going to feel embarrassed about her apartment or anything else.

"What's up?" she asked.

"I came to apologize."

That was not what she'd expected him to say.

"For what?"

"Lying to you."

She tucked her hands into her apron pockets and watched him. Here it came, whatever he'd been keeping from her. She was pretty sure she knew what it was. Her stomach clenched, and she realized her heart was pounding.

God help me, I've been lusting after someone else's husband.

He stepped closer and gazed down at her, and her heart pounded harder. He'd shaved, finally, and she caught the faintest whiff of cologne. Had he actually cleaned up before coming over here?

"I'd like to start over," he said.

"How do you mean?"

He pulled a leather folio from his pocket, flipped it open, and set it on the table.

Leyla frowned as she stepped over for a closer look.
Her gaze jerked up. "You're with the FBI?"

S EAN NODDED, WATCHING her eyes closely.
     She crossed her arms—not a good sign—and a worry
line appeared between her brows.

"You're a special agent?"

He nodded again.

"Why didn't you just say so?"

"It's complicated."

Anger sparked in her eyes.

"I couldn't go into it," he said. "I still can't. But I wanted
you to know."

Her gaze narrowed. "You're being evasive again. This
doesn't feel like starting over."

He sighed and glanced around. Her apartment was even
smaller than his closet-like place in D.C. Two armchairs
dominating the living area, leaving no room for a couch,
and the kitchen didn't have a bar, much less any stools.

He reached for a wooden chair by the drop-leaf table.
"Mind if I sit down?"

"Sure." She gestured at the table. "Make yourself at
home. How about something to drink?"

He lowered himself into the chair as she strode—a whole
five feet—into the kitchen.

She yanked open the fridge. "Do you want a beer? I'm
having one."

"Sounds good."

She took out a pair of beers from some brewery he'd
never heard of. Pulling a tool from the pocket of her apron,
she popped the tops off, expertly catching the caps and
tucking everything into her pocket in one smooth motion.
She placed a bottle on the table.

"Thanks."

She eyed him over her beer as she took a sip. Then she set her bottle on the counter and leaned against it. "Okay, talk. I'm listening."

He took a tentative sip, stalling for time. "What is that?" He looked at the label.

"A Belgian hefeweizen."

"It's good."

"I know." She crossed her arms. "Now, talk. You were explaining why you felt compelled to lie to me earlier?"

He set the bottle down and looked at her. This was the part he had to finesse. And he knew that if she *realized* he was trying to finesse it, she'd get even more pissed off.

"I can't really talk about my work. That's the first thing. But I wanted to at least tell you I *am* working. You were right—I didn't come down here to fish."

"So, the lie was that you're here on vacation?"

"Sort of."

Her blue eyes sparked again.

"I came down from Washington, D.C., for the wedding. But the reason I'm staying is for work."

She studied his face, and he could tell she was trying to judge his truthfulness.

"So, that's it. That's all I can really say about it, but I wanted you to know. And I'd appreciate it if you wouldn't let other people know."

She tipped her head to the side. "Know what? That you're a federal agent?"

"Yes. That's not a secret or anything, but I don't want to draw attention to the fact that I'm down here working on something."

"Hence, the fishing vacation BS."

"Yeah."

She gave him a long, measured look. Then she turned

and opened the fridge again. He watched as she took out a bundle of greens wrapped in paper towels. She pulled several sprigs from the bundle and rinsed them under the faucet, then shook them out and placed them on a cutting board.

"What about Joel?" she asked.

"What about him?"

"Do you even know my brother, or was that crap, too?"

He smiled. "Of course I know him. He invited me to his wedding."

She shot him a glare. "Not 'of course.' You lied to me about him, too. You said you guys worked the vice squad together in Houston."

"Oh. Right." He sighed. He'd forgotten about that particular lie.

"What else?" She folded her arms over her chest.

"What do you mean?"

"What else did you lie to me about?"

Sticky question. He couldn't actually remember, and he'd probably lied about something over their three conversations—four if you counted the first one where she'd shouted at him like a drill sergeant and he'd been instantly turned on.

"Hello?" She leaned forward. "You really have to think about it?"

"Nothing."

Her gaze narrowed.

"Is there something specific you want to know?" he asked, turning the tables.

"Why?"

He shrugged. "Ask me whatever you want. I'll answer it if I can."

She watched him, seeming intrigued by this new game.

"All right. Did you or did you not work with Joel in Houston?"

"We went through the police academy together. We lost touch for a while after that. I applied to the Bureau, and he moved down here after your father died—"

She arched her eyebrows, clearly surprised that he knew that personal detail.

"—and then we crossed paths again later, through work."

"The task force Joel's on."

Sean didn't respond. He'd reached the limit of what he was prepared to discuss with her, so he let it go, hoping she'd drop it.

She pulled a gleaming knife from the wooden block on the counter. Her hands became a blur as she started chopping.

"So . . . I'm guessing the rest of it's top secret, right?" She didn't look up. "Joel doesn't talk about his work anymore. I don't even think he tells Miranda about it."

Sean wasn't working with Joel's task force on this particular case. But that was one more detail he didn't want to get into, so he stayed silent.

She sent him a sideways look. "I'll take that as a yes."

She lifted the lid off the pot on the stove. A cloud of steam rose up, and Sean's stomach rumbled. Using the blade of the knife, she scraped the herbs into the pot, then she replaced the lid and turned to look at him.

"How'd you get into the FBI? I thought they took mostly lawyers, accountants, and computer geeks."

He smiled. "Guess I'm lucky." Plus, he had some computer geek in him, but she didn't need to know about that.

She folded her arms and watched him. The kitchen was warm and steamy, and a lock of hair clung to her neck. She looked amazingly sexy, standing there glaring at him.

"Are you single? Or was that a lie, too?" she asked.

"No."

"No, you're not single or—"

"I'm single."

He held her gaze, and he could have sworn her cheeks flushed a little more.

She turned away and took the lid off the soup again. She added a bowl of raw shrimp to the pot, then stirred it with a long wooden spoon.

"So. Washington, D.C., huh?" She shot a glance at him. "You like it there?"

"It's all right."

"I assume you're from Houston. Do you ever miss Texas?"

"Sometimes."

He leaned back in the chair and picked up the beer. Whatever test she'd just given him, he seemed to have passed it, and it felt like they were having an almost normal conversation.

"What do you miss?" she asked.

"My family. My parents are in Houston still and my sister lives in Austin."

She nodded.

"And Mexican food."

She lifted an eyebrow. "Mexican or Tex-Mex?"

Being a foodie, she probably considered them completely different.

"Tex-Mex."

She added some seasonings to the pot. "I spent four years in New York."

"Oh yeah? College?"

"Culinary school. Then working in restaurants." She shook some more seasonings into the pot. "I was *desperate* for good Tex-Mex."

"Don't they have any places up there?"

"Yeah, but it's not the same. The tortilla chips are off. Also the salsa." She shrugged. "I learned to make my own."

She grabbed a dish towel from the oven door and wiped her hands.

"So. Can I offer you some gumbo?"

"Thanks, but I didn't come here to mooch dinner."

"I know. I'm inviting you."

Sean wanted to stay. Having beer and gumbo around her cozy little table sounded good, better than any invitation he'd had in a very long time.

But he had to get back to work.

He stood up and stepped closer to her, taking care not to hit his head on any of the pans hanging from the ceiling.

"I wish I could, but I have to go."

"Work?" she asked.

He nodded.

She gazed up at him with those ice-blue eyes that looked so much like Joel's, it kept freaking him out. Sean wasn't sure what his friend would have to say about him standing in his baby sister's apartment, thinking about getting her naked.

Leyla's eyes heated, as though she'd just read his thoughts, and her gaze dropped to his mouth.

Time to leave.

"Thanks for the invite," he said. "Sorry I can't stay."

She eased around him and led him to the door.

He looked at her. "Some other night, maybe?"

She pulled the door open. "We'll see."

CHAPTER

SEVEN

EXCITED BARKS GREETED Leyla as she hiked up the stairs to her brother's house on the bay. One of the kayak slips was empty, and it looked like someone was out for a morning paddle. Before Leyla could knock, Bailey Rhoads peered through the window and then opened the door.

"Hi there. Wow, what's all this?" she asked as she stepped back and ushered Leyla inside.

"Just a little dinner for you guys. Can I set it in the kitchen?"

"Sure."

Miranda and Joel's excited brown dog jumped around at Leyla's feet.

"Benji, calm down," Bailey said, tugging him away.

"He's fine."

Leyla followed Bailey into the kitchen. Miranda's sister wore a T-shirt and shorts, and with her dark hair up in a ponytail, Leyla could see the family resemblance.

"It's seafood gumbo." Leyla set a paper bag on the counter. "And some baguettes that just came out of the oven."

"Oh my gosh, you *made* all this?"

"Yes, on the gumbo. The bread is from Rogelio, who does a lot of our baking." She unzipped an insulated tote and took out two quart-size travel containers of soup. "These are microwave safe, so you can just pop them in. Or heat it in a pot on the stove, whatever's easiest."

"Gosh, *thank you.* Jacob's going to be thrilled. He absolutely loves gumbo. Benji, *no.*"

The dog was in the living room now with one of the sandals that had been sitting beside the door. Bailey rushed over to rescue it.

"Sorry." She smiled at Leyla. "I think he gets excited for visitors."

Leyla walked over to pet him.

"Can I get you some coffee or anything?" Bailey asked. "We're fresh out of soft drinks."

"I'm good. I just had an espresso back at the shop." She watched Bailey play with the dog. "How's the house sitting going?"

"Great. Jacob's out in the kayak right now. He's been out every day this week. We watched the sunset last night from a cove not far from here."

"Sunset Cove."

"I don't know what it's called. There were lots of boats."

Leyla smiled. "It's a popular spot."

"It was beautiful. I can see why Miranda loves it here."

Leyla noticed the wall of pictures on the far side of the room. "That's new."

Bailey turned around. "You mean the photo wall? Yeah, Joel did that for her. He painted it black and installed the spotlights."

Leyla walked over for a closer look at the framed photographs that made a striking display against the matte black backdrop. There were four rows of four. Some were bird close-ups, others were landscapes, some were fishing boats. Leyla zeroed in on a photograph of a great blue heron silhouetted against a fiery orange sky.

"These are amazing," Leyla said.

"I know."

"I'm surprised she didn't stay with nature photography."

Miranda had originally moved to the island to do nature shots and take a break from photographing crime scenes.

"She can't stay away from CSI work," Bailey said. "I don't know why when it's so gruesome. But that's Miranda. She's really passionate about it."

Bailey's expression grew serious, and Leyla braced herself for what she knew was coming.

"I was so sorry to hear about Amelia Albright," Bailey said.

Leyla nodded.

"What a terrible *shock*."

Leyla's throat felt tight. "Yes. It's really . . ." She shook her head. She still didn't have words for it. Nothing seemed adequate.

"Have the police made any progress?" Bailey asked.

"I don't know. They're not really keeping me in the loop."

Bailey sat on the sofa arm. "I've been reading everything I can get my hands on about it. But the coverage has been light, honestly. I'm surprised."

Bailey was a reporter for a newspaper in Austin. Leyla remembered now hearing how Bailey had broken a big story related to a brutal murder up there. Leyla didn't recall all the details, but she remembered that Bailey's reporting had uncovered the critical fact that the victim had been in the witness protection program. So, like her sister, Bailey was no stranger to the aftermath of violence.

Leyla had a sudden flash of memory: a stark white face in the glare of a flashlight. She had dreamed about that face last night. *Amelia's* face. And Amelia's outstretched hand.

"Leyla?" Bailey leaned forward. "Are you all right?"

"Yes. Sorry." She forced a smile. "I keep . . . tuning out lately."

Bailey watched her. She had to know all about what had happened. Not only had Bailey been following the story in the news, but she'd probably heard details from Miranda.

Leyla turned away and her gaze fell on the coffee table, which was blanketed in Polaroid photos.

"Are those from the wedding?" She stepped over for a closer look. The wedding coordinator had put Polaroid cameras on some of the cocktail tables so guests could snap candids throughout the reception.

"I've been sorting through them for Joel and Miranda. There are some fun shots."

Leyla peered down at the array of pictures, smiling as she recognized friends and cousins, most with drinks in their hands, hamming it up. Her gaze settled on a picture of Joel feeding Miranda a bite of wedding cake. There were dozens of shots of the cake-cutting moment. One showed them beside the cake table as Miranda smiled and held up a champagne glass, and Joel watched her with a look that could only be described as adoring.

"Your brother's a good guy."

Leyla glanced up. "He is. And Miranda's good *for* him. I've never seen him so happy."

Her gaze settled on another photograph. This one was of the cake, too, but what caught Leyla's eye was Sean standing off to the side. He held a drink in his hand and talked to someone whose back was to the camera. Leyla leaned closer. Sean was a striking man, no doubt about it. The dark suit, the straight posture, the confident smile. It was the smile he'd given her less

than an hour later when he'd found her alone on the beach and
tried to charm her into leaving the party with him.

"Take one. Take as many as you want," Bailey said.
"They've got *hundreds*. And that's not even counting the
professional photos."

Leyla picked up the snapshot of Joel and Miranda in
front of the cake she'd made for them. She'd felt so proud in
that moment, and so happy for her brother. He'd had a bad
breakup before he met Miranda, and Leyla had once worried he wouldn't give relationships a chance again.

"Benji. *Ugh.*" Bailey got up as Benji scratched at the
door. "I think he needs his walk now."

"Well, I should get going," Leyla said, tucking the picture into her bag.

"I'll walk you down."

Bailey clipped a leash to Benji's collar as Leyla stepped
out of the house. It was a clear day, and the sun sparkled off
the water in the canal beside the house. Leyla spied a kayaker
in the distance, possibly Bailey's fiancé on his way back.

"Thanks again for the dinner," Bailey said as they
tromped down the stairs.

"Sure thing. Have you talked to the newlyweds?"

"I've been trying to leave them alone. I had to call yesterday. We blew a fuse, and I couldn't find the electrical
panel. Other than that, I haven't wanted to bug them. They
really need this vacation."

"Yep."

"You know, they almost came back early. But the police
chief—what's his name?"

"Chief Brady." Leyla stopped at the base of the stairs and
looked at her.

"He talked them out of it. I think he basically told Joel if
he came back early he could consider himself on permanent
vacation."

"He threatened to *fire* him?"

"I don't know if he was serious, but"—Bailey shrugged—"it worked. They decided to stay."

"Good. There's nothing Joel can do anyway. He and Owen are sidelined because of me."

Bailey lifted an eyebrow. "Well, I'm not sure how *sidelined* they are. Miranda tells me they've been on the phone together quite a bit."

That didn't surprise Leyla at all. Joel was a control freak, and there was no way he and Owen were going to sit out a murder investigation right in their backyard.

"I'm not sure who they've got in charge now, but I hope they make an arrest soon." Bailey slid her feet into sandals. "Everyone can sleep easier."

Leyla didn't think she'd ever get a normal night's sleep again.

"Do you know who it is?" Bailey asked.

"Who, the detective in charge?"

Bailey nodded.

"Nicole Lawson. You probably saw her at the wedding. She's smart. And she has a good team working with her."

"You think they'll get it solved? The department's so small here, I'm a little worried about whether they're up to the task," Bailey said.

"They're up to it."

"You sound confident."

"I am. We're small, but we're also a tight community." Leyla looked out over the water. "That makes this personal."

NICOLE SHUT DOWN her computer and grabbed her car keys.

"Heading out?"

She glanced up to see McDeere striding through the bullpen.

"About to."

He stopped and leaned an arm on the top of her cubicle. McDeere wore street clothes today because he was technically off duty. But he was here anyway. The chief had given him an opportunity to help with the Albright case, and he seemed eager to prove himself.

"How'd it go at Playa del Rey today?" he asked.

"Not great. I asked around, but no one recognized her photo, so she's probably not a regular."

"You thought she would be?"

"I don't know. Maybe if she was moonlighting as an escort or something."

Following up on the matchbook lead had been a long shot. But Nicole had spent time on it anyway because she still hadn't figured out why the feds were nosing around her homicide case. The only thing that made sense was that they had some reason to believe the victim might be involved in something linked to organized crime—something like maybe sex work or drugs.

"How's it coming with the phone records?" she asked. Emmet had enlisted his help combing through them.

"Still coming. Nothing interesting yet, but I've still got some more records to go through."

"Don't stay too late. There's always tomorrow."

"I know. You're covering the funeral, right? Isn't it in the afternoon?"

She nodded. "I need to see the family. I already did a video interview, but I want to meet them in person." She also wanted to see who showed up for the service.

"Good luck," he said, looking relieved to skip that particular detective responsibility.

"Thanks."

Nicole crossed the bullpen, thinking about how much she was dreading the service. It was a two-hour drive to Port O'Connor—which would crush her afternoon—and she'd have to dress up. But worse, she'd have to talk to the victim's parents, and she didn't have any big developments to share. It had been four days since their daughter was viciously murdered, and Nicole's team didn't even have a person of interest yet.

Frustration welled inside her as she passed through the empty waiting room. She pushed through the front door and stepped into the warm evening air.

"Detective Lawson?"

She turned around, instantly wary.

A man approached her from the parking lot. Dark hair, dark eyes, medium build.

"You're Detective Lawson, right?"

"Who's asking?" she said, although she had an idea, based on the lanyard around his neck that looked like a press pass.

"Miguel Vidales with the *San Antonio Tribune.*"

"I have no comment."

He smiled slightly as he stopped in front of her. "I haven't asked for one."

"Well, don't bother. All press inquiries need to go through our public information officer."

They didn't actually have a public information officer. The closest thing was Denise, their receptionist, who screened calls and passed everything on to Brady to handle.

"You're the lead detective on the Amelia Albright case, correct?"

"Did you hear what I said? You need to direct your questions to our PIO."

He sighed and looked her over. "I'm not here to ask questions."

"Why are you here, then?"

He glanced around. "Is there somewhere we can talk?"

"Not really."

"Could you just give me a minute? I drove all the way down here to speak with you."

She looked him over, annoyed. But also curious. How did he know she was the lead on this case? She hadn't been quoted in any articles on this thing. At least, she didn't think she had. She hadn't intentionally talked to any reporters.

He tucked his hands into his front pockets. He wore jeans and an army green jacket with worn black sneakers, and he looked way more casual than the TV reporters who'd been down here covering the story. Of course, most of them had already left town, and she didn't expect to see them back again unless something dramatic happened, such as an arrest. Barring some huge break in the case, Nicole wasn't anticipating that anytime soon.

"Five minutes." He rocked forward on the balls of his feet. "That's all I need."

A uniformed officer stepped through the door and cast a glance at her before heading to the parking lot. The last thing she needed was to be seen giving an interview to a reporter in front of the police station.

"Five minutes." She checked her watch and then nodded toward the corner of the building. "This way." She led him around to a side courtyard where there was a picnic table illuminated by a floodlight. She leaned against the table and checked her watch again, just to make the point that she was timing him.

He glanced around. "Mind if I smoke?"

She shrugged. "It's your lungs."

He reached into his jacket for a pack of Marlboros and tapped out a cigarette. He lit it with a cheap lighter and watched her as he blew out a stream of smoke.

"I take it this is your first homicide case to lead?" he asked.

In response, she glanced at her watch.

"I haven't seen your name in the news," he added.

"Yeah, well. I try to avoid reporters."

The side of his mouth quirked up.

"I'm surprised your paper sent you all the way down here," she said, happy to burn up his time with small talk. "What is that, a three-hour drive?"

"Three and a half." He flicked ash on the pavement.

"Long drive when you could have called."

He took another drag. "So, how's the case going?"

"It's going." She checked her watch again. "I'm curious why you're covering it. A city that size, don't you guys have enough crime of your own to cover?"

"I'm not really covering it."

"No?"

"Not yet, anyway." He took another drag.

"Then why are you here?"

He blew out a stream of smoke. "You heard of Jose Rincon?"

"No."

"Sandra Massey?"

"No."

"Both lived in San Antonio."

"Lived?"

"They were murdered—six weeks apart—last fall."

She watched him.

"Both cases are still open. The police haven't announced any suspects, but I happen to know that they've been zeroing in on a few leads."

"Good for them. Why are you telling me this?"

"Thought you might want to call SAPD. Maybe compare notes. Both victims were stabbed."

She watched him, growing more irritated by the minute. "Well, I hate to tell you this, but fatal stabbings aren't exactly unheard of. Especially in a city as large as yours."

He nodded. "Both victims were left in an alley, too. And both had their hands bound."

She tensed.

"Blue cordage." He tossed his cigarette down and gave her a sharp look. "Sound familiar?"

Nicole didn't move, didn't even blink.

"I can see from your expression that that's a yes."

Her throat tightened, but she didn't respond.

"It's okay. I don't need you to confirm or deny anything," he said.

"Where are you getting your information?"

"Does it matter as long as it's true?"

She didn't have a reply to that, so she looked away. It had to be someone in the medical examiner's office. That's where Sean Moran had gotten his info, so why not this reporter, too? They needed to patch up their leaks over there.

"Look, I'm still not clear on what exactly you want," she said to him.

"Isn't it obvious? I want to help you. I just gave you a major lead."

"Why?" she asked, then immediately regretted the question. She didn't want him to think she was confirming or denying any of the details he'd shared with her. She didn't want her name, or sensitive info about her case, turning up in some news article. And the blue cordage detail certainly qualified as sensitive. Aside from investigators, only someone involved in the murder should know about that. Nicole herself hadn't even known until she'd read the preliminary autopsy report, which mentioned tiny blue splinters in the abrasions on the victim's wrists.

She looked Miguel Vidales over, taking in the longish hair, the scruffy clothes. He definitely had the casual attire of a print reporter, versus a television personality. But that didn't put her at ease. In Nicole's experience, print journalists tended to dig deeper and be more tenacious. The TV ones often just wanted some dramatic video footage and a pithy sound bite, and then they moved on to the next story.

He still hadn't answered her question about why he'd come here to tip her off.

"Didn't you just tell me you're not covering the Amelia Albright case?" Nicole asked.

He nodded. "Like I said, not yet. If it turns out to be related to what I'm working on, that could change."

"And what is it you're working on, exactly? You never specified. Are you on the crime beat or—"

"Bigger than that. I'm on a team investigation. We're working on a series about the Saledo family."

She drew back. The Saledos had their hands in everything from drugs and prostitution to gun running. Like several other organizations south of the border, they'd been making inroads here lately as the population grew. Nicole had heard talk that the Saledos were buying off border agents here and there as they expanded their reach.

A ball of dread filled her stomach. The last thing she wanted was a newspaper running a string of stories about organized crime taking root in her idyllic little beach town.

She cleared her throat. "Why did you drive all the way down here to tell me this?"

"I wanted to talk face-to-face."

"Why else? You don't expect me to believe you came all this way just to help me out, do you? I mean, you obviously want something in return."

He nodded. "You're right, I do."

"I already told you I can't—"

"I don't need a comment right now."

She watched him warily.

"If and when your department makes an arrest—"

"We will."

"—I'd like a heads-up before it's announced. That's it."

"That's it?"

"Yep. That's all I'm asking for."

She highly doubted that.

"You have your phone on you?" he asked. "I'll give you my number."

"Why don't you give me your business card?"

"I don't use business cards."

She waited a beat and then pulled out her phone. He rattled off a number with a San Antonio area code.

"Just so we're clear, I'm not making any promises here," she said. "I'm not agreeing to give you some scoop on a story just because you show up and drop a supposed 'tip' in my lap. How do I even know it's legit?"

"It is," he said, watching her enter his number. "Text me later and I'll send you a link to an encryption site. We'll get you set up so you can message me when you have something."

"Encryption? Is that really necessary? Why don't I just call you?"

"Don't."

The sharpness of his tone startled her.

"This way is better. Trust me."

She slipped her phone back into her pocket, studying his face carefully. The grim set of his jaw told her he meant it about the encryption thing. And for the first time since they'd started this conversation, she was starting to believe he really was a serious investigative reporter.

He took out his phone and checked it. "Well, my five minutes are up. Thanks for your time, Detective."

"Don't thank me yet. I didn't make any promises, remember? You may have wasted your trip."

He tucked his phone away. "I didn't."

LEYLA STARED UP at the building and wondered which window was Sean's.

She shouldn't be here. She knew that. She'd been gone all day, first at the funeral and then at the Windjammer store placing a food order and working on the schedule. What she needed to do was go home and wash the day off and then sit down and catch up on the emails she'd been avoiding all week.

But she didn't want to do any of that. After leaving the coffee shop, her car had steered itself here, as though it had a mind of its own.

Leyla glanced down at the phone in her hand.

"Screw it," she muttered.

She scrolled through her text messages until she found the one he'd sent the other night. She started to write back but then stopped herself. Her stomach knotted as she tried to think of what to say.

Thump thump.

She jumped, startled, and turned to see a man beside her car.

Sean.

Her stomach did a little somersault as she buzzed the window down.

"Hey," she said, looking him over. He wore jeans and a T-shirt and had his hands full of plastic grocery bags.

"Hi. What's up?" he asked, probably wondering why she was sitting in the parking lot staring at his building.

"I was looking for you." She swallowed. "I thought I'd see if you wanted to have a drink."

He leaned closer and gazed down at her curiously. She was still in her funeral clothes—a black skirt, blouse, and heels. "What, you mean right now?"

"Sure. Or later. Whenever. Or if you haven't already eaten yet, we could get dinner." Now she sounded desperate. "I was just on my way home so—"

"Let me drop these off. You mind?"

"Not at all."

He shifted the bags to one hand and opened her door. "Come on up."

She hesitated for a moment, then raised the window and turned off her car. She swung her legs out, careful to keep her knees together, and he watched as she stood up and then reached in to grab her purse.

She stepped back, and he closed the door.

"Thanks," she said, locking the car with a *chirp.*

"I was just stocking up on some things."

She eyed the plastic bags in his hands as she followed him to the sidewalk. He'd been to Marcel's Grocery on the corner, where tourists got gouged for beer, sunblock, and microwaveable burritos.

He reached the door to his condominium and pulled a key card from his pocket. The door buzzed, and he held it open for her. She stepped into the air-conditioned lobby, where a seventies-era tile mural of dolphins decorated the wall.

"You been here before?" he asked, leading her to the elevator bank.

"Not since prom night."

He laughed. "I won't ask."

"It was nothing too crazy," she said, stepping onto the elevator. "Some of my friends rented a place for the weekend. What floor?"

"Four."

She tapped the button, and the door whisked shut. "We basically drank and played poker."

"Uh-huh."

It had been slightly more eventful, but nothing compared to the kind of wild partying her brothers were known for.

The door dinged open, and she stepped out first.

"To your left," he said.

She walked left, and he stopped in front of room 404 and used the key card again. When she'd gotten up this morning, the last place she'd expected to end up was Sean's rental condo. Butterflies filled her stomach as she followed him inside.

The place was small and generic-looking, with oversize leather sofas and seashell-themed décor. A bar separated the living room from the kitchen, and a laptop sat open on the counter beside some paperwork and an empty plate. He deposited the grocery bags on the counter.

"So, you were at the funeral today, I take it?" He closed the laptop and started unloading drinks into the fridge.

"It was this afternoon." She stepped over to the sliding glass door that opened onto a balcony with a surfboard propped against the wall. "Nice view," she said, peering out at the beach. The sun had just set, and the waves were a dusky lavender.

"Beats my view back home."

She turned to look at him. He was still unloading, and she moved back into the kitchen. "Need a hand?"

"I've got it."

His phone buzzed, and he pulled it from his pocket to check the screen. His brow furrowed.

"I need to take this. You mind?"

"Go ahead."

"Want some water or anything?"

"I'm fine."

He eased past her and opened the sliding door, confirming her suspicion that the call was probably work-related.

Unless it was a girlfriend. But he'd told her he was single, and she believed him.

He slid the door shut and leaned on the railing as he took the call.

She unloaded the last of the groceries. He'd bought a meat-lover's pizza, which she stashed in the freezer beside a selection of burritos. Then she added a six-pack of Gatorade to the fridge, which was empty except for some beer and a few packets of ketchup. Sighing, she turned around.

The laptop caught her eye. He'd been very smooth about closing it when he walked in here. She glanced at the balcony, where he stood facing the beach with his phone pressed to his ear. A pile of papers peeked out from beneath the computer, and Leyla stepped closer. The top page was a printed news article from the *Seattle Times*.

TECH MOGUL ACQUIRES RIDESHARE APP, read the headline.

Leyla nudged the laptop aside and skimmed the first few paragraphs. She glanced at the balcony and gathered up the empty grocery bags as he opened the door and came back in.

"Sorry. Work." He darted a look at his computer.

"You keep these?" she asked, holding up a bundle of bags.

"Drawer by the sink."

She stashed the bags and checked her watch. "So, what sounds good? Did you eat dinner yet?"

"Yeah. You?"

"Yeah." If a zucchini muffin could be considered dinner.

"How about a drink?" he asked. "There are plenty of places on the beach I haven't tried."

"Sure."

He grabbed his keys off the counter. No leather jacket tonight to conceal a holster, but she noticed the bulge above his boot, which told her he was armed. She wouldn't have expected otherwise.

They rode the elevator down in silence, and she could feel his gaze on her. He smelled good again—some kind of bodywash or aftershave. But he had a day's worth of stubble along his jaw, so he hadn't shaved recently. Maybe he'd showered after a run.

The door dinged open, and they stepped out. He held the elevator as a woman with two little boys in swimsuits got on, dragging a turtle-shaped float behind them.

"This way," Sean said, leading her to the lobby door that faced the beach. The passed a smallish pool surrounded by faded lounge chairs and rusted umbrella tables. Leyla still didn't know what precisely Sean's job was, but the government clearly wasn't splurging on his accommodations.

He opened the metal gate that led to the wooden bridge over the dunes. She looked out at the beach, where night was falling and people strolled along the shoreline.

A gust whipped up, and Leyla twisted her hair into a knot at the top of her head as they crossed the bridge.

She looked at him. "Did you run today?"

"This afternoon. You?"

"No."

As usual, exercise was the first thing to fall off her list when things got hectic. They reached the beach, and she paused on the stairs to take off her heels. She tucked them into her purse and stepped onto the cool sand.

"Where to?" he asked, looking north, toward the high-rise hotels. "There's Buck's Beach Club."

She made a face.

"Okay, how about the sports bar? O'Toole's?"

O'Toole's was better than Buck's, but there was a chance she'd run into Owen there.

"How about the Hut?" she said. "It's a dive, but you can hear yourself talk."

"Sounds good."

She nodded in the opposite direction. "It's just past the next bridge there."

"Guess we could have taken the street."

"This is better," she said, looking out at the water. She liked the wind against her cheeks, and the sand felt good between her toes as they walked.

Like the Island Beanery, the Hut had a wooden deck that looked out over the dunes. Unlike the Beanery, it had a liquor license. A small bar sat beneath a brown thatched roof. The place was busy as always, but she spied an empty table.

"Do they have table service?" Sean asked as they stepped onto the deck.

"Nope."

"Why don't you snag that free table and I'll get the drinks?"

Leyla didn't want him paying again.

"Why don't *you* snag the table and I'll get the drinks?"

The side of his mouth ticked up. "Because I don't know what I want yet."

She gazed up at him. He seemed amused that she'd stepped right into this trap.

"All right." She reached for her wallet. "I'd like a mojito, please. Dark rum."

"Got it."

He headed for the bar before she could offer him money. Sighing, she turned and wended her way through the crowd to claim the empty table before someone could pounce. It was the best spot out here, with an L-shaped bench tucked into the corner of the deck overlooking the beach. The table consisted of a wooden whiskey barrel.

Nerves fluttered inside her as she sat down and looked across the dunes. Clumps of tourists congregated on the sand and couples walked hand in hand along the water's edge. It was a clear night, and stars were already appearing in the purple sky.

What was she doing here?

She and Sean had butted heads and then patched things up, and she could have left everything right there, with his apology as the defining moment of their brief relationship.

But now she'd invited him out for drinks, essentially hitting reset. She was giving him the do-over he wanted, and she had no idea why. She didn't date tourists. It was her rule. He wasn't a tourist, but he was still a transient. He lived on the *East Coast*, for God's sake, and she had no idea why she would want to get involved in anything when he would obviously be leaving town soon. She didn't. She needed to keep this to drinks, full stop, and then get back to the work she had waiting for her at home.

Sean appeared at the table with a highball glass and a bottle of Corona.

"Dirty mojito," he said, setting the glass in front of her.

"Thank you."

He sat down and watched as she picked up her drink.

"She used Bacardí Black," he said, poking his lime into the bottle.

"That's perfect." She took a cold sip. It was tart and minty.

He sipped his beer and set it beside her glass. "This place is popular," he said, looking around.

"The locals like it. It's not as trendy as the other places on the beach. You been to any yet?"

He smiled. "No." He raked his hand through his hair. "I've been a little sidetracked."

With work, he meant. Again, she wondered what sort of investigation had brought him all the way down here from Washington. His unwillingness to talk about it had only piqued her curiosity.

She looked out at the beach.

"How did it go today?" he asked.

She took another sip, thinking of how to describe it. "Basically, it was horrible. The church was packed. I've never been to a funeral with so many young people."

He watched her, his brow furrowed with concern. "Did you meet Amelia's parents?"

"Briefly. They were inundated with people."

Amelia's mom had had a dazed, glassy look, and her husband and son had had to practically hold her up as they walked her down the aisle.

The sour ball of guilt that had been in Leyla's stomach for days was back now. She gazed at the water.

"Leyla?"

She looked at him.

"Don't do that."

"What?"

"Look guilty, like somehow this was your fault. Or there was something you could have done."

"Of course there was something I could have done. It was *my* place where she was attacked. I should have had better lighting, or security cameras, or—"

"And it could have happened anyway." He leaned closer. "You didn't cause this. Someone else did."

She folded her arms over her stomach and looked away. She disagreed wholeheartedly. But there was no point in arguing.

"Did any of your employees go?" he asked.

She nodded. "Four of them. They drove together." She stirred her drink with the bamboo swizzle stick. "Siena read a scripture during the service."

"Siena?"

"My assistant manager. You probably saw her at the wedding. She helps me with the catering business."

"The tall one."

She nodded. "And Amelia's best friend from high school read a poem. Then her twin brother gave a eulogy."

"She had a twin?"

"Yes. He was very poised. I don't know how he got through it." She shook her head. "They were really close, evidently."

Watching Amelia's brother had been the hardest part. The man was clearly devasted, but he got up anyway in front of all those people and talked about his sister.

"Did you see a boyfriend there?" Sean asked.

She looked at him, studying his bland expression. It was the second time he'd asked about a boyfriend.

"I don't think she had one," she said.

"No?"

"Not that I've heard about. Why?"

"Just curious."

She watched his eyes, somehow certain there was more to the question than simple curiosity. But he clearly didn't want to go into it with her.

She stirred her drink and looked away. "So, how was *your* day? You get any work done?"

"Some."

"I noticed the article on your counter about Luc Gagnon, the tech mogul."

His guard went up, and she could tell he didn't like this topic either.

"You know he has a house down here?" she asked.

"I'd heard that, yeah."

"He paid three-point-eight million and then gutted the whole thing. I hear he put in a rooftop deck with a pool. And a sauna. And he added a movie theater."

"Sounds expensive." Sean sipped his beer.

"Some people have way too much money."

She watched him, wondering if he'd expand on the topic of Luc Gagnon, but he didn't—which confirmed her suspicion that the man was somehow mixed in with whatever Sean was doing down here. Now she was even more intrigued than before.

"So, you heard from the newlyweds?" Sean asked, changing the subject.

"I talked to them briefly. Why?"

"Just wondering if they're liking Costa Rica."

"They've been doing some diving, which is good. Joel hasn't been on a vacation since—" She squinted. "Come to think of it, I can't even remember the last time it was. It's good for them to get away."

Sean nodded. "He's a workaholic."

"Yep."

Maybe Sean knew her brother better than she thought.

"Are you guys close?" he asked.

She shrugged. "We were close growing up. Not so much lately."

"How come?"

She sipped her mojito, debating how much to tell him. "Ever since my dad died, I don't know. My brothers and I have kind of drifted in different directions. I mean, I still *see* them and everything. Everyone but Alex lives here on the island, so there's no avoiding it. But . . . I guess we're all wrapped up in our own things."

He watched her, appearing interested in her family dynamics. Whether he really was or not, she couldn't tell.

"Anyway, Joel's with Miranda now. Owen's with Macey. Alex . . . Well, who knows about Alex? I'm sure he's got a string of girlfriends." She shrugged. "We don't spend that much time together anymore."

"And your mom?"

"She rounds everyone up for family stuff from time to time. You know, birthdays and holidays, things like that. But even then, cops don't exactly work regular hours, so work tends to get in the way. I'm sure you know how that goes."

He nodded. "I do."

Leyla picked the mint leaf from her drink and put it into her mouth. "You said you have a sister in Austin. What does she do?"

"She runs a software startup."

"Oh yeah? Good for her."

"Fifteen employees. She basically works twenty-four seven." He leaned back. "She reminds me of you, actually. She's pretty intense."

"*I'm* intense?" She laughed. "I think you mean Joel. And Alex. They're the intense ones in the family."

"What about Owen?"

"He's a little mixed." She took a sip of her drink.

"Mixed?"

"He *pretends* to be chill about everything, but really he's a workaholic, too."

He nodded. "You're lucky."

"I'd have to agree. But why do you say that?"

"You have family around."

And Sean didn't. He lived several thousand miles away from his family.

"So, what do you do for fun when you're not working?" he asked.

"Me?"

He smiled. "Yeah, you. Do you ever get a day off?"

"I try to take Mondays." Which only worked out about half the time. "And occasionally, I'll get Siena to cover for a weekend if I need to leave town. But, you know, it's hard to get away. That's one of the things about running a small business."

He looked interested. "Do you like it?"

"Yeah, actually. Even with the crazy hours, I like it a lot."

"How come?"

"I don't know. The autonomy. The creativity. Being my own boss."

"That cuts both ways, though, doesn't it?" he asked. "It's a lot of responsibility."

"I don't mind." She leaned closer. "Honestly, I'm not great at having a boss."

"You don't like people telling you what to do."

"Basically."

He smiled, and she felt warmth blooming deep inside her. His eyes creased at the corners, and it suddenly hit her that he was older than she was—Joel's age. He had life experience and maturity, and she found that appealing.

"How do you like *your* job?" she asked.

He arched his eyebrows, looking surprised she would ask. "It's good."

"Hmm. Very descriptive."

"It's challenging. I like that. And there's a lot of variation, so I don't get bored."

Challenging had to be an understatement. She'd been doing a little poking around, and she'd learned that just getting into the FBI Academy to begin with was an impressive accomplishment. And then the program was a rigorous combination of academic and physical requirements. Plus, there were the mental demands of a career in law enforcement—which she'd seen firsthand through her brothers.

But despite all that, she got the feeling Sean excelled at his job. He seemed very capable.

"What's that look?" he asked.

"Nothing."

"What?"

She shrugged. "It's just an interesting career path, that's all. I'm glad you like it. It took me years to figure out what I wanted to do."

"Oh yeah?"

"I bounced around awhile before landing at culinary school. I think my parents thought I was crazy, but it turned out to be a fit."

"Why'd they think you were crazy?"

"Probably because I could barely make a sandwich growing up." She smiled. "I was kind of a tomboy, always trying to keep up with my brothers. I didn't take much interest in whatever my mother and grandmother were doing in the kitchen."

"So, how'd you get interested in being a chef?"

"Long story."

He arched his eyebrows.

She sighed. "I started seeing this guy who ran a restaurant.

He began teaching me to cook—just some knife skills, basic sauces, stuff like that. It all came very naturally to me so"—she shrugged—"that's it. Here I am."

"That's not really a long story. What happened with the guy?"

She grimaced. "It ended. Badly. But, hey, I learned a lot."

He picked up his beer, watching her, and she felt suddenly self-conscious that she was sitting here talking about Derrick, a man who'd cheated on her and jerked her around and turned her off relationships for years. And did he even want to hear about this? Most guys wanted to talk about themselves all the time.

She glanced down and noticed her glass was down to ice cubes and mint leaves. And he'd finished his beer.

"Want another drink?" he asked.

"I should get home." She checked her watch. "I have to be up early."

He held her gaze for a long moment but didn't say anything.

She stood and collected her purse. They had barely stepped away from the table when a couple swooped in to get it.

Sean walked beside her at a leisurely pace as they crossed the bridge spanning the dunes again. Going back on the street would have been faster, but not nearly as scenic. And she got the sense he wasn't in a hurry to end their evening.

The sand felt cool and cushiony beneath her feet as they headed toward his condo. She glanced up and counted the windows to find his balcony.

"Is that your board, or did it come with the unit?" she asked.

He looked up. "The surfboard? It's the owner's. Or someone left it there. It's not mine."

"Do you surf?"

"No. You?"

"I go when I can." Which was hardly ever anymore. "Have you been snowboarding?"

"No."

"Ever skateboard?" she asked.

"Not since I was a kid."

"Well, you could probably pick it up pretty fast anyway since you're athletic."

He cast a sidelong look at her at the vague compliment.

They strolled in silence, and she looked out at the water, where the waves were silver and shimmery under the moonlight. Several wade fishermen stood in the surf. The tide was changing, and it was a good time for fishing. Not that Sean cared. He hadn't come here for vacation. That had been a lie, like the thing about working vice with Joel in Houston. He'd lied to her, and that should have been it. No second chances. Yet he'd somehow charmed his way back into her good graces, and she was actually having a nice time. Sean was attractive and easy to talk to, and when he looked at her with those eyes, she felt a deep, warm buzz that she hadn't felt in ages.

"So, what time does a pastry chef have to get up?" he asked.

"Three."

"Three?"

"But I don't make the pastries. Or at least, not all of them. That's Rogelio. I get up at four and try to get to the shop by four thirty."

"Damn."

They reached the bridge leading to his condo and crossed back over the dunes. She stopped beside the gate.

"One sec." She dropped her shoes to the ground and rested her hand on his arm as she slid her feet back into her shoes. When she looked up again, he was still taller, but she was closer to eye level.

His gaze dropped to her lips, and anticipation rippled through her as he leaned down to kiss her.

His mouth was warm, and his hands slid around her waist as he pulled her against him. She went up on tiptoes, her heels coming out of her shoes as she reached up to glide her hands over his shoulders. His tongue tangled with hers and heat flooded through every part of her body. She pressed her breasts against him and combed her fingers into his hair as she pulled his head closer.

Damn, the man could *kiss*. And she should have known it. All that life experience coming through again. Everything about him seemed so capable, as though he'd taken the time to learn how to do things well.

She slid her fingertips over his jaw, feeling that rough stubble as his mouth explored hers. He knew what he was doing, setting off little tremors inside her with every stroke of his tongue. His palms slid over her butt, pulling her against him, and she rocked her hips.

"Leyla." He trailed kisses along her throat, and she tipped her head back to let him. "Come upstairs."

She kissed his mouth again. She didn't want to talk just now. She wanted to feel his body pressed against hers and his hot, avid mouth as he kissed her deeply. He tilted her head to the side to get a better angle, and the kiss went on and on, getting more and more insistent. She nipped his bottom lip, and he made a low groan and pulled her in tighter, surrounding her with his heat.

He stepped back. "Come upstairs."

Her heart clenched as she gazed up at him. She gave a tiny shake of her head.

She eased back, stumbling as she tried to get her foot back into her shoe, and he caught her arm to steady her.

"Sorry." She pulled back and smoothed her blouse. "I shouldn't have done that."

He just looked at her, a combination of lust and confusion in his eyes, and she felt a twinge of regret.

"Sorry," she repeated, stepping away.

He released her, gazing down at her as if to see what she would do next. She glanced around.

"Here, let's . . ." She motioned toward the gate.

He took out his key card and opened the gate. Silently, they walked past the pool to the narrow sidewalk along the side of the building.

"I think I can cut through here," she said.

He rested his hand lightly at her waist as he walked her down the shadowy path to the parking lot. He glanced around with those cop eyes, taking in their surroundings as he walked her to her car.

Emotions warred inside her. She wanted to go upstairs with him. And yet she didn't. And she shouldn't have kissed him like that if she didn't know what she wanted. Although, she *did* know what she wanted—she just wasn't going to let herself have it. She had more self-control than that.

She dug her keys from her purse and clicked her locks open.

"Thank you for the drink," she said.

He looked down at her, his gaze still heated. He rested his hand on her shoulder, and she thought he might kiss her again. And she wasn't sure if she could resist another onslaught. But instead he dropped a soft peck on her forehead.

"Text me when you get home." He pulled the door open for her.

She slid behind the wheel and looked at him. "Why? I'll be fine."

"Humor me."

CHAPTER

NINE

NICOLE STEPPED INTO Amelia's closet and flipped on the light switch. Scanning the racks, she immediately spotted the dress she was looking for. She reached for the hanger and held the dress up to the light, running her gloved hand over the rose gold sequins. The dress had a halter neckline and a plunging back. Nicole checked the tag. Size four. It smelled faintly of perfume, and the smudge of makeup on the neckline suggested the dress had been worn.

Nicole hung the hanger from a hook on the wall. She reached for a shoebox on the top shelf but couldn't get it. She spied a plastic stool on the floor and moved it into place, then climbed up and tried again.

"Find something?

She whirled around, nearly losing her balance.

"Damn it! Don't sneak up on me."

Emmet stepped into the closet. "I didn't sneak. What are you doing in here? I thought you guys came over to check out the storage locker."

"McDeere's going through it now."

After learning that the tenants in Amelia's apartment building each had access to a locker on the premises for surfboards, bikes, and other equipment, they had come by this morning to make sure they hadn't overlooked any clues among the victim's possessions.

Nicole reached for the top shelf again, but still the box she wanted was too high. She stepped down.

"Here, get up there and grab that pink shoebox, would you?"

He reached over her head and handed it down.

"What are you looking for?" he asked.

"I'm not sure."

She took the lid off the box and lifted out a pair of rose gold stilettos. She held them up to the dress. They were a perfect match.

"What do you think of this outfit?" she asked.

"Looks expensive."

"It does, doesn't it?"

He leaned against the doorjamb. "So, did you hear back from that detective in San Antonio?"

"Not yet." Nicole poked through the shoebox, hoping to find a receipt. "I left him a message."

She'd left two messages, actually, but so far the detective handling the two homicide cases Miguel Vidales had told her about had yet to return her calls. In the meantime, she was pursuing every other lead they had come up with.

"Where on the island can you even *wear* an outfit like this?" Nicole asked. "Everything's casual."

"Maybe a wedding? Or a private party?"

"These are Stuart Weitzman." She held up the sandals.

"Who?"

"A designer. These probably cost five hundred dollars. A little pricey for a barista attending community college, don't you think?"

He nodded.

"Same for Playa del Rey."

"Just because she has a matchbook from somewhere doesn't mean she stayed there," Emmet said. "Or even had dinner there. She could have just met someone for a drink."

"I'm beginning to think she was supplementing her income somehow. Maybe selling drugs or working as an escort or something."

Nicole checked the soles of the shoes. They were scuffed, indicating they'd been worn out at least once.

"Or maybe she had a rich boyfriend," Emmet said.

She glanced up. "I thought you didn't like my boyfriend theory?"

"I didn't at first. But there could be more to it."

"Oh yeah? What?"

He leaned against the doorframe again, blocking the opening with his wide shoulders. He was standing close enough for her to smell his cinnamon gum. She looked at his mouth, then turned away.

"I've been working on that phone number we haven't been able to identify," he said. "The one that was in her phone records and also written on that matchbook? I think it was a no-contract phone."

She replaced the shoes in the box. "So, someone was calling her on a burner."

"Looks like. A total of eight calls, starting with the night of Saturday, February sixteenth of this year."

"Maybe it's a drug connection," she said. "Or a pimp. Who else would need a burner?"

"Someone who's married? Maybe he's got a phone his wife doesn't know about?"

"Hmm."

"Also, most of the calls were at night on a Friday or a Saturday, some of them late."

"So, booty calls."

"Could be."

"Interesting."

"I think we should interview some of her girlfriends, see if we can get more details about her social life," Emmet said.

"I already interviewed them."

"Let me take a crack at it."

She bristled. "You're saying I missed something?"

"Don't get defensive. It never hurts to talk to people a second time."

She looked at him without responding. She knew he was right. She also knew that he had a knack for getting female witnesses to open up. It was a certain brand of easygoing charm that—when combined with his surfer-boy good looks—some women found irresistible.

Emmet's talent with witnesses was an asset she shouldn't ignore. Still, it was going to really irk her if he managed to get something she hadn't.

But whatever. At this point, she needed all the help she could get, especially with Owen barred from helping with the investigation.

"Fine," she said. "Talk to them again. See what you find out."

He nodded. "I'll make the rounds this afternoon."

She replaced the top on the box and slid a look at him. This was the longest conversation they'd had in days, and she felt like things were almost normal again.

"So . . . are you still pissed at me?" she asked.

"Who said I was pissed at you?"

"You've had a chip on your shoulder ever since Brady made me lead on this."

"I haven't had a chip on my shoulder."

She rolled her eyes.

"Okay, maybe I have. But it's not about you," he said.

"Then what is it about?"

"Well, maybe it is about you, but I'm not pissed at you. I'm pissed at Brady."

"Why?"

"Because. I've been busting my ass in this job three years longer than you have, and with Owen and Joel sidelined this should have been my case to lead. I earned it."

"Well, don't take your frustration out on *me*. I didn't tell him who to put in charge of this thing."

"Sorry." He frowned. "I didn't mean to take it out on you."

"I don't need it. I've got enough crap to deal with."

"I said *I'm sorry*. I know I've been a dick."

"You have."

He sighed. "Don't you even know how to accept an apology?"

She just looked at him. She'd never been particularly good at letting go of things.

She cleared her throat. "Thank you for apologizing for being a dick."

He shook his head and walked away.

L EYLA SHIELDED HER eyes from the sun as she watched the man atop the ladder.

"Can you go a touch *higher*?" she called out. "I want to make sure we cover the entire parking lot."

"It's covered," he said.

"Are you sure?"

"I'm sure."

Siena stepped through the back door of the coffee shop. "There you are. I couldn't figure out where you'd gone." She glanced at the workman on the ladder and did a double take. The guy was tall and muscular and had a leather tool belt slung around his waist.

"Oh my *Lord*," Siena murmured as she sidled up beside Leyla. "Why didn't you come get me?"

"For what?"

Siena gave her a *get real* look.

Leyla smiled. "I thought you were in a relationship?"

"Oh, please. And speaking of hotties, your brother just showed up."

As if on cue, Owen stepped outside. He glanced at the ladder as he walked over to join them. "What's all this?"

"Our new security system," Leyla said.

He stopped beside her and rested his hands on his hips. He wore his typical Lost Beach PD golf shirt, brown tactical pants, and all-terrain boots, which told her he was on duty right now.

"I'll go help Rachel," Siena said. "See you around, Owen."

"Later."

"I'll be in in a sec," Leyla said as Siena walked away.

Owen watched as the workman used a drill to install a metal bracket.

"I didn't know you were doing this now," Owen said.

"Yeah, you did. I told you about it Tuesday."

"I thought you were still taking bids. I didn't know you'd decided already."

"I wanted to get it done," Leyla said. "This system includes cameras at both doors, and one inside that covers the register. And it's synced to my phone, so if anything comes up, I get an alert."

"You went with the expensive option."

"Yep." She looked at Owen. She couldn't see his eyes well behind his sunglasses, but she sensed something was on his mind. "So, what brings you here?"

"I stopped by to say hi." He turned to her. "I wanted to see how you were doing."

The tone of his voice put her on guard.

"You're just in time," she said. "I need a hand with the dairy delivery." She strode over to the sidewalk beside the door, where a delivery truck had just unloaded a trio of milk crates. She grabbed the top one. "Can you get the other two?"

"Sure."

Owen stacked the two remaining crates, and Leyla propped hers on her hip as she opened the door and held it for him.

She followed him down the hall to the kitchen, which smelled like rosemary. All the staffers were out front, and a tray of fresh focaccia bread sat on the work island.

"Put it over there by the reach-in," she told him.

Leyla set her crate on the island and started unloading jugs of milk into the fridge.

"So. How are you doing?" Owen asked, handing her a jug.

"Fine. Busy." She arranged the containers by fat content. "We suddenly got slammed with calls, and now I've got two events lined up next week, plus six new cake orders."

She turned, and Owen was watching her, his brow furrowed. "I meant how are *you*?"

She grabbed a carton of half-and-half. "I need to take this out front. One sec."

She strode to the front, where the tables were packed with lunch customers. Siena was on the register, and Wade and Rachel were busy at the espresso machine. Rachel's cheeks were flushed, and she had a line of shot glasses in front of her.

"Oh, good," she said when Leyla set the carton on the counter. "I need to fill the carafes."

"Thanks. Hey, do we have any jalapeño-cheese croissants left?"

"They're eighty-sixed." Rachel glanced over her shoulder. "We still have some ham-and-cheese, I think."

Leyla scooted past her to the pastry case. She grabbed some tongs and plucked the second-to-last ham-and-cheese croissant off the tray and dropped it into a pastry bag.

She returned to the kitchen, where Owen was looking at his phone.

"We're out of jalapeño," she said, handing him the bag.

"Thanks."

He set the bag on the counter and tucked his phone away while Leyla stacked the empty milk crates by the wall.

"So, are things going okay or—"

"Fine." She reached around him and opened the fridge again. She grabbed a block of butter to soften for the frosting she planned to make later.

"Leyla."

She turned to him.

"Stop. Jesus. I'm trying to talk to you."

She took a deep breath and nodded.

"How *are* you?" he asked.

"I'm okay."

He just looked at her, those blue eyes pinning her in place. Her father used to look at her that same way when he interrogated her about her activities the previous night.

"Really, Owen. I'm fine."

"Then why do you keep dodging my calls?"

"I've been busy."

"Well, we're worried about you."

"We?"

"Me. Macey. Mom," he said. "You're avoiding everyone."

"I'm not avoiding anyone."

He shook his head and looked away.

"Really. I've just been swamped with everything going on right now. You're swamped, too. You can't tell me you don't get it."

"No, I get it. Just—" He folded his arms over his chest,

and she could tell he didn't like how this conversation was going. "I've been worried that this thing with Amelia might be bringing up some stuff for you."

She stiffened. "No."

"No?"

"No. I'm fine."

"Are you?" He watched her. "Because, you know, you never really told me what happened when you were mugged in New York."

"Yeah, I did. *I was mugged in New York*. That's what happened."

He stared at her, as if willing her to say more.

Leyla stared right back. He was determined to get her to talk about this. She was determined to avoid it. And she had the advantage here because the topic of her assault at knifepoint five years ago was way, way out of her brother's comfort zone.

And the fact that he'd brought it up anyway put an ache in her chest.

She reached over and squeezed his arm. "I'm okay. Really."

He didn't look convinced.

"How's Macey doing?" she asked.

"You're changing the subject."

"It's called *deflection*. Get your terms right." She scooted around him and grabbed another block of butter from the fridge, then took her biggest mixing bowl from the baker's rack. "Seriously, if I need to talk about this, I'll call my therapist, okay? You don't have to worry."

She unwrapped the butter and dropped it into the bowl to soften.

She turned around, and Owen was still watching her. She hoped mentioning her therapist would get him off her case.

"So, I heard you had a date with Sean Moran," he said.

"Where'd you hear *that*?"

"Did you?"

"No."

"Macey saw you two leaving the Hut last night."

She tossed the wax paper in the trash and wiped her hands on her apron. "We grabbed a drink." She tipped her head to the side and looked at him. "Is *that* why you stopped by? To ask me about Sean?"

"Partly." He kept his arms crossed.

"Why do you care if I have a drink with him?"

"Why are you defensive?"

She felt a surge of irritation. "Because you're butting into my personal life."

He laughed. "You butt into mine all the time."

"What have you got against Sean Moran? I thought he was Joel's friend. You barely know him."

"I don't think it's a good idea for you to get involved with the guy."

Leyla didn't either, but probably for different reasons.

Owen rested his hands on his hips. "You know he's a fed, right?"

"So?"

"So . . . his work is dangerous. I don't like you hanging around him."

She closed her eyes and tipped her head back, so annoyed by that statement she didn't even know where to begin.

"Owen. Oh my God."

"What?"

"You sound like Dad. Or Joel. And do you even *get* the irony of what you're saying?"

He frowned.

"Anyway, what do *you* know about his work?" she asked.

"Nothing."

Leyla highly doubted that. And she felt another dart of irritation. Joel knew about Sean's work. Owen knew about Sean's work. But for some reason, Leyla had to be kept in the dark. It was more of the macho bullshit she'd been dealing with all her life.

She looked at Owen and clenched her teeth, trying to tamp down her temper because she knew he meant well. He was just being the overprotective older brother—the role usually reserved for Joel.

She took a deep breath. "Look, I appreciate your concern about . . . everything. But I can handle it."

He just stared at her.

"Is there anything else you want to interrogate me about?" She checked her watch. "Because we're slammed, and I've got things to do."

He watched her for a long moment. "I mean it about Moran. You need to be careful."

"Uh-huh."

"Don't blow me off, Leyla."

She handed him the pastry bag and smiled sweetly. "When have I ever blown you off?"

S EAN POUNDED ALONG the sand, skimming his gaze over the houses on stilts. A four-story Victorian came into view. It was covered in scaffolding as a team of workers painted it pistachio green. Not Sean's color, but hey. To each rich idiot his own.

He kept on jogging, past the Victorian, past a yellow Tuscan villa, past a Nantucket-style bungalow with gray shingles and crisp white trim. Then came a modern gray stucco with lots of glass and right angles. Sean ran another fifty yards and then slowed to a walk and turned around. Stretching his arms over his head, he studied the gray stucco box. The water-facing side was almost all windows, which took full advantage of the house's beachfront lot. The reflective glass had been specially selected to block out not only heat but the prying gazes of curious beachcombers.

Not to mention the telephoto lenses of an FBI surveillance crew. Luc Gagnon was a lot of things, but he wasn't stupid.

Sean surveyed the top level, where a palm tree peeked up over a tall wall—presumably the location of the swimming pool Leyla had mentioned. The house's four stories encompassed a whopping twelve thousand square feet of living space, most of it on levels two through four. Aside from stilts, the first level consisted of what appeared to be storage closets and a six-car garage.

And what was behind those six garage doors? Sean didn't know, but he intended to find out. On his last few trips to the island, Gagnon had flown into the private airport and been delivered to his house by limousine. He'd only emerged twice during those trips—both times in a red Tesla Roadster—to drive to the marina where he kept his boat.

Nearing the house, Sean looked out at the water, searching for the catamaran the surveillance team had been using to keep an eye on the house. No sign of it. Maybe they'd called it a day. The wind was up and so was the surf, so conditions were less than ideal.

Sean's phone buzzed, and the sight of Leyla's number sent a shot of lust straight to his groin. His pulse sped up. Unbelievable. He'd barely known her a week and she had him feeling like a desperate teenager.

"Hey," he said.

"Hi." She paused. "What's that noise?"

"Seagulls." He glanced up at the circling birds. Some kids down the beach were tossing potato chips at them. "I'm finishing a run. What's up?"

"I'm returning your call."

The formality in her tone didn't bode well for what he wanted to ask her.

He cleared his throat. "I was calling to see if you'd like to have dinner tonight at the Nautilus."

Silence.

"Leyla?"

"That place is really nice."

"I hear they have a new head chef. I thought maybe you'd want to stop in, check out the competition."

She laughed. "We don't exactly play to the same audience."

He smiled, happy to have made her laugh.

"Yeah, well, I'm guessing you're competitive anyway. Or at least curious."

"Well. You're right on both," she said. "And I appreciate the invitation, but I can't make it tonight. I'm going to be here late working on a cake order."

"How about tomorrow?"

Now he sounded as desperate as he felt. And he didn't care. He wanted to see her again, soon, and he was willing to resort to manipulation and flat-out bribery to get her to say yes.

"Tomorrow's busy, too."

"Okay, what about a drink when you knock off? Or dinner Sunday?"

She sighed. "I don't know, Sean."

"What don't you know?"

"Whether this is a good idea. Dinner at the Nautilus sounds a lot like a date."

"And?"

"I don't date tourists."

"Didn't we establish that that's not why I'm here?" He kept his tone light, hoping to keep her in an agreeable mood.

"You know what I mean."

He was pretty sure he did, but he didn't want her to spell it out for him. Once she put it out there, it might be harder to get her to change her stance.

Sean stopped and looked out at the water, where a pair of kayakers were cutting through the surf. Just hearing her voice made him feel good. He hadn't realized he'd been so worried these past few hours that she wasn't going to call him back.

"I've been thinking about you all day, Leyla. I'd really like to see you again."

His heart was thudding now, even harder than it had been when he finished his run.

"I've been thinking about you, too."

Relief flooded him. He wasn't the only one who'd been distracted as hell today, thinking about that kiss. At least he'd gotten her to admit it.

Now he wanted to push his luck. But he sensed the better strategy was to leave the ball in her court. She liked to be in control.

"We don't have to do the Nautilus if you'd rather keep it causal," he said. "We could grab a beer somewhere."

"Let me think about it."

"Okay."

"I'll give you a call, all right?"

"Sounds good."

"Bye, Sean."

He watched the kayakers for a moment, then started running again, needing to get rid of his pent-up energy. He couldn't remember the last time he'd felt this way. It was crazy. And frustrating. And he knew Leyla's instincts were right—getting involved *wasn't* a good idea for either of them. He was going back to D.C., probably sooner than later if this operation went as planned, and he couldn't afford to let himself get distracted right now.

But he was going to anyway. Leyla was a beautiful, fierce distraction, and he was dying for more of her, if he could just convince her to give him a chance.

His phone buzzed, and he answered it without looking.

"Yeah?"

"Sean?"

It was a woman's voice, but not Leyla's. He slowed his pace and checked the number.

"Hi, Nicole. What's up?"

"We've had some new developments."

He stopped running.

"We need to meet," she went on.

"When?"

"The sooner, the better."

NICOLE PULLED UP to Sean Moran's condominium in an unmarked police unit, and he slid into the passenger seat. His hair was wet, and he wore a leather jacket again, despite the balmy weather.

"You might try getting some of those Hawaiian shirts," she suggested as she pulled away.

"Hawaiian?"

"You know, loose-fitting cotton? Guys wear them untucked? You can carry concealed without having a heat-stroke."

He darted a look at her and rested his arm on the door. "Where are we going?"

"You been to Josie's yet?"

"No."

"It's the juice place over on Third."

She hung a right onto Second and cut through an alley to avoid the Friday-evening traffic on Main Street. She pulled into the drive-through and looked at the menu board.

"What would you like?" she asked.

"I'm good."

"Oh, come on. My treat."

He ordered a lemonade, and she got a mango smoothie, which was going to have to count as her nutrition for the day. It had been one of those hectic afternoons, and she'd skipped lunch.

They pulled up to the window and waited in silence.

"Thanks for meeting me," she said finally.

"How's the investigation coming?"

"Okay. How's yours? Anything new?"

The attendant reached out to give them their order, and Sean ignored the question. He wasn't going to talk in front of other people. Nicole handed him his drink and then pulled into an empty parking space facing the dancing-pineapple mural on the side of the building. She rolled up the window and took a long, cold slurp. Then another. She settled the cup into the holder and turned to face him.

"I have some stuff for you." She reached into the back and grabbed a manila file folder off the floor.

"What's this?" he asked as she handed it to him.

"Autopsy reports from the Bexar County Medical Examiner's Office."

He opened the folder and skimmed the top page.

"Jose Rincon and Sandra Massey." She paused, watching his expression as he read. "Both were murdered in San Antonio last fall, six weeks apart. Both had their hands bound with blue cordage at some point."

He glanced up.

"Both victims were stabbed and left in an alley in what initially looked like a robbery."

His brow furrowed as he flipped the page.

"Did you know about this?" she asked.

"No." He rubbed his jaw as he read. "I should have."

She studied his face, trying to gauge whether he was being honest with her. He looked up.

"What? I didn't know," he said.

She decided she believed him.

He closed the folder. "How'd you find this?"

"A reporter tipped me off."

His eyebrows shot up. "A reporter? Who?"

She shook her head. "He's paranoid about his safety. I had a phone call today with the San Antonio detective in charge of the cases. Rincon—the male victim—was a low-level distributor for the Saledo cartel. And Massey was the former girlfriend of one of their dealers. She was set to testify about her ex at a trial this winter, but she turned up dead behind her apartment building before she could make it to court." Nicole nodded at the folder. "There's a news clip about her murder in there behind the autopsy reports. The detective told me both victims' valuables were stolen to make it look like a robbery, but the autopsy revealed tiny blue splinters in the abrasions on their wrists, indicating they'd been bound and likely held at a different location than the place where the bodies were dumped."

Sean sighed and flipped to the article she'd printed for him. It was an AP story, and the byline wasn't Miguel Vidales. She was trying to keep his name out of this.

"You don't look surprised by the link to the Saledos," she said.

"I'm not."

She crossed her arms, trying to rein in her temper. "But you *didn't* know about these two homicides?"

"I didn't."

She sighed. "So, if you're here investigating a drug cartel, why isn't the DEA involved?" she asked. "Why'd they send you?"

"That's not what I'm investigating."

"No?"

"I'm not here about the Saledos. They're only involved tangentially."

Fuming, she looked out the window and shook her head.

"You know what? I'm ready for some straight answers," she told him. "I can't lead an investigation this way."

He looked at her for a long moment. Then he opened the folder again and shuffled through the paperwork she'd pulled together for him. He rubbed his chin and seemed to be debating something in his mind.

"We're on the same side," she said. "I want to help you, and I want you to help *me*. But I don't know what it is you're doing here in Lost Beach."

He looked up. "Have you heard of Luc Gagnon?"

"The software mogul."

He nodded.

"Yeah, I've heard of him. He recently bought a big place down here." She leaned forward. "Are you telling me Luc Gagnon's running drugs with the Saledos?"

"No."

She arched her eyebrows. "What are you telling me?"

"He's working with them in a different capacity."

And suddenly she got it.

"Technology."

He nodded.

"What's his company do again?" She snapped her fingers. "The phone thing?"

"GhostSend. It's a next-generation encryption app."

She sat back and blew out a sigh. "He's providing encryption software to the Saledos?"

"That's what we're investigating."

Investigating. He was being cagey again about whether or not they had it confirmed.

"Gagnon's company makes a range of different messaging

apps, and not all of them are sold on the open market," Sean told her.

"Sounds like a big business."

He nodded. "Extremely."

"For drug dealers, mafia, practically any criminal enterprise."

Sean nodded. "This stuff is mission-critical. Without secure comms, half these guys would be rotting in prison right now."

"So . . ." Her mind was spinning as she tried to digest the implications. "You're here about Luc Gagnon. Are you trying to arrest him for something? Or get him to inform on his clients?"

"Something like that."

Frustration welled up inside her. She was losing patience with these half answers.

"What does Amelia Albright have to do with any of this?" she asked, circling back to the whole reason she was here right now.

"I don't know."

"Oh, come on."

"I have some ideas," he said, "but nothing confirmed. I believe she was connected to Gagnon."

"You think she was romantically involved with him?"

"That, or maybe working for him in some capacity. Or both."

"You know, her phone is still missing, but we collected a tablet from her apartment," Nicole said. "Maybe she had some communications with him on it. The tablet's at the state crime lab waiting to be analyzed by their cyber team."

"Not anymore," he said.

"What?"

"It's at Quantico."

Her anger bubbled up. "Now you're moving my evidence around? You guys have a lot of nerve, you know that? I should have been informed."

"I agree."

She shook her head and looked away.

"I'm not the only one involved here," Sean said. "My project's being run by the FBI's cyber section chief."

She looked at him. "Does Brady know?"

"He knows the general gist of it, but there's a lot we can't disclose. He's agreed to keep his focus on the Albright homicide and share anything relevant with us if anything comes up."

Nicole wondered what else Brady had been withholding from her. Were his hands really tied here? Or had he been fine to keep his lead detective in the dark about all this? In the past, she'd known Brady to be territorial. He didn't like other law enforcement agencies horning in on his investigations. So maybe keeping her out of the loop hadn't been his choice. But it bothered her all the same.

"So, what's the theory here?" she asked Sean. "You think some thug working for Saledo killed Amelia?"

"I don't know."

"Or are you saying Gagnon did it? I really don't see some rich tech geek stabbing this young woman in the back and dumping her body in an alley."

"Neither do I," Sean said. "Anyway, he was at a conference in San Jose the weekend of the murder, so we know he didn't actually do it."

"So, you think it was a hired hit?"

"Could be. The fact that she had her hands bound— that's what first got our attention. It suggests someone held her somewhere and questioned her before she was killed, maybe to find out something she knew or something she'd done."

"Then . . . possibly she had some sensitive information about Gagnon's business or his clients, either something she came across by sleeping with him and working for him?"

"It's a possibility."

"Maybe she tried to extort someone," Nicole said. "Or maybe someone thought she might go to the police."

"Or maybe someone wanted to eliminate a risk to a major deal going down."

Nicole tensed. "Something's going down? When?"

He shook his head. Another topic that was off-limits.

"What you're telling me is that you think either Luc Gagnon or someone in the Saledo organization had Amelia questioned and killed." Her chest got tight just thinking about it. A young woman's entire life snuffed out, just to eliminate a risk to some guy's business.

Sean watched her, not confirming or denying anything.

"I can only imagine Gagnon's clients are like a who's who of dirtbag criminals," Nicole said. "They probably cover the whole spectrum. And cross borders. You must really want this guy."

"Oh yeah."

"Good." She nodded. "I want the doer."

Sean raised an eyebrow. "You mean—"

"You're focused on Gagnon. I'm focused on the person who killed Amelia." She leaned forward. "Someone ambushed and terrorized this girl, then killed her and dumped her in an alley. People can't come to our town and murder someone with impunity. Whoever the hell this guy is, I want him. You guys can have the bigger fish, but I'm going to keep working this case until we get this assailant, and we're not leaving it to some outside agency."

"We have more resources," Sean pointed out.

"This one's ours. I'm sure Brady told you the same thing,

didn't he?" Nicole didn't even have to ask. "Whoever this guy is, we're going to figure it out, and he's going down."

S EAN LOOKED AT her, wondering if he was going to regret bringing her into the loop—even though he'd barely scratched the surface of what he was doing here.

"What?" she demanded.

"I admire your determination."

She rolled her eyes.

"But ultimately, it's not up to me. I'm not the one running things."

"Okay. But I'm just telling you how it is. I'm trying to be *clear*," she added. "We are not just going to sit here and wring our hands and hope the feds solve this case for us. I mean, I'm sure one woman's murder is just a blip on the radar to you people in Washington when you've got some massive criminal conspiracy you're trying to roll up. But to us it's major. This is a small town, and this young woman was murdered right here." She gestured to the window. "We're talking four blocks from here."

"I know."

"Which reminds me of why I called you. I need a favor."

She took the file from his lap and shuffled past the autopsy reports. A slip of paper was clipped to the back of the folder.

"This is a number from Amelia's phone records." She tapped it. "We haven't been able to trace it. We also found this number written—in what looks like Amelia's handwriting—on a matchbook recovered from the pocket of her work apron. The matchbook is from the Playa del Rey golf resort."

"Any prints on the matchbook?"

"Just Amelia's."

"The number could be from a burner phone."

"It probably is, and we need your help," she said. "You can use some of those 'resources' you mentioned that we don't have in our quaint little police station."

She was chiding him for being condescending toward her. Maybe he deserved it.

But Sean didn't mind. He was glad to have her input, even if it was limited. Nicole Lawson was sharp, she was energized, and she had local connections. But even more important, she cared about bringing someone to justice for Amelia Albright's killing. Her read of the situation was right on target—the array of federal agencies involved in this thing were focused on Gagnon and the international network of criminals he was aiding and abetting with his technology. Amelia's murder wasn't the focus.

She closed the folder and held it out to him. "That's for you. Consider it a trade."

He took the folder. "I'll see what I can do."

LEYLA CREATED A perfect petal, and then another and another. She finished piping the flower on the square of parchment paper and then examined her work.

Fifty-two down, forty-eight to go. She set the blossom beside the other buttercream flowers on the baking sheet. Then she shook out her sore arm and started again.

She could be at the Nautilus right now, drinking wine and sampling Anton Devereux's supposedly "innovative" Texas-Creole cuisine. A teeny, tiny part of her regretted her decision not to go. She'd been wanting to try the place for months. Sean had guessed right. *Of course* she wanted to see what one of the island's few classically trained chefs was doing.

But it wasn't a guess. Sean knew she was competitive, and he had no qualms at all about using that knowledge to try to get her to go on a date with him. She was impressed by his tenacity and his ability to read people. Or at least, to read *her*. He'd been doing it since that first night on the beach.

But maybe she wasn't hard to read. It wasn't like she tried to hide the fact that she was competitive. She took pride in it. Growing up with three brothers, it was either compete or get left behind, and she'd carried that attitude into adulthood. It was her competitive nature that had led her to rent out a shuttered ice cream parlor and turn it into one of the island's most popular cafés. And then she'd aggressively grown the business, expanding to a second location and then starting a catering firm, all in a matter of four short years. None of that would have happened without her competitive streak, and she was proud of how far she'd come. While some of her friends from culinary school were still toiling away as line cooks in Manhattan, Leyla was running her own company, calling her own shots in a place all her own.

Of course, her place wasn't exactly in a trendy location. Some people might even consider it a backwater. But she'd grown up here, so it was *her* backwater, and she felt a sense of excitement watching Lost Beach transform from a sleepy shrimping town into something more eclectic. Her hometown was changing every day, gaining restaurants and bars and food trucks. They even had their own microbrewery now.

And then there was the true *pull* of doing what she did.

She loved it.

She loved the beautiful chaos of a busy kitchen. She loved the smell of fresh bread dough, the clatter of pans, the hiss and groan of the espresso machine. She loved the subversive comradery of cooks and servers bantering back and forth. She loved the pure, simple pleasure of making something good with her hands, something pretty and delicious and—on a good day—maybe even inspiring. Leyla took pride in her work, and she knew that it showed, and that it was the reason people came back to her humble little café again and again.

A blur of motion caught her eye, and she noticed Siena waving from the doorway.

Leyla plucked out her earbuds.

"She had her music in," Siena said over her shoulder. Then she turned to Leyla. "You have a *visitor*," she told her, lifting an eyebrow.

Sean stepped into the kitchen, and Leyla felt a rush of giddiness.

"Hi." She set down her piping bag. "What brings you here?"

"Just dropping by."

Siena was watching them with a curious smile.

"Siena, did you meet Sean at Joel's wedding?"

"I did *not*." She turned to him. "It's a pleasure to meet you, Sean."

"Likewise."

"Well, I'm all done out there." She grinned at Leyla. "See you in the morning, Ley."

Siena vanished, leaving Leyla alone in her kitchen with the one man she'd ever known who could turn her knees to Jell-O with a single kiss.

He stepped over to the counter. "Damn, that's a lot of roses," he said.

"I'm about halfway done," she said. "And they're cherry blossoms."

He tipped his head. "Okay. I see it now. We get those in D.C. every spring. They have a festival on the Mall."

"Yes, I know." She smiled. "This bride is from Virginia, so this is her theme."

He glanced at the five-tier cake in the refrigerated display case behind her. Leyla had frosted it with buttercream earlier. "So, these go on the wedding cake?"

"That's the plan."

"Mind if I watch?"

A little tingle went through her. "Not at all."

She picked up a flower nail and secured a square of parchment to it with a dab of icing. Then she started a new flower, glad for something to do with her hands. She piped each petal, rotating the nail as she worked.

"I saw that I missed your call earlier," Sean said.

"Yep." She added the new blossom to the baking sheet. Each flower had five petals made of pale pink icing, so five hundred petals for the entire cake. It was completely over the top, but so was this bride.

She glanced up, and Sean was leaning against the counter, watching her.

"You didn't leave a message," he said.

"Yeah. No, I wanted to talk to you in person."

She set her bag down and grabbed a towel.

"Everything okay?" he asked, looking worried.

"It has to do with the investigation, so I didn't want to leave it in a message."

He looked guarded now.

"You've asked me several times whether Amelia had a boyfriend. I gathered it wasn't just a casual question, so I did some digging."

His eyebrows tipped up.

"I chatted with one of my baristas this afternoon—a girl who had a lot of overlap with Amelia's schedule. I asked some questions about boyfriends, and she mentioned something I thought you'd find interesting." She set the towel down and rested her hand on her hip. "Amelia didn't have a boyfriend *per se* in the last year or so, but this spring she went on a couple of dates with a guy from Seattle."

Interest sparked in Sean's eyes. "Who?"

"This friend didn't know his name. Amelia had mentioned he owned a tech company, and this girl got the impression it was a startup."

Sean pursed his lips.

"I know what you're thinking. Gagnon's company isn't exactly a *startup*. It's worth, like, two-point-four billion dollars."

"Where'd you get that?"

"I looked it up. But anyway, it just so happens that Gagnon is from Seattle, so I thought you might be interested."

Sean didn't respond.

"Seeing as how you're *investigating* the man?"

Again, no response.

She rolled her eyes. "Are you seriously going to pretend you're not?"

"This isn't a conversation I want to have with you."

"Okay, fine. Just take the tip and do what you will with it." She slid the sheet of flowers into the fridge and then stepped over to her standing mixer. Using a spatula, she spooned pink icing up the sides of the piping bag and then added a scoop of white, which would create the gradient effect she wanted.

She looked over at Sean. "What?"

"I don't like that you're going around asking people questions about this."

"It was just a casual conversation with someone who works for me." She shrugged. "So what?"

"So, you shouldn't be involved."

"Well, I care about Amelia, so I am involved."

"You need to drop it."

She searched his face, wondering if he realized how much his reaction revealed.

"You do know that you're confirming what I thought, don't you?"

"What's that?" he asked.

"You believe Amelia's murder is somehow linked to that thing you're here for. Your secret project."

Now he rolled his eyes. "Leyla . . ."

"Why can't we just talk about it? I'm trying to help you."

"Thank you. But I don't want you involved. At all. You need to leave it to the investigators."

"Sure. I just thought you'd want to know." She watched his eyes, looking for clues that she was on the right track here. "Are you aware Luc Gagnon used to stay at the Windjammer Hotel? He was there all the time while his place was under construction. He'd fly down on his private plane and check on his house between fishing and rounds of golf."

"What's your point?"

"We have a location at the Windjammer. Gagnon used to come in for coffee. We even catered an event for him."

Sean frowned. "When?"

"Earlier this year. It was nothing big. He did a breakfast meeting in one of the hotel conference rooms, and we took in pastries and coffee. My point is, Amelia could have met him at the Windjammer during one of his trips."

Sean clearly didn't like the direction the conversation had taken—which told Leyla she was onto something.

"This is all conjecture," he said. "The guy Amelia dated could be anyone."

"Yes, because we have *so many* Seattle tech CEOs hanging around Lost Beach. They're everywhere."

He folded his arms over his chest. "Leyla . . ." His voice was full of warning now.

"Fine. Let's talk about something else."

The room fell silent except for the low hum of the refrigerator. She reached over and tapped her phone to switch her music to speaker mode. Latin jazz drifted from the phone, and she resumed her piping. She focused on her work and tried to ignore the sudden tension in the room. It was the tension more than anything that told her that her instincts were right, and Sean had more than a passing interest in whether Amelia had had a boyfriend. Well, Leyla had gotten an answer for him, and now he wanted her to kindly butt out.

That wasn't happening. Leyla was interested now and determined to learn more. She had contacts Sean didn't. Just because he was some hotshot FBI agent didn't mean he couldn't use her help.

He walked up beside her, and she felt a shiver of excitement. She ignored it. He smelled like that cologne or body-wash she remembered from last night, and she ignored that, too. Obviously, he was trying to distract her from their conversation.

"How do you get those so perfect?" he asked, leaning his hand on the counter.

"Practice." She finished another blossom and added it to the baking sheet. "Would you like me to teach you?"

"I'm not artistic."

"Everyone's at least a little artistic."

"Not me."

"Want to try one?"

"Sure."

She peeled a flower from a parchment square and turned to face him, lifting it up. He held her wrist and licked it off her fingertip.

She turned around.

"That's good," he said.

"Yep."

"It just dissolves."

His hands settled on her waist, and she turned to face him again.

"I can't concentrate when you do that."

"I know." He gazed down at her, giving her a chance to push him away. When she didn't, he dipped his head down.

His mouth was warm, and she tasted her icing on his tongue. Nerves shot through her as he leaned into her, pinning her against the counter with his hips. She tossed the piping bag aside and slid her hands into his thick hair.

Desire surged through her, and she thought about how much time she'd wasted today thinking about last night's kiss on the beach and how hard it had been driving home alone afterward. She'd thought she'd made progress today shaking this off. But now she knew she hadn't made any at all. She was right back where she'd been last night, wanting to throw caution to the wind for once. His hand slid up her side and grazed her breast.

"Damn it." She kissed his mouth, his jaw, his neck. "I wasn't going to do this tonight."

"Why not?"

She pulled back and looked up at him, and the intensity in his eyes sent a jolt of yearning through her. She was so ridiculously attracted to this man, even when he ticked her off, like he was doing right now.

She kissed him again, pulling his head down as she pressed against him, probably getting sugar and butter all over the front of his clothes.

"Leyla."

She didn't stop, afraid if she let him talk, she'd remember why this was a bad idea.

"Leyla?"

She jerked back.

"Someone's here, babe."

"What?"

He nodded over her head.

She whirled around and heard a *rap rap rap* coming from the front of the shop. "Damn. It's Rogelio."

She rushed out, straightening her apron. Rogelio stood at the door with his silver cart. He wore a white chef jacket and checked pants—the required uniform for the Windjammer Hotel kitchen.

She unlocked the door, then remembered to tap in her code before opening it.

"Hi," she said, stepping back.

"My code didn't work," he said as he wheeled in the cart.

"I had to reset everything. I'll give you the new one."

Rogelio looked behind her. "Who's here?"

"Just . . . a friend."

He glanced at the kitchen again. Then he shot her a knowing look with those brown-black eyes. "You're pink, *chiquita*."

"Oh, whatever." She waved off the comment, but her cheeks warmed as she followed him into the kitchen, where Sean leaned against the counter.

"Hi. Rogelio." He reached out a tattoo-covered arm. "You must be . . . ?"

"Sean."

They shook hands, and then Rogelio started unloading trays filled with biscotti.

"Vanilla, chocolate, and amaretto," he said. "I still have to dip the vanilla ones."

"I've got some Ghirardelli chips in the back," Leyla told him.

Sean caught her eye. "I'll head out."

She felt a stab of disappointment. Followed by relief. Then disappointment again as she walked with him to the door.

He stopped beside it, glancing at the brand-new keypad on the wall.

"New system?" he asked.

"Just got it today."

"It's a good brand."

"That's why I got it."

She held the door open for him, and humid air wafted inside.

"You plan to be here late?" he asked.

"Not too much longer. I need to get home. I've got an early start tomorrow." She nodded back toward the kitchen. "We both do."

He held her gaze. Then he tilted her chin and kissed her mouth. "Be careful," he told her.

"I will."

CHAPTER

ELEVEN

NICOLE TURNED OFF Palmetto Drive into the pitted parking lot. It was mostly full, but she found a space at the very edge of the lot next to a dinged pickup even older than hers. Cutting the engine, she stared up at Amelia's building. Lights glowed in many of the units, and several tenants stood out on their narrow balconies, either smoking or talking on the phone.

Nicole slid from her truck and locked it. A stench hit her—like rotten vegetation and sewage, and she pinched her nose as she walked across the spongy lawn. A man watched her from a second-floor balcony, the orange glow of his cigarette moving through the darkness as he leaned against the railing. She reached the corner staircase and trudged up the steps. On the landing she encountered a pair of teen boys who stuffed something under their shirts as she passed them.

Nicole walked down the open breezeway to Amelia's second-floor apartment, then pulled out the key and let herself in. The scene had been released, but the victim's family hadn't been here yet. From her conversation with them after the funeral, Nicole had gathered that Amelia's parents didn't know when they'd come down to pack up their daughter's apartment. They had seemed too overwhelmed to think about it.

Nicole locked the door behind her and flipped the light switch. A fluorescent fixture flickered on in the kitchen, and she stood still for a few moments, just surveying the room. This was her fourth trip here, and she wasn't quite sure what she expected to find. Clues suggested that Amelia had had a wealthy, possibly shady, man in her life. Maybe the tech mogul from Seattle. Maybe someone affiliated with the Saledo cartel. If so, Nicole wanted to find evidence of him. A number from a burner phone wasn't enough. She needed a receipt, or a gift, or maybe a note—*something* she could use to prove this phantom boyfriend existed.

Nicole grabbed a pair of gloves from the box that had been left by the door. She tugged the gloves on, then toed off her dirty sneakers and pulled paper booties over her socks. She stepped into the kitchen and took a cursory look around. It had been thoroughly searched already by a pair of county CSIs. Her gaze fell on the class schedule taped to the fridge. Above it was a slip of paper with a printed quotation that Nicole remembered without having to look. It was a Bob Ross saying about no mistakes, just "happy little accidents."

Nicole headed into the bathroom first. She pulled back the shower curtain and scanned the items lined up on the side of the tub. Razor. Loofah. Hair and skin products galore, but nothing that looked like it had been taken as a souvenir from a ritzy hotel.

Turning to the medicine cabinet, she noted the smudges of fingerprint powder as she opened the mirrored door. The prints they'd lifted from here hadn't come back yet, but Nicole wasn't optimistic about getting anything useful. This dingy apartment didn't seem like the place for a romantic rendezvous. The medicine cabinet contained the typical stuff—makeup, sunscreen, whitening toothpaste—and Nicole had been through it all before. She moved to the cabinet beneath the sink, crouching down on the old linoleum floor.

A dark spatter along the baseboard caught her eye. She pulled the Mini Maglite from her pocket. Her pulse quickened as she shined the flashlight on the reddish-brown dots that looked like blood. How had the CSIs missed this? She opened the cabinet. Inside was a jar crammed with paintbrushes and a shoebox filled with watercolors. She blew out a sigh. *Paint.* One of the CSIs had mentioned something about paint in the bathroom, but at the time Nicole had been distracted by the discovery of Amelia's iPad.

She stood up and looked around the cramped space. On the counter beside the sink was a sunflower-shaped jewelry box. Nicole lifted the lid and poked through. Lots of earrings and necklaces, a few woven bracelets, but nothing that looked like a gift from a boyfriend, wealthy or otherwise.

Something skittered across her foot. Nicole yelped and jumped back as a giant roach darted behind the toilet.

"*Ick!*" She shook her foot and glanced around, shuddering as she imagined more jumbo-size roaches crawling up her leg.

Grabbing her flashlight off the counter, she went into the bedroom.

The nightstand had been almost empty, but Nicole rechecked it anyway. Once again, nothing of interest, just a cheap lighter and a tube of lavender-scented lotion. She looked under the bed. Dust bunnies. She moved into the closet and flipped the light switch.

Nothing.

Of course, the one time she'd come here at night, the light was burned out.

Muttering a curse, she turned on her flashlight and swept it over the rack of clothes. Zeroing in on jackets, she started searching pockets. She was looking for ticket stubs, matchbooks, bar receipts—anything that might connect Amelia to a date with someone—especially anything that her date might have touched at some point, leaving behind a fingerprint.

She moved on to a shelf of purses. She went through all of them but found only some loose change and a pack of Tic Tacs. She grabbed a pink tote bag with "Aloha" scripted across the front. Inside was a bottle of sunscreen and a pair of sandy flip-flops. The bag felt heavy. She checked the inner pocket and found a small black sketchbook.

Tucking the flashlight under her chin, Nicole pulled out the sketchbook and flipped through the pages. The drawings were in heavy pencil with lots of shading. Some looked quick and unfinished, others showed more detail. Nicole turned the pages, finding a range of subjects—the lighthouse at the tip of the island, a beach umbrella, two toddlers digging in the sand, a sleeping man.

She stopped on the sleeping man and sucked in a breath. He wasn't at the beach. He was stretched out in bed, with sheets tangled around his waist. He had muscular shoulders and his head was on a pillow with his hands tucked beneath.

Turning the page, she found a profile of a man's face and neck. A lock of hair hung over the eyes, but the picture wasn't finished. No mouth, and the nose was only a faint pencil stroke.

She flipped back to the previous page. No face visible. But the drawing definitely depicted a muscular, naked man lying prone on a bed. Could the sketch be from a life drawing class, maybe? But the rumpled sheets looked so real Nicole could practically smell the sex on them. She studied the lines, the shading, the contours of the muscles. Plenty of detail on the body, but the background consisted of only a few charcoal smudges. Frustrated, she flipped to the picture of the face again. Dark hair, long bangs, a faint line that suggested the barest hint of a nose . . . but that was it. Nothing definitive.

A soft *thud* had her glancing up. Was that a neighbor? Or someone outside?

Clink.

That noise was closer. She switched off her flashlight and held her breath, listening. Her heart started to race as she heard shuffling near the door. Could it be Emmet? Or McDeere?

Hearing a muffled voice, she stepped to the door of the closet.

"Yeah, I'm in," someone said quietly. "Gimme ten."

That voice was *not* Emmet or McDeere. Her pulse was racing now. She shouldn't have come here alone.

Silently, she set down the sketchbook and eased the weapon from her holster. She should announce herself. It could be Amelia's brother. Or maybe her landlord.

But something—some inexplicable, deep-rooted instinct—told her it wasn't. Should she confront them or wait?

She remembered her shoes beside the door, and her heart skittered.

No more shuffling. The place had gone silent. Had the person spotted her shoes and realized someone else was here?

Gun raised, she crept silently across the bedroom to the door. A wedge of light spilled in from the kitchen, but she stayed in the shadows.

The apartment was quiet. Not a sound.

Creak.

"Police!" she yelled, whipping around the doorway.

The front door slammed shut.

She raced across the living room as footsteps pounded down the walkway. She yanked open the door and lunged out just in time to see a dark figure darting into the stairwell.

"Police! Stop!" She dashed after him.

A weight slammed into her, sending her to the ground with an *oomph!*

Her breath whooshed out, but she managed to hang on to her gun. She rolled to her back as what felt like a sledgehammer crashed into her ribs. Pain rocketed through her. Another blow to her ribs, and she hunched into a ball as a blur of black hurdled over her. Gasping with shock, she heard footsteps thundering down the stairs.

Nicole rolled to her back, wheezing and gripping her weapon. Her side was on fire, and pain pulsed through her body. She managed to get to her knees, then grabbed the railing along the walkway and pulled herself up. She peered over the rail, searching the shadowy lawn. But she didn't see or hear anything—just the distant buzz of cicadas in the marsh.

She staggered down the walkway, dizzy and gasping for breath. No one in the stairwell.

In the distance, a car door slammed. Someone fired up an engine. Clutching her side, she heard a squeal of tires as they peeled away.

W HERE ARE YOU?" Moore asked Sean over the phone.
"Just getting home."

"Home?"

"The condominium."

"Listen, Gagnon's on the move."

Sean had been about to turn into a parking space. Instead he pulled over.

"He just passed through the gates at the front of his subdivision," his boss said.

"Red Tesla?"

"Negative. He's in a black Jeep hardtop. The team got a plate. It's Echo, Charlie, Foxtrot—"

"Wait." Sean grabbed a napkin from the cup holder and dug a pen from the console. "Okay, go ahead."

Moore recited the license plate as Sean jotted it down. Then he drove to the edge of the parking lot.

"They said he just turned west on Driftwood. Can you catch up to him?"

"Yes." Sean exited the parking lot.

"This is the first time he's left since he got here this trip. We need to see what he's up to."

"Roger that."

Sean checked the gas gauge. Only a quarter tank. Not ideal, but this was a small island.

"Keep your distance," Moore said. "We don't want to put him on alert."

"I won't."

N ICOLE LET HERSELF into her apartment. Not bothering with a light, she went straight into the kitchen and dropped her plastic bag on the counter. She crouched down, wincing as pain shot up her side. Tears burned her eyes and she paused for a moment before opening the cabinet and taking out the dusty bottle that she hadn't touched in years. She didn't want to reach for a glass, so she grabbed an empty mug from the sink and poured a shot of bourbon. Scrunching up her face, she took a tentative sip.

A rap on the door had her whirling around, and she gasped as pain zinged through her. She carefully set the mug down and went to check the peephole.

Shit.

Nicole took a few shallow breaths—deep ones were out—and smoothed a hand over her hair before opening the door.

"What the hell, Nicole?" Emmet stepped past her.

"Please come in."

"Why didn't you call me?"

She closed the door and locked it, then walked past him into her kitchen.

"Why'd you go over there by yourself?" he demanded.

"I was looking for evidence."

"At eleven at night?"

"Sure, why not?"

He folded his arms and leaned back against the kitchen counter. He wore jeans and a T-shirt, and the hair gel told her he'd been out at a bar earlier. Unlike her, Emmet attempted to have a social life on the weekends.

"Tell me what happened," he said.

"You already heard, obviously, or you wouldn't be here." She leaned against the counter opposite him and tried not to wince.

"I heard you got your ass kicked."

"Who told you that?"

"Someone at the clinic."

Emmet was friendly with several of the nurses there. He was friendly with a lot of people and caught gossip with annoying regularity.

"Nothing broken," she said. "Just some bruised ribs."

"Let me see."

"No."

His face darkened. Then his attention went to the bourbon bottle. He grabbed the plastic bag on the counter and peered inside it. Nicole had gone by the pharmacy on her way home for some ibuprofen.

"Couldn't they give you any real meds?" he asked.

"I don't need any. I'm fine."

His gaze narrowed. "Why are you downplaying this?"

"I'm not."

He held her gaze for a long moment. Then he shook his head and looked away. "What the hell were you doing at a homicide victim's apartment at eleven at night?"

"Searching for evidence."

"Of what?"

"Amelia's mystery man."

"We went through the whole place multiple times already. What could we have missed?"

She watched him for a moment. Then she slid her phone from her pocket and pulled up the photos she'd taken before dropping the sketchbook into an evidence bag.

She handed him the phone. "I found this in her beach bag. It's a sketchbook."

Emmet studied the photo. Then he flipped to the next one and the next. She'd taken two shots of the man on the bed and one of the unfinished profile.

"You can't see who it is," Emmet said as he scrolled through the pictures again. "And there's no date or anything."

"Correct. But there *is* a date on the drawing right before these. That one's a picture of kids playing at the beach, and it's dated March twenty-first."

He lifted an eyebrow and handed the phone back.

"That's four weeks ago," she said. "Which suggests the other sketches were done since then."

He just looked at her.

"Wouldn't you agree?"

He folded his arms over his chest. "What'd you do with the sketchbook?"

"Sent it to the lab. Who knows? Maybe he touched it and we'll get a print."

Emmet shook his head.

"What?"

"You left out the part of the story where you got jumped by two men."

"Where'd you get that?"

"Callahan and Flores. Where do you think?"

The two patrol officers had responded to Nicole's request for assistance after she was attacked. They had interviewed Amelia's neighbors—none of whom had seen anything—

while Nicole had collected her new evidence and resecured the apartment.

"It was *one* guy who jumped me," she told Emmet. "The other one ran off."

"Who do you think they were?"

Sighing, she reached for her mug. "Want some?"

"No."

She took a sip. The previous sip was already hitting her, probably because she'd skipped dinner tonight. She set the mug down.

"I don't know," she said. "Someone doing what I was doing, maybe?"

"Which was?"

"Searching for something that would connect Amelia to the man who killed her."

Emmet's gaze narrowed. "I thought your current theory is that the tech bro from Seattle had something to do with it? Luc Gagnon?"

She'd shared her theory with Emmet while being careful not to reveal that the name had come from Sean Moran.

"I think he might have been *dating* her, but I doubt he actually killed her," Nicole said. "If he's involved, he probably hired someone to handle it."

"And that's who you think was at the apartment," he stated. "A couple of hired goons."

"Maybe."

It sounded far-fetched when she said it out load. Nicole finished off the bourbon and set the mug in the sink.

Emmet eased closer. "Let me see."

She gazed up at him, and the look he was giving her sent a warm ripple through her body. Or maybe it was the booze. Gingerly, she pulled up her shirttail, revealing an angry red bruise at the base of her rib cage. It was already turning dark in places.

He sucked in a breath and stroked a finger up her side. "Damn, Nicole."

She tugged her shirt down.

"You sure they're not broken?"

"I'm sure."

She leaned against the counter, and Emmet held her gaze for a long moment.

"You should have called me," he said.

"You'd left already. Anyway, it was a spur-of-the-moment thing."

He eased closer, and the intensity in his eyes made her stomach flutter. He rested his hand on the counter beside her, and she still felt the burn of his fingertips on her skin. They stared at each other, and the moment seemed strange, even stranger than standing in that closet and realizing someone had just entered the apartment.

"Shit!" Emmet jumped back and looked down.

Nicole's cat rubbed against her ankle, purring.

"Damn it, Lucifer."

"It's *Lucy*," she said. "And she's a sweetheart."

Emmet scowled down at the skinny black feline that had once clawed him to pieces. The cat had been orphaned at a crime scene. When the local shelter couldn't take her, Nicole had reluctantly become a cat owner.

"She eaten?" Emmet asked.

"No. I just got home."

He stepped over to the utility closet and grabbed the plastic bin of cat food off the washer. He dug out a scoop and bent down to pour it into Lucy's bowl—a movement that would have been agony for Nicole.

Lucy dashed over and knocked Emmet's hand out of the way with her head.

"Thank you," Nicole said.

"Sure."

He replaced the scoop. Whatever weird moment had just happened between them was over now. Or maybe she'd imagined it.

Emmet pulled his phone from his pocket and frowned at the screen. Someone was texting him. Someone from the bar, most likely.

He slid the phone into his back pocket. "I should go."

"Yeah."

She led him to the door, and he paused beside it.

"Bruised ribs are a bitch," he said. "I used to get them in football. You should use an ice pack."

"The doctor recommended two ibuprofen."

"Which won't do shit." He smiled. "Unless you chase them down with some more bourbon. That might help."

"Maybe I will."

His smile faded as she opened the door.

"Next time call me," he said. "Or call someone. You shouldn't have gone over there alone."

"Sure, whatever."

He stepped out and turned around. "I mean it, Nicole."

"Next time, I will."

CHAPTER

THIRTEEN

SEAN DROVE DOWN the two-lane highway, keeping his gaze trained on the Jeep's taillights. He checked the gas. He was down to an eighth of a tank, which wasn't good. He'd meant to fill up after dinner tonight, but he'd gotten sidetracked going to see Leyla.

The low gas tank was sloppy. Normally during an op, he was on top of details like that. But nothing about this op had been normal, starting with meeting Leyla Breda on day one and then kissing her tonight in her kitchen. He shouldn't get involved with her. And *she* sure as hell shouldn't get involved in anything he was doing. But Leyla was stubborn, and she seemed to have a burning need to jump right into the middle of everything.

He focused on the Jeep two cars ahead of him. He'd been tailing Gagnon for sixty-five miles, which was much farther than Sean had expected when Gagnon pulled out of his neighborhood for a little late-night drive. Where the hell was he going? He'd crossed the causeway to the mainland more than an hour ago and was now deep into the Rio Grande Valley, a region made up of ranches and citrus farms and the occasional ag town.

The Jeep's turn signal went on. Sean tapped the brakes.

Gagnon turned onto a narrow road, and Sean had no choice but to sail right past it or else risk drawing attention. He drove about a hundred yards farther before making a U-turn and heading back.

Sean turned onto the road. No sign of the Jeep now, and Sean consulted the map on his phone. The road was a winding cut-through that crossed a creek and connected two state highways. Sean drove through a couple of bends, then dipped down over a low-water bridge. He came up a rise and spotted the red taillights again. They glowed brightly as the Jeep slowed and turned left.

Sean pulled over and cut his headlights. Consulting the map, he saw that the Jeep had turned down what appeared to be a private driveway.

Sean waited a few minutes, then followed the Jeep's path, slowing at the turnoff. As suspected, it was a driveway. Sean passed it, taking note of the electronic gate and keypad set back from the road. Sean curved around a bend and pulled his SUV over beneath the shadow of a gnarled oak tree.

Using his phone, he checked his location. He was at about the midpoint of the cut-through that connected the two highways. Judging from the terrain and the barbed wire fencing, the property on both sides of the road was private ranch land.

Sean pulled up a satellite map of the area. The roads were visible, but there wasn't a house or any other building nearby. The place where Gagnon had turned was a short dirt road that dead-ended at a circular clearing and what appeared to be a pump jack. How old were these satellite images? Sean had no idea whether any more roads or buildings had been added since these pictures were taken.

Sean screenshotted his location and forwarded it to Moore with a text. Then he grabbed a flashlight and his binoculars and slid out of his truck. The air smelled of dust and juniper. Emerging from the shadow of the tree, he put his flashlight on dim mode and used it to light his path as he jogged back to the turnoff. He stopped shy of the driveway and looked around for security cameras or motion-sensitive lights. Now he had a decision to make. Go in or wait for instructions?

Patience wasn't Sean's strong suit. And anyway, whatever was going down right now could be over by the time Moore got back to him.

Sean ducked between the barbed wire, snagging his T-shirt. He jerked it free, then crept toward a clump of mesquite. His eyes were adjusting to the dark now, and he could make out the shadowy silhouettes of bushes and scrub trees. Due north of him, he spied a faint glow over a clump of trees. Sean knelt down and pulled his Sig from his ankle holster. He tucked the pistol into the back of his jeans and then moved toward the glow. He heard a low hum of something mechanical in the distance. A generator? He moved steadily through the darkness, taking care to keep his steps soft and not rustle through the trees.

Suddenly, a light flashed on. Sean ducked behind a mesquite tree and peered through the branches at a distant pump jack illuminated by a spotlight. Tucking his flashlight away, Sean crept through the scrub brush and approached the oil well. Beside it was a metal shed, along with some tanks surrounded by chain-link fencing.

Through the foliage, he spotted the Jeep, headlights off. It was backed up to the shed, facing out, and Gagnon sat behind the wheel, his face illuminated by the glow of his cell phone. Creeping closer, Sean spied a second vehicle—a white pickup truck. No lights on. It sat on the opposite end of the fenced-off area from Gagnon. A shadowy form leaned against the tailgate, and Sean caught the glow of a cigarette.

Edging closer, Sean lifted his binoculars and studied the white pickup. It was a Ford F-150 with an extended cab. Sean wanted to get the license plate, but that was impossible in the dark from this distance. He wished he had a camera right now with a zoom lens, so he could at least get a shot that someone might be able to enhance later. But he was out of luck tonight.

Sean shifted his attention to Gagnon. Still no movement. Still waiting.

He peered through the binoculars again and studied the silhouette leaning against the tailgate. The man looked around six feet tall, medium build, baseball cap. Suddenly, a phone glowed in his hand. As he lifted it, Sean got a look at his face in the bluish light. Pale skin, brownish goatee. The man stared down at this phone, scrolling through. Something about him looked familiar. He tossed his cigarette away and then picked up a can from the bumper and took a long swig.

Sean adjusted the binoculars, wishing the light were better. He studied the guy's face—the goatee, the prominent cheekbones. Sean felt like he'd seen him somewhere before, but he couldn't place it.

Sean shifted his focus to Gagnon again. He and this guy seemed content to sit out here, fifty feet apart, not talking, clearly waiting for someone. Sean pictured the satellite image and tried to imagine which direction someone might come from. He'd only seen one road leading onto the property.

A distant grumble pulled Sean's attention north, the

opposite direction of the road he and Gagnon had used. It was a heavy-duty engine, probably a V-8, and the noise changed pitch as the truck bumped over the rugged terrain. Sean searched the scrub trees and spotted the glare of headlights through the foliage. Two thick beams, high and wide apart. The truck bumped closer, and Sean saw that it was a black dually with a big grille guard. It was coming in fast, mowing down everything in its path, including flimsy scrub trees. Sean darted his gaze around, looking for better cover. The only thing sturdier than mesquite was a scraggly juniper, and Sean rushed behind it.

The truck roared past him and stopped beside the pump jack. Sean crouched at the base of the juniper and watched.

The Jeep's interior light went on as Gagnon slid out, leaving the door open. The goatee guy took one last swig of beer and tossed his can away, then slid his phone into his pocket and walked over.

The dually had two occupants, but only the driver got out. He was tall and potbellied and wore a cowboy hat that seemed pointless out here in the dark. He stalked around the front of his truck. Everyone shook hands and nodded, and Sean got the impression this was a business meeting of sorts.

Sean looked around for a better vantage point. He wanted those license plates, but he might not have time to get both. The white pickup was closest, so he ducked low and made a run for a clump of trees behind it. Then he crept around a bush, all the while keeping an eye on the meeting.

The black truck's door opened, and the passenger handed something out to the cowboy. Sean stopped and lifted the binoculars.

The package was dark and flat—about the size of a brick—and the cowboy said something as he gave it to the goatee guy. Next, the cowboy handed Gagnon a small black duffel with a Nike swoosh on the side. The bag didn't look full or heavy. Gagnon grabbed it with one hand and tossed it into the Jeep. Then he turned to leave. Pausing beside the Jeep's door, he said something over his shoulder before hitching himself behind the wheel.

Meanwhile, the goatee guy was already back in his truck, starting the engine. The taillights glowed as he backed away from the fence.

Cursing, Sean lowered the binoculars and darted behind some scrub trees. He swung his attention to the black dually just as it lurched backward. Another throaty growl, and the truck lurched backward again. Then the engine changed pitch, and the headlights swung straight toward him.

Sean's pulse jumped. He glanced around and dove into a shallow ditch beside some trees. The truck roared toward him, and for a deafening moment, he didn't breathe, just flattened himself to the ground as the noise reverberated around him like an earthquake. Sean's heart skipped a beat as the truck raced right past his head, pelting his face with gravel.

Fumes burned his eyes. Grit clogged his nose, his mouth, his throat. Finally, he lifted his head. Choking on dust, he squinted into the darkness as the taillights faded away.

A LOUD THUDDING DRAGGED Nicole from sleep.
　　She squinted at her mini-blinds. What time was it? It was light out, although it seemed like she'd just barely gone to sleep. She'd finally drifted off after watching a movie while propped against a stack of pillows. Slowly, she sat forward and looked at her clock. Who would show up here at eight on a Saturday? She grabbed the phone from her nightstand and figured out the answer as she saw a string of missed messages.

Coming, she texted back.

She got out of bed and shuffled to the chair where she'd left her jeans. Slowly and carefully, she pulled them on. Putting on a bra at the moment was well beyond her pain threshold, so she grabbed a button-down flannel from her closet and made a quick bathroom stop. Then she crossed her living room and opened the door for Sean Moran.

"Morning," she said.

He looked immediately apologetic. "Damn. Sorry, I thought you'd be up by now."

"Yeah, well. Late night." She stepped back to let him in. "You had coffee?"

"No."

She led him into her kitchen and gestured at a bar stool. "Make yourself at home."

He eyed the bottle of bourbon as he sat down. Emmet had been right. The ibuprofen had done zip for her pain, and she'd ended up making herself another stiff drink before bed.

She warmed up the coffeemaker and then turned to look at Sean. He wore jeans and his leather jacket again. Apparently, he wasn't a fan of her Hawaiian shirt idea. His hair was damp from a shower, and he looked way too alert for this early in the morning.

"What happened to your face?" she asked.

He rubbed his cheek. "Caught some gravel."

She looked at him with suspicion as she retrieved some coffee pods from the pantry. Thankfully, there were two left because she couldn't bear the thought of giving away her last cup. She reached for the Keurig and hissed out a curse as pain darted up her side.

"I heard about Amelia's apartment." Sean got up and walked around the counter. "Mugs?"

"Upper cabinet."

He took down two mugs and put a coffee pod into the machine. Then he turned to face her.

"Who told you?" Nicole asked.

"Brady."

She lifted an eyebrow. Evidently, the chief was keeping their FBI friend very much in the loop.

The first cup of coffee finished brewing, and she handed it to Sean.

"I hope you like it black," she said. "I'm all out of sugar."

"Black's good." He put another pod in and started a second cup. When it was done brewing, she picked it up and watched him over the rim as she took a sip. The coffee was hot and strong, and she was going to need a lot of it today.

"Tell me something." She set the cup down. "Does Luc Gagnon have any kind of private security working for him?"

Sean nodded. "He travels with a two-man detail. Why?"

"Just wondering. What do they look like?"

"Couple of tall blond guys. They look Scandinavian, but they're from Serbia." He paused. "You get a look at who attacked you?"

"No. It happened really fast. And it was dark." She took another sip and set her cup down. "But one of them was definitely tall. And it felt like he had on steel-toed boots. Of course, I could be imagining that part."

Sean's brow furrowed. "You shouldn't have gone over there alone."

"Thanks for the tip." She leaned back against the counter. "So, what brings you here? I'm guessing you didn't track down my home address just to say hi."

"I'm hoping you can do me a favor." He pulled a plastic bag from his jacket pocket and set it on the counter. Inside the bag was a Budweiser can with dirt and grass clinging to it. "I need you to run this for fingerprints."

"Why?"

"Gagnon had a meeting with someone last night. I'd like to know if he's in the system."

"Why can't you run it?"

"I could," he said. "It's better if it doesn't come from me."

"Why?"

He just looked at her, not answering her question, and she got an uneasy feeling in the pit of her stomach.

"Can you run it?" he asked.

"Sure. But you know, it's going to take a lot longer if I send it to the county lab. You're the one with all the *resources* at your fingertips."

He just stared at her.

"By the way, how's that phone number coming?" she asked him.

"I haven't heard back yet."

"No?" She tipped her head to the side, watching him. She was putting a lot of trust in this federal agent. And so far, their "cooperative" relationship had been exactly what she'd expected: a one-way street.

"When do you think you'll hear back?" she asked.

"I don't know. Soon, I hope."

"So, here's another question," she said, purposely leaving him hanging about his beer can.

"Yeah?"

"Who is Virgil?"

That got his attention. "Where'd you hear about Virgil?"

"Around."

"Around where?" The sharp edge in his voice told her Virgil was important.

"I overhead the chief talking to someone about him in his office yesterday."

"Who?"

"I don't know. They were together in there for a while. I think he may have been one of you guys."

"What did he look like?" Sean asked.

"Big. Around six four. Black. Probably midforties."

"That's Dwight Moore, my boss."

"You still haven't answered my question. Who is Virgil?"

He looked at her for a long moment, and she could tell he was debating—once again—how much to tell her. But she still hadn't agreed to handle his evidence for him, and she wasn't going to unless she got something in return. He wasn't the only one running an investigation here.

"Virgil isn't a person," he said.

"No?"

"It's an op. It's the reason I'm down here."

She hadn't expected that.

"So, why is it called 'Virgil' if the target is Luc Gagnon?"

"It's named after a Roman poet. And Gagnon's not really the target. We're focused on his company."

She watched him, trying to fill in the gaps with what she already knew. "The company makes software that encrypts communications."

"Yes. And he also makes a line of super secure encrypted devices."

"He does?"

"For some VIP clients, yes. We have reason to believe he's getting a shipment of those devices soon. That shipment is very important. We're trying to intercept it."

"And *that's* the major deal that's going down," she said, suddenly catching on. "The thing you mentioned yesterday. You're trying to intercept the shipment before all these preloaded devices go out to drug cartels and mafia people and so on."

He nodded.

"When is it happening?" she asked.

"That's what I'm trying to figure out."

"And where is it happening?

"Again, I don't know yet. I wish I did. It's a little challenging to investigate someone when *all* their sensitive communication is done on encrypted devices. Not only that, every person using these devices is difficult to investigate. Many of our usual tools and methods are useless. I mean, we arrest somebody with one of these phones, and suddenly all their messages are wiped clean before we can even get a look at anything."

"They can wipe them remotely?"

"Yes," he said, clearly frustrated. "This technology puts a major dent in our ability to build cases. And we're talking about criminal operations all over the globe that utilize this software."

She sighed. "Damn."

"Exactly."

She watched him, thinking about what he'd said as something niggled at the corner of her brain.

"If I'm remembering my freshman lit class correctly, Virgil wrote about a Trojan horse," she said. "You know, the wooden horse the Greeks used to sneak into Troy?"

Sean didn't respond.

"So . . . you're not just trying to intercept these devices. You want to corrupt them or something. That's why you need Gagnon. You want to convince him to give you guys a back door?"

He lifted an eyebrow, and she felt a rush of adrenaline because she could tell she was on the right track.

"Not a bad plan, assuming it works," she said. "It sounds risky."

He sipped his coffee, not confirming or denying anything. But she knew her guess was at least in the right ballpark. She could tell from his body language.

Sean checked his watch. He was getting antsy to leave, and she still hadn't agreed to run his evidence for finger-prints.

Nicole debated what to do. He'd just shared some very sensitive information with her, and she knew it was a trade. Which made her think this beer can had to be important. Why he couldn't run it through the FBI, she had no idea. His channels were faster than hers, but clearly it was more important that the evidence not link back to him. She'd have to think about what that meant, but in the meantime, she wanted to keep the flow of information going.

"I'll take care of the beer can for you," she said.

"Thanks."

"I know someone at the lab up there. I'll put in a call, see if I can get a rush on it."

"I appreciate it." He checked his watch again. "I'd better go."

She led him to the door.

"Thanks for the coffee," he said. "I needed it."

"Sure." She glanced at him. "Not as good as Leyla's, but it does the job."

He nodded, keeping his face carefully blank.

She stopped by the door. "I hear you've been spending time with her?"

His eyebrows tipped up. "Where'd you hear that?"

"Small island. You know, you want to be sure to keep her out of it."

"Out of what?"

"This operation you've got going here. It sounds dangerous." She reached for the door. "If you value your friendship with Joel, you'll want to keep his sister way the hell away from it."

LEYLA MET SEAN on the bridge spanning the sand dunes. Today she wore white jeans and a tight black T-shirt, and the breeze off the water whipped her ponytail around her shoulders.

She smiled as she neared him, and Sean's pulse sped up. That was all it took. One smile, and his whole body reacted.

He held out the drink he'd brought her. "Lemonade," he said. "I stopped at the juice place."

"Aww, thanks." Her smile fell away as she took the cup. "What happened to your face?"

"Caught some gravel," he said, because he seemed to have lost the ability to lie to her.

"How?"

"Don't worry about it." He took her hand to distract her as they walked to the end of the bridge.

She slid him a look, not distracted at all. "Are you all right?"

"Fine. Thanks for taking a break with me."

"I only have twenty minutes or so. Our event starts at five."

They walked together down the stairs, and she dropped his hand to remove her sandals. She'd painted her toenails pink, he noticed. The other night they'd been silver.

She left her shoes at the base of the steps.

"Thanks for the drink." She sipped from the straw and then offered him the cup. "Want some?"

"I'm good."

They walked toward the water, passing a beach blanket where a family had set up for the afternoon with what seemed like a crazy amount of gear: three umbrellas, two coolers, six beach chairs, plus a wagon filled with foam pool noodles. A group of kids ran back and forth between the water's edge and a giant pit where they were building a sandcastle.

Leyla sipped the lemonade and stopped to gaze at the surf. "Tide's out." She glanced at him. "You get a chance to fish today?"

"Nope."

They started walking, and she looked at him, clearly hoping he'd elaborate on what he'd been up to since she'd last seen him.

"I spent the day inside, mostly," he said. "Online, on the phone. It's been pretty tedious. How about you?"

"Saturdays are always busy. After the lunch rush, I decorated a cake for a christening that's tomorrow." She handed him the cup and then bent to roll the cuffs of her jeans. "And then I fried forty crab cakes and made a remoulade sauce for tonight's gig." She straightened. "So, if I smell like cooking oil, that's why."

He stepped closer and tucked a lock of hair behind her ear. "You smell amazing."

"Right."

He gave her back the lemonade. Then he took her free hand again and they strolled down the beach, passing a boy and his dad trying to get a shark-shaped kite into the air. Most of the families out today had small children who were probably still too young to be tied to the school calendar.

They walked along in companionable silence. His condo was just up ahead, and he had the urge to take her upstairs and make her late for her event. Sean was dying to get her alone. Truly alone, where they wouldn't be interrupted by crowds or co-workers or cell phones. Maybe when this op wrapped, he could tack on some vacation time. He wanted a real vacation, where he could turn his phone off and give Leyla his undivided attention.

He wanted to get to know her. *Really* get to know her, beyond the stuff she'd been willing to share so far. He already knew she kept her guard up with most people, and he got that, but he wanted to be different. He wanted to learn what made her happy, and frustrated, and turned on. He wanted every detail. He'd never been so intrigued by anyone, and he was trying not to feel bitter over the fact that they lived so far apart. He was trying to focus on *her* instead, but the logistical stuff kept eating away at him. He couldn't help it. That was how he was. When he saw a problem, he homed in on it.

She looked at him. "What's wrong?"

"Nothing. Just thinking."

"About?"

"Stuff I don't want to talk about right now." He squeezed her hand, and she gave him an amused smile.

"So"—she sipped her lemonade—"you know there's a golf tournament tomorrow over at Playa del Rey? It's this big event for charity."

Something in her voice put him on guard. "What about it?"

"Luc Gagnon's assistant called me. Her name's Jillian."

Sean halted.

"She asked if we might be able to cater a dinner party after the tournament," Leyla said.

"She just called you out of the blue?"

"I've worked with her before. Remember I told you about the breakfast meeting at the Windjammer?"

Sean stared down at her. "And she just randomly called you?"

"Well, she was returning my call. I'd left her a message yesterday letting her know our catering firm was officially launched and then I sent her a menu."

Sean's gut tightened. "You're actively marketing to him?"

"I'm marketing to everyone at the moment. I'm trying to get my business off the ground."

"I can't believe you did that."

"Anyway, it's a small group for dinner. Jillian said she was glad to hear from me because the headcount unexpectedly jumped from twelve to twenty at the last minute so—"

"*Where* is this dinner?"

She pulled back, clearly startled by his tone. "At his house."

Sean shook his head and looked away.

"What? I thought it might be a good opportunity."

He glared down at her. "How's that?"

"Well . . . it's his big new house, and almost no one's been inside," she said. "He brought in an architect and a decorator from Seattle. He travels with his own staff. I thought, I don't know, this might be a good opportunity for someone to poke around a little and maybe eavesdrop."

"Are you serious right now?"

"Yes."

"You're not an agent, Leyla."

"Not me. I meant you could send someone in. They could pretend to work for me."

"No."

She huffed out a breath. "You won't even *consider*—"

"No."

"Fine." She started down the beach again.

"And you shouldn't consider it either," he told her. "Luc Gagnon is not the kind of client you need."

"What, you mean wealthy people who entertain? That's exactly the kind of client I need."

Sean gritted his teeth. Now she was just trying to piss him off. He couldn't believe she'd come up with this scheme.

But then again, he could. She'd been nosing around his work ever since she'd figured out about the possible link between Amelia and his investigation.

"Forget it," she said now. "It was just an idea. I haven't even accepted the job yet. I can always tell her it's too last-minute and we're booked."

"That sounds good. Tell her that."

"I hate leaving people in the lurch, though."

What she probably hated more was sending people to her competition. Sean glanced at her. She seemed annoyed by his reaction, but he didn't give a damn.

She pulled her phone from her pocket and checked the screen. "Siena's texting me. I need to get back."

They turned around and headed back toward the bridge in silence. He trudged through the sand, absorbing everything she'd told him. All of it made him extremely uneasy.

Luc Gagnon was a thirty-six-year-old jet-setter who routinely did business with some of the most notorious lowlifes on the planet. Sean didn't want Leyla anywhere near the man, or near anyone in his orbit, for that matter. Just the idea of her inside Gagnon's house, waiting on a bunch of rich assholes who'd been getting loaded all day, put a tight knot in the center of Sean's chest.

"It was just an idea. Relax."

"I am."

"Sean, I can *hear* your teeth grinding."

They neared the bridge and she veered away to toss her drink into a trash bin. Watching her, he wondered whether she'd really had a text from Siena. Maybe she just wanted to get away from him because he'd pissed her off again.

They reached the steps, and she unrolled her cuffs and slipped on her sandals.

"So . . . I was thinking." She smiled up at him. "Does that dinner invitation to the Nautilus still stand?"

"Yes."

"How about Monday night?"

She gazed up at him with those big blue eyes, and he considered how to respond. He couldn't believe he'd even hesitate. Since the moment he'd met her, he'd been on a mission to get her to spend time with him.

But the more she did, the more she became intrigued by his work. Leyla wouldn't even know about a possible link between Amelia and Luc Gagnon if she hadn't been at Sean's place the other night. Leyla was observant, she was intuitive, and she was deeply interested in the case he was working on. It was a dangerous combination.

And to make things worse, Sean continued to show bad judgment. He'd allowed himself to get distracted, resulting in dumb mistakes. Letting the gas tank get low. Inviting Leyla up to his apartment when he'd left his computer out. Bottom line, he was distracted as hell by everything about her. He needed to get his head in the game before he did something really stupid that couldn't be undone.

She looked up at him expectantly.

"I'll let you know," he said. "I may have a late-day meeting at the Brownsville office."

"Oh."

It was a lie, but that was too bad. Giving her the truth—even little scraps of it—had backfired.

She dusted the sand from her palms and tucked her hands into her back pockets. She looked at him, and he got the distinct feeling the whole dinner-date conversation was an attempt to change the subject.

"What are you going to tell Gagnon's assistant?" he asked.

"I don't know." She shrugged. "I'll probably just tell her we're booked."

Probably.

He gritted his teeth, and the knot in his chest was back again.

She reached up and stroked her fingertip over his jaw. "Don't clench. It's bad for you."

"I'm not."

She went up on tiptoes and kissed him, and he slid his arm around her waist before he could stop himself.

She eased back, smiling. "Thanks for the lemonade. Let me know about Monday night."

NICOLE HURRIED PAST the reception desk, where Denise was filing her nails.

"They started yet?"

Denise buzzed the door open. "Five minutes ago."

"Crap," Nicole muttered, rushing through the bullpen. Brady's office was empty, and so were most of the desks, including the ones for Emmet, McDeere, and Lopez, who was the rookie they'd pulled in to help with some of the legwork.

Nicole was thirsty from being in the sun all afternoon, plus she was hungover from her little bourbon binge last night. She swung into the break room and grabbed a bottle of water from the fridge before hurrying into the conference room.

All heads turned her way as she walked in.

"Hi. Sorry I'm late."

No one responded, and she took the closest empty seat. It was next to Lopez, and he eyed her curiously as she set her stuff down and slowly lowered herself into the chair.

"I was just filling them in on Luc Gagnon," Brady said.

Nicole looked at the chief, surprised. "All right."

"And the possible connection with the two Saledo hit jobs back in the fall." Brady leaned back in his chair. "Anything new from the lab?"

The chief had sent her on yet another squeaky-wheel mission, but this one had been more successful. The lab supervisor had given her a preview of several results that had just come in. She'd also had a chance to personally drop off the beer can Sean had asked her to run for him.

She cast a glance at Emmet. His cool gaze told her he'd picked up on the fact that she'd had some inside info that she'd neglected to share with him. How much had Brady revealed to the team? And how much did he even know? Nicole hadn't discussed Operation Virgil with anyone here. She'd gotten the distinct impression from Sean that she wasn't supposed to know about it.

"Some interesting updates." She scooted her chair in, wincing as fire shot up her rib cage. Biting back a curse, she opened her file folder.

"The tox report came in," she said. "No drugs in her system. Also, the rape kit came back. Nothing there, no foreign DNA or anything."

Whatever terrors Amelia Albright had been subjected to before her death, they hadn't included sexual assault.

"They *did* come up with some interesting DNA evidence, though. This is from the swab the ME took from the site of the knife wound." She looked at Brady. "The swab shows a second DNA profile that doesn't match the victim."

"Like, the killer nicked himself?" Emmet asked.

That's what Nicole had thought, too. A knife handle could get slippery during a bloody struggle, and it was possible the perpetrator could cut himself and leave blood on the victim.

"Weirder than that," she said. "The DNA profile matches Jose Rincon."

Brady's eyebrows arched. "*Rincon?*"

"Sorry. Who's Jose Rincon?" the rookie asked.

"One of the two San Antonio victims," she said. "The other one is Sandra Massey."

"Wait. Back up. *How* would some dead guy's DNA end up on Amelia Albright?" McDeere asked.

"The murder weapon," Emmet said, staring at Nicole. "He didn't clean it."

"Didn't clean it enough," she said. "Some trace amount of a previous victim's blood was transferred to our victim."

"Interesting." Brady steepled his hands together under his chin.

Nicole felt a swell of pride that she'd managed to get a decent lead. And on a Saturday, no less. The squeaky-wheel strategy seemed to be working, and she was developing a good rapport with the lab supervisor.

She cleared her throat and continued. "Combined with the blue cordage—which isn't totally *conclusive* evidence. I mean, that could have been a coincidence—but combined with *that*, we can now confirm that whoever carried out the hits in San Antonio is responsible for Amelia Albright," Nicole said.

"Well, at least we know they used the same murder kit. Same knife, same bindings. Could have been a different hit man," Emmet pointed out.

Nicole nodded. She hadn't thought of that, but he was right.

"At any rate, it definitely connects the three crimes," she said. "So, that's big." She glanced at Brady, looking for confirmation.

He was still watching her over his steepled hands.

"The San Antonio detective, he give you any details about the MO?" the chief asked. "Besides the killing itself?"

"What do you mean?" she asked.

"How did they track the vics?" he asked. "The Massey woman was dumped behind her apartment building, right? But the other guy—Rincon—he was ambushed after leaving a bar. How'd they know he'd be there?"

"Yeah, I asked that," Nicole said. "The detective told me they assume whoever carried out the hit had been following the guy around. It wasn't a place Rincon frequented, so they figured he must have been followed there. And based on some fiber evidence, they believe he was picked up while walking to his car, then bound, beaten, and questioned in the back of a vehicle before being stabbed and dumped in the alley behind the bar."

"Fiber evidence?" Emmet asked.

"Yeah, some carpet fibers," Nicole said. "And that's a good detail for us to be aware of, too. San Antonio recently got the lab results back on the carpet fibers. They were run through a national database, and the fibers came back to a Dodge minivan. We don't have an exterior color, unfortunately, because a lot of the vans have black carpet inside. But that's where they think someone held Rincon and questioned him."

"The van could have been a rental," McDeere said.

She nodded. "True. Also, we don't have any reason to think Amelia was held inside a vehicle. Based on the blood traces inside the coffee shop storeroom, it looks like she was held in there."

Silence settled over the room as she looked around.

"Where are we on those security cams?" Brady asked, turning to McDeere.

"I've talked to every business in the area," McDeere said. "Surf's Up, the gas station across the street, the souvenir shop, even the grocery place three buildings down. No one had any outdoor cameras that picked up anything near the alley or the parking lot behind the Island Beanery. We're out of luck on that front. Too bad the Beanery didn't have any cameras."

"They do now," Emmet said. "I was in there yesterday. Leyla just had some installed."

"Okay, what about the boyfriend angle?" Brady asked Emmet. "You were going to reinterview some of her friends."

"I did. One of them told me Amelia went on a few dates with some tech CEO who was down from Seattle," Emmet said. "We're assuming that's Luc Gagnon."

"Who is this friend?" the chief asked.

"One of the baristas she worked with. I hadn't interviewed her before. Turns out they had a bunch of shifts together, so they talked a lot."

"She say where Amelia met this guy?" Brady asked.

"She didn't know," Emmet responded. "Could have been at the coffee shop or a bar or anywhere. We know from Amelia's friends that she liked to go out a lot."

"So far, nothing on the sketchbook. I mean, in terms of fingerprints or whatever." Nicole opened her file again and shuffled through until she found a printout of the sketches she'd discovered in Amelia's apartment. She'd also found some photos online of Luc Gagnon. She'd printed several shots, including profiles and straight-on angles. "Here are some pictures for comparison." She slid the printouts across the table to Brady and Emmet.

They leaned forward to study the pictures, and Nicole

waited expectantly. She knew what Brady was going to say even before he said it.

Brady looked up. "Inconclusive."

"He has dark hair," Nicole pointed out. "And a similar body type." She nodded toward the sketch of the man stretched out in bed. If she'd been in a room full of women, she would have made the obvious observation that the guy in the drawing was hot. "The sketch shows someone muscular, and we know Luc Gagnon is athletic."

"How to we know that?" Emmet asked, and she detected a trace of snark in his voice.

"According to *People* magazine, he does mountain biking. And surfing. And he plays golf."

Emmet rolled his eyes.

"You're right, though," she said, turning to Brady. "There's nothing conclusive in the sketch. No tattoos or anything, and the face is barely filled in. All we know is the guy in her sketchbook has dark hair."

"Okay, I think we can disregard the sketchbook for now," Brady said. "Unless we get a fingerprint."

Nicole sighed with frustration. She'd gone over to that apartment and had the shit kicked out of her, and she had nothing to show for it.

"Let's focus on San Antonio now that we have a confirmed link," Brady said. "Nicole, I want you to juice that connection."

"Juice it?"

"The detectives you're talking to up there—keep working that. They've been on this case much longer than we have. They've got leads that would take us months to develop, like the carpet fiber thing. They've completed tons of interviews, and all their lab work has already come back. We should take advantage of that."

"So, you want me to circle back with them?" she asked.

The San Antonio detectives hadn't exactly prioritized her calls. She'd had to hound them for days and make a pest of herself.

"Yeah, and do it in person," he said. "Drive up there. Get them talking. Take them out for beers if you have to. Find out what they have that they're not saying."

"You think they're holding out on us?" she asked.

"Hell yes. They're San Antonio. We're not," Brady said. "The last thing they're going to do is share everything they have and watch some beach town police department crack their case for them."

CHAPTER

SIXTEEN

SEAN WAITED FOR an empty elevator and got on by himself. He was sweaty, smelly, and his muscles were on fire. He'd spent ninety minutes in the building's windowless fitness room trying to work out his frustration with Leyla. But it hadn't helped because he knew she was going to ignore his advice and take that catering job. He didn't doubt it for a minute.

Stepping out of the elevator, he smelled deep-fried shrimp coming from one of the units. His stomach began to rumble. He was starving, but he'd finished off the last of his frozen burritos and his fridge was empty.

Sean paused at his door, and his pulse picked up. A TV was on. He leaned close to listen. *His* TV.

He reached under his T-shirt for the Sig tucked in the neoprene holster around his waist. Who the hell was here?

Leyla.

Still holding his gun in case he was wrong, he slipped

the key card from his pocket, unlocked the door, and eased it open.

Dwight Moore sat on his couch, feet propped on the coffee table, watching a baseball game. He glanced over his shoulder.

"Hey," he said in his deep voice.

"Hi." Sean turned and tucked his gun away before walking into the kitchen. "How'd you get in here?"

Moore got up and came over, and the smirk on his face told Sean he'd noticed the Sig. "They gave me two keys when I rented the place."

Sean grabbed a dish towel from the oven door and wiped his face as he looked at his boss. A former Naval Academy defensive end, Moore was six four and outweighed Sean by about sixty pounds. Sean always felt small in the guy's presence.

He tossed the towel on the counter. "Want a beer or anything?"

"I got one." Moore's brow furrowed, and Sean could tell he was noticing the cut on his cheek.

"What's up?" Sean asked.

"We think we IDed the cowboy."

"Oh yeah?"

"Greg Tillman. He has a black dually pickup truck and owns the cattle ranch where you were last night." Moore leaned back against the counter. "He keeps a small herd, but all his money is in oil and gas."

"Okay."

"At least until recently. He may have started a side business running guns into Mexico."

"To Saledo?"

"Maybe."

"Where'd we get this?"

"ATF."

Sean crossed his arms. It was the first involvement he'd heard from the Bureau of Alcohol, Tobacco and Firearms. Sean could only assume this meant that they knew about Operation Virgil.

"Also, we got a bead on that shipment, and we think it's coming in soon. It could be on the island as early as this week. Maybe even Tuesday. The big question is *where*."

Moore walked over to the coffee table and grabbed a cardboard tube, along with a half-empty bottle of beer. Sean watched as he unrolled an aerial map of the island. He used the bottle to weigh down one of the corners and Sean grabbed some coasters to weigh down the other three. Then he stared at the map. He'd spent a lot of time studying a version of it on his computer.

"All depends whether it's coming by yacht, speedboat, fishing boat," Moore said. "It's a small island, so that limits the options."

"Not as much as you'd think," Sean said. Having been here more than a week, he'd seen all sorts of possibilities for a person wanting to smuggle goods here under the radar.

"We've got eyes on the marina," Moore said, tapping the bayside location where Gagnon kept his thirty-two-foot Boston Whaler. "They're taking a close look at any unfamiliar boats coming in."

"What about the airport?" Sean pointed to the private airstrip that Gagnon used for his Cessna.

"We're set up there, too. But we don't have the staff to cover both these locations, plus the house, twenty-four seven. We need intel. We need to know where, and *when*, this is happening so we can focus our resources and get our cyber team in place to respond quickly."

Moore looked up.

"I'm working on it," Sean said.

"So are we. But so far, it's mostly guesswork."

Sean stared down at the map of the island that he'd scoured from top to bottom. He'd driven it, jogged it, walked through most of downtown. The place was wide open, with access points by car, boat, and plane. Lost Beach was only a stone's throw from the border. The island's tourism—plus the new airport—made it a smuggler's dream, which was why the Saledos liked it and also probably why Gagnon had wanted a foothold here. The place was fast becoming a hot spot for criminals, and law enforcement hadn't caught up yet.

An uneasy feeling settled in Sean's stomach as he studied the map.

"What's on your mind?"

He glanced up, and Moore was watching him intently.

"I was just thinking . . ." Sean shook his head.

"What?"

"There's a chance we're too late."

His eyebrows arched. "Why do you say that?"

"I've been thinking about last night. You know, Gagnon's midnight drive into the valley."

"What about it?"

"What if that was a decoy?"

Moore just stared at him.

"Maybe he figured out he's under surveillance and he wanted to lure us off the island so the handoff could go down while he was gone." The knot in Sean's stomach tightened as he said the words out load. "If that was his plan, then it worked perfectly."

Moore shook his head. "I don't think that was it."

"No?"

"No. In fact, I'm sure of it. Based on his history, we believe that he intends to personally take possession of this shipment. That's why he's here. And the intel we have on the container ship is solid. They haven't off-loaded anything yet, and we've been watching."

"Okay, what about the rest of our intel?" Sean asked. "How solid is that?"

Moore frowned. "What do you mean?"

"Well, do we have an inside guy working with Saledo? Or with this rancher, Tillman?"

"No."

"Are you sure?" Sean asked.

"I'm sure."

"What about ICE or DEA or ATF?"

"We don't have any undercover agents with Saledo or Tillman. I would know about it. Anyway, why are you asking?"

"Just wondering."

"What's with the paranoia?"

"Nothing," Sean said. "I'm just being cautious."

Moore watched him skeptically.

And he was right. Sean *was* paranoid. There wasn't one specific reason he could pinpoint. It was more a cluster of small things—none of which he was ready to disclose to anyone, even Moore. Not that Sean didn't trust him. Moore was a straight arrow, and Sean didn't have even the smallest doubt about his integrity. But Sean had felt edgy for days now, and his feeling was only heightened after last night's little field trip.

"If you know something I don't, let's hear it," Moore said.

"I don't. Yet."

Moore gave him a long, hard look. "Keep me informed. I can't have your back if I don't know what's going on."

"I will."

Moore checked his watch. "I need to go." He nodded at the map. "You keep that. I've got another one back at the office."

Great. One more thing to keep out of Leyla's sight if she ever came over again. Which would obviously be a bad idea, for many reasons.

"We're going to keep watching and listening," Moore said. "Hopefully, something will pop soon. Keep your phone charged and be ready to execute the plan as soon as it's a go."

"I will."

"Cheer up." Moore slapped him on the shoulder. "This thing's moving faster than we thought. With any luck, we'll get this thing wrapped and be out of here soon."

CHAPTER

SEVENTEEN

Leyla's phone chimed as she turned onto Driftwood Avenue. Sean again. She let it go to voicemail.

"You want me to grab that?" Siena asked from the passenger seat.

"He'll leave a message."

And Leyla knew what it would say. Sean had left a message earlier telling her that if she wasn't working tonight, he'd love to meet her for a drink at the Windjammer.

It was his not-subtle way of finding out whether she'd taken the catering job at Luc Gagnon's.

Well, she had. And she didn't care to hear his opinion about it. It was her business, and she'd take whatever jobs she wanted—especially ones that paid big bucks for a few hours of work. She'd been shelling out a fortune on startup costs, including a website, kitchen supplies, serving equipment. She needed a delivery van, too, but as of this week, every dime she'd been saving for that had gone to pay for a new security system. Bottom line, she was strapped for cash and needed to take every job she could get for the foreseeable future.

Leyla rolled to a stop at the wrought iron gate, and a young man stepped out of the guardhouse. She flashed him a smile.

"Hi, I'm with Just In Thyme Catering, going to the Gagnon residence. It's me and the Subaru behind me."

The guard checked his clipboard. "Uh . . . Leyla Breda?"

"Yep."

"I've just got the one name down."

"Well, it's me and my staff."

"One sec." He stepped into the guardhouse and made a phone call. A few moments later he nodded. "Okay, you're good."

The gate lifted and Leyla rolled through. Wade followed in the car behind her. They hung a left onto a palm-lined street with three- and four-story houses that faced the beach.

"Damn." Siena gaped out the window. "These places are enormous."

"Have you ever been back here before?"

"No. You?"

"I walked through a few sites when the subdivision was under construction. It's been years, though." She surveyed the manicured tropical landscaping and expensive cars in several of the driveways.

"Look how many places are empty." Siena sighed. "What a waste. People spend a fortune and don't even come down here."

Leyla pulled up to a modern gray stucco with six garage doors. Gagnon's assistant stood at the base of a grand staircase leading up to the double front door.

"Welcome," Jillian said with a smile as Leyla got out and Wade pulled into the space beside her. "Any trouble finding us?"

"Not at all."

Jillian wore flowy white pants and a jade green blouse that tied at the waist. Her blond hair was pulled back in an elaborate twist that somehow managed to look messy and perfect at the same time.

"I'm glad you're here," she said. "Everyone should be arriving any minute now."

Leyla gasped. "I thought you said six?"

"They're coming early." Jillian rolled her eyes. "No worries, though. We're pretty well set up already."

Leyla's head spun with logistics as Siena and Wade began unloading supplies.

"We're eating poolside on level four," Jillian told her. "You can use the elevator to unload. The kitchen's on two and there's an interior staircase, plus one outside connecting the decks. What else? If you need extra fridge space, there's one in the utility room off the kitchen." She smiled broadly. "Let me know if I can help with anything."

"Thanks! We got it."

Leyla hurried to help unpack. They had four foil trays and three plastic tubs filled with preprepped food and supplies. They squeezed most of it into the elevator and left Wade behind with a giant cooler.

Siena shot Leyla a look as they rode up together. "An *hour* early? What the hell?"

The elevator door slid open, and they stepped into a living room that had a soaring ceiling and a wall of glass facing the beach.

"Wow," Leyla said, taking in the view.

She had expected something impressive, but nothing quite like this. The windows had to be thirty feet tall.

The interior décor was modern and minimalist, with lots of stone and glass everywhere. As opposed to the bright Caribbean colors that were so common throughout the island, the palette here consisted of muted grays. Tropical plants in the corners gave a few splashes of green.

Leyla reached the kitchen and stopped short.

"Damn." Siena looked at her, wide-eyed.

A gigantic marble island divided the kitchen from the living area. Top-of-the-line appliances lined the walls, including a Sub-Zero refrigerator and a wine cooler.

Siena set her stack of bins on the counter. "Look," she said, nodding at the La Marzocco espresso machine that was nicer than the one at the Beanery.

But it was the Viking range that made Leyla ache with envy. It had six burners, a built-in grill, and a copper hood. Best of all, it was gas—a feature prohibited in her tiny apartment because of the fire code.

She deposited her trays on the island and went back to the elevator, taking a curious look around as she did. Off the living area was a hallway and the door to what appeared to be a home office.

"Want me to go check out the deck setup?" Siena asked.

"Yes. Thanks. I'll be up in a minute."

Leyla returned to the elevator for the last bin as the front door opened. Wade bent down and lifted the heavy cooler.

"You could have waited for the elevator," she said.

"I'm fine." He glanced around. "Where to?"

"This way." Leyla grabbed a tub filled with utensils and led Wade into the kitchen. She left him to begin unpacking and took the elevator to Gagnon's rarely seen, much-talked-about rooftop pool.

The door whisked open, and she stepped into what looked like a tropical oasis. Lush vegetation surrounded a Buddha statue overlooking a rectangular swimming pool with a waterfall on one side. At the far end of the deck was a roof-covered living area and bar. Pink oleanders lined the walls and wooden planters brimming with yellow hibiscus flowers filled the corners. Strangely, the view of the ocean was mostly blocked by a high stucco wall that had only one rectangular window. Evidently, Gagnon cared more about his privacy than about being able to see the beach from his pool.

As promised, the area had already been set up for the party. A trio of high-top tables stood near the bar, and soft Hawaiian music played in the background. Alongside the pool were two long dinner tables set with black linens. Leyla counted the chairs to make sure the number hadn't changed.

Jillian caught her eye from the far end of the deck and strode over.

"I knew it. Our votives won't stay lit." She glanced at the bar. "Not even under the covered area."

"I've got some hurricane lamps in my car," Leyla said.

"Hurricane lamps?"

"Tall glass candle holders. They're wind resistant."

"Oh God, you're a *lifesaver*. Can we use them?"

"Sure."

"Need a hand?" Siena asked.

"I've got it."

Leyla rode the elevator down. Nearing the ground level, she heard voices and laughter, and her nerves did a little dance before the door slid open.

Luc Gagnon stood at the base of the grand staircase. He wore a black golf shirt and sun visor with his company logo scripted across it. He had a cell phone pressed to his ear and an arm draped around a slender blond woman in a clingy white microdress. She swayed on her feet as she moved toward the staircase, and Gagnon steered her toward the elevator.

Leyla scooted out of the traffic flow. The driveway quickly filled as guests spilled out of luxury cars and SUVs. A red Porsche whipped into the drive, and Leyla jumped out of the way. She dug her car keys from her apron and rushed to move her Toyota before someone blocked her in. Who knew how late this party would go, and some people might even be spending the night.

By the time she made it back to the pool with the hurricane lamps, the tone of the party had shifted. The soft Hawaiian guitar had been replaced by up-tempo club music, and women in thongs sashayed around the pool.

Wade walked up to her. "Need help?"

"Yes." She handed him the box. "Put two of these on each dinner table, one on each cocktail table, and one on the bar."

"Got it."

"Where's Siena?"

"Filling trays downstairs," he said. "Did we bring any peaches?"

"Peaches? No."

"What about the fruit kebabs?" he asked.

"They're pineapple, mango, and watermelon. Why?"

"He wants to make Bellinis."

"Who does?"

"Him." Wade nodded over her shoulder, and Leyla turned to see Gagnon behind the bar. He had a silver cocktail shaker in his hand and was pouring drinks for a couple of women in cowboy hats and bikinis.

Jillian stepped off the elevator and waved across the deck at her boss. "Phone call," she mouthed, holding up a cell.

Gagnon shook his head at her.

Sighing, Jillian walked over and whispered something in his ear, then handed him the phone. He said something to the women and then strode inside the house.

"Leyla?"

She turned to Wade. "What?"

"Peaches. Are you sure there aren't any here somewhere?"

"I'll check," she said.

The elevator was busy again, so Leyla took the stairs. She found Siena in the kitchen arranging skewers of barbe-cued shrimp on trays.

"The host wants peaches," Leyla said.

Siena didn't look up. "What for?"

"Bellinis."

"I'll check the back fridge. It looked pretty stocked." She wiped her hands on her apron and went into the utility room.

Leyla turned her attention to the trays filled with shrimp skewers and spring rolls. She glanced across the living room to the hallway. She could hear Gagnon's muffled voice from behind the closed office door. She'd noticed a bath-room down that same hallway, and if she went to use it right now, she might be able to overhear some of the conversation that had pulled him away from his party.

"You know we're up three, right?" Siena called from the back.

"What's that?"

"We're up *three guests.*"

The office door opened, and Gagnon walked out, slip-ping a phone into his pocket.

Leyla quickly turned away, and Siena stepped into the kitchen with a bag of frozen peaches.

"Oh, good," Leyla said. "Could you take those up to the bar?"

"Sure."

"Who told you we were up three guests?"

"The assistant was just in here. Jillian. Evidently, they picked up some strays at the club."

"Women?"

"I assume."

"Well, they probably won't eat much. Everyone here looks like they're a size zero." Leyla grabbed a jar of maraschino cherries and handed it to her. "Take those up, too. He probably needs them."

"Be right back. The short ribs are warming."

Leyla checked the oven. Then she stepped to the island again and counted the apps on each tray. They were going to have to pace things.

She took a deep breath, trying to calm her nerves. The house was quiet, with only the faint thud of bass drifting down from upstairs. She glanced across the living room at the hallway. The door to the office was open now.

Leyla heard heels clomping down the inside staircase, and a moment later Jillian breezed into the room.

"How's it going in here?" she asked.

"Good. Perfect. We're about to serve the apps."

"Listen, I have to run back to the club. Desiree left her Ray-Bans in the bar. I'll be back in a few minutes."

"Sure."

"Call me if you have any questions while I'm gone."

"No problem. Oh, is there a guest bathroom I can use?"

"Down that hall on your left." She nodded across the living room. "And there's one up by the pool, too, if anyone asks." She checked her watch. "Call me if you need anything, okay?"

She rushed out, and Leyla waited until she heard the front door shut. Then she wiped her hands on her apron and crossed the living room to the hallway. She walked to the bathroom, glancing at the office on her way.

She shut herself in the bathroom and looked at her reflection in the mirror.

She felt stressed, and it showed. Her cheeks were flushed. Her mascara was smudged. Strands of hair had come loose from her bun and clung to her sweaty neck. She grabbed a tissue from the marble holder on the vanity and dabbed her forehead. Then she tossed the tissue into the wastebasket and washed her hands with an expensive-looking bar of verbena soap.

She dug a lipstick from her apron. Leaning over the sink, a thought hit her like a slap. Had Amelia ever stood at this same mirror? Had she washed her hands with French-milled soap and maybe changed into a bikini and gone up to join Luc Gagnon in his pool?

Shuddering, Leyla tucked her lipstick away and walked out of the bathroom. The office beckoned her, and she glanced around before taking a tentative step through the open door. A glass desk and leather chair occupied the center of the room. The floor-to-ceiling window looked out over the beach, where dusk was falling. Leyla's attention returned to the desk. A big map covered most of the surface beside an open laptop computer.

She stepped closer and saw that it wasn't a map, but a schematic diagram of some kind. She studied the drawing, then glanced at the glowing green light on the laptop. If she tapped the mousepad, would the screen come to life? Probably not a good idea.

She glanced at the diagram again. On impulse, she pulled out her phone and snapped a photo of it. Why? She had no idea.

Although, she did. Whatever was on Gagnon's desk, and on his computer, whatever his phone call had been about—all of it would be of interest to Sean. He would kill to be in her shoes right now. And why waste an opportunity to get a glimpse into Gagnon's private sanctum?

Leyla's phone vibrated, and she jumped, startled. She stepped to the door and peered into the hallway before returning to the bathroom to check her phone. Rogelio's number showed on the screen. Probably something about the pastries for tomorrow. She let it go to voicemail, then reviewed the photo she'd just taken. The light wasn't great, but she wasn't going back in there.

Leyla stepped over and flushed the toilet, then turned on the faucet and let the water run for a minute. Eyeing her reflection one last time, she took a few calming breaths before stepping into the hallway.

It was quiet, with only the faint din of music coming from upstairs. Not a sound from the living room or the kitchen. She passed Gagnon's office without looking this time and paused at the end of the hallway beside a row of photographs. Each picture was dramatically lit with an individual spotlight. The first picture showed a desert landscape and a climber scaling a sheer rock face. The second showed a skier atop a mountain, pole lifted in the air and pointed toward a helicopter. Leyla leaned closer. The skier was Gagnon. The third photograph showed a surfer cutting through the curl of a big blue wave.

"See something you like?"

She whirled around.

Gagnon sauntered down the hallway, highball glass in hand. Where had he come from? Her shoulders tensed as he stopped beside her and smiled. He smelled like weed, and his eyes looked dilated.

"You're the caterer, right?"

"Leyla Breda." She stuck out her hand. "Just In Thyme Catering."

He shook her hand, smiling slyly as he looked her over. He had longish dark hair and more of a tan than she would have expected for a tech executive. But then, he clearly spent a lot of his time outside the office.

He turned to the pictures. "You like these?"

"Yes."

"Ever been to the North Shore?"

She glanced at him. Was he screwing with her?

"That's in Oahu," he added.

"I haven't," she said. "Looks beautiful, though."

He tipped his head to the side, still giving her that cocky smile that she was used to seeing in bars.

"Sex on the Beach?"

"Excuse me?"

He lifted his drink.

"I'm good," she said. "Thanks."

"I insist."

He offered her the glass again. Annoyed, she accepted it and took a small sip.

"Not bad," she said.

"Have the rest."

"Thanks, but I can't. I'm working."

"Can't you take a break?"

"Nope."

"Not even with the host of the party?"

"Especially not with the host."

He sighed and shook his head. "Too bad, Leyla."

"Well." She forced a smile. "I'm sure your friends are hungry. I should get dinner out."

"You do that." He smiled. "And hit me up later if you want a drink."

S EAN SPOTTED THE light glowing in the shop and whipped into the parking lot. He pulled into a space near the door beside an old Subaru. As Sean slid from his car, the door to the coffee shop opened, and a skinny man in black walked out.

"Hey, is Leyla around?" Sean asked, catching the door before it closed.

"She's in back with Siena."

"Thanks."

Sean walked in and cut through the eating area into the kitchen. Siena stood at the sink with her back to the door.

"Hi."

She turned around. "Oh, hey, Sean." She smiled. "Leyla's still unloading."

"Thanks."

Sean walked down the hall, frustrated. What good was a top-of-the-line security system if no one used basic common sense? He found Leyla alone in the parking lot dragging a big plastic tub from the back of her SUV. At least her new floodlights were working. Someone would have no trouble choosing the perfect moment to ambush her while she had her hands full.

"Hi."

She jumped and turned around. "Oh, hey. You scared me."

"Sorry." He took the tub from her hands.

"Thanks." She wiped her forehead with the back of her arm. She wore all black, including tight-fitting jeans and high-heeled ankle boots. It wasn't chef's attire, so he guessed she'd had to double as a server tonight.

"How'd it go?" He didn't bother to ask where she'd been.

"Fine," she said, grabbing another tub from the back. She set it on the ground and then closed the hatch.

"Stack that on mine," he said.

"I can get it."

She hefted her tub and led him to the back door. Leaning the load against the wall, she tapped a code into the panel beside the door. A light flashed green.

Sean opened the door and held it for her.

"Thanks. We can just put these down here."

"You don't want them in the kitchen?"

"I'll deal with them tomorrow. Here, come into my office."

They set the tubs down, and she led him into a window-less room with a small wooden desk and a pair of metal file cabinets. Squeezing around the desk, she pulled open a drawer. She dropped an envelope inside—probably her payment—and then glanced up.

"How was your night?" she asked.

"Boring. How was yours?"

She walked around the desk and propped her hip on the corner. "Long." She blew out a sigh and rubbed the back of her neck. "I thought we'd never get out of there."

He stepped closer, gazing down at her. Her makeup was smudged and some of her hair had fallen out of her bun.

"I've driven by here about ten times."

Her brow furrowed. "Why?"

"It's late. I was worried." He tucked a lock of hair behind her ear. "Who was at the party?"

"Golf people." She rolled her eyes. "And a bunch of women mooching drinks and coke." She tugged her hair loose and it fell in waves around her shoulders. "God, I need a drink. And a shower. It was hot as hell outside. All I wanted to do was jump in the pool."

"What was your impression of Gagnon?" he asked.

"*My* impression?"

"Yeah."

She tossed her hairband onto the desk. "He was just what I expected. Big money. Big ego. Cringey pickup lines."

"He hit on you?"

"He hit on everyone, even his assistant." She stood up and pulled her phone from her back pocket. "Here, I want to show you something."

Sean's irritation with Gagnon morphed into dread as Leyla unlocked her phone.

"What did you do?" he asked.

"Nothing. I just took a picture you might be interested in. So, at the beginning of the party his assistant brought him a phone call."

"What do you mean *brought* him a phone call?"

"She brought a phone out to the pool. It wasn't his, because his phone was black, and this was a silver one. Maybe it was hers, I don't know. Anyway, I think it might have been an important call, because she whispered something in his ear, and then he took the call downstairs, away from the party."

"You saw all this?"

"Yeah."

"Don't even tell me you followed him."

"I didn't."

Sean studied her face, and he goddamn *knew* she was lying to him.

"What? I *didn't*," she insisted. "I was busy in the kitchen."

He looked down at the phone in her hand. She'd probably fucking recorded him. And this was exactly why he hadn't wanted her going over there.

"Here." She handed him her phone. "That's a picture of the desk in his office."

"You *went through his office*?"

"I didn't go *through* it. I just stepped inside for a sec on my way back from the bathroom. I wanted to snap a picture of whatever he was looking at when he took that phone call." She tapped the screen, enlarging the photograph. "See?"

Sean bit back a curse as he stared down at the screen. "What is this?"

"It was some kind of map rolled out on his desk. Or it

looks like more of a diagram. I don't know. I thought you might know what it is."

Sean set the phone on the desk. "Leyla. *Shit*." He took her hands and pressed them against his chest.

"What?" she asked.

"Did anyone see you?"

"No."

"Are you sure?"

"Yes."

He stared down at her, not reassured at all.

"Sean, it's fine. Anyway, everyone there was either drunk or high. No one saw me step into that room for, like, one-point-five seconds. And if they had, I would have just said I was looking for the bathroom." She pulled her hands free and picked up the phone. "Now, aren't you going to look at this?"

Sean stared down at the photo. The lighting was terrible, and it took him a second to orient himself. It was a schematic diagram of a factory. The notations in the margins appeared to be in Chinese. He zoomed out. The photo showed the diagram spread out over a large glass desk. Sean studied the other items on the desk, and his blood ran cold.

"Sean?"

He looked up.

"What's wrong?"

"Nothing."

She crossed her arms. "You know, for a cop, you're pretty bad at lying."

"Can you text me that picture?"

"Sure." She plucked the phone from his hand and started tapping. "Okay, it's sent."

Sean's phone buzzed, and he pulled it from his pocket.

He'd received the photo. He put his phone away and then he took hers from her hand.

"Did you get it?" she asked.

"Yeah."

"So, why are you sending it again?"

"I'm not. I'm deleting it."

CHAPTER

EIGHTEEN

THE ISLAND BEANERY was packed when Nicole walked in. She peeled off her sunglasses and tucked them into the collar of her shirt. Scanning the café, she saw Leyla Breda standing at a table talking to a customer. She waved Nicole over.

"Hey," Leyla said with a smile. "Did you meet Miranda's sister Bailey at the wedding? She's visiting from Austin."

The woman looked up at her with a smile. She had wavy dark hair and gray eyes, and the bridge of her nose was sunburned.

"Hi, I'm Nicole Lawson."

"Nice to meet you," she said, glancing at the gun on Nicole's hip.

"Nicole is a detective with Joel," Leyla said.

Nicole turned to Bailey. "Looks like you decided to stay in town awhile?"

"My fiancé and I are house-sitting and taking care of

Miranda and Joel's pup. And making use of their boat, too, since they were kind enough to offer."

"Good for you. They get back tonight, right?" Nicole asked, just to be friendly. She knew exactly when they were getting back, and she was counting the minutes. With two people out, the department was feeling the pinch.

"That's the plan," Bailey said. "Unless they decided to extend the honeymoon. I don't see that happening, though. My sister's a workaholic."

"Joel, too. I'm surprised they've managed to stay gone this long." Leyla turned to Nicole. "Are you picking up lunch, or—"

"Just coffee."

Leyla glanced over Nicole's shoulder, and her expression changed. Nicole turned to see Sean Moran walking into the shop. His attention settled on Leyla.

"Well, be sure to come see us before you leave town," Leyla told Bailey. "I'll send you back with some pastries."

"Thanks."

Leyla excused herself to talk to Sean, and Nicole could see that her advice for Sean to keep his distance from Joel's sister had gone right out the window. The look he gave Leyla when she walked up to him could have melted butter.

"Wow. Who is *that*?"

She glanced at Bailey. "Him? A friend of Joel's."

"I didn't know Leyla was seeing someone."

Nicole glanced back, noting the casual way Sean rested his hand on Leyla's waist.

"Would you like to sit down?" Bailey nodded at the plate in front of her containing two double-chocolate-chip muffins. "She brought me way more than I can eat here."

Nicole pulled out a chair. "Thanks. I'll sit for a minute until the line dies down."

"She really does have a booming business." Bailey popped

a chunk of muffin into her mouth. "So, if you're a detective here, then I assume you're working the Albright homicide?"

Nicole studied Bailey's expression, surprised by the question. Her guard went up as she remembered someone mentioning that one of Miranda's sisters was a newspaper reporter.

"I'm not covering the story, don't worry," Bailey said, evidently reading Nicole's reaction. "I'm just curious how it's coming."

"It's coming," Nicole said, feeling awkward now.

"No arrests yet, I take it?"

"Not yet."

"I get that you can't really talk about it," Bailey said. "I bet you're sick of reporters calling you for quotes. Like I said, I'm just asking out of curiosity. I can't believe something like that happened here." She looked out the window at the sand dunes. "I always thought of this place as a quiet beach town. But it seems like you guys have had one thing after another recently."

"Yeah."

"It's like that in Austin, too. Growth is up. Crime is up. I guess there's no avoiding it—the two go hand in hand."

Nicole nodded, feeling awkward again. Bailey seemed like a nice person, but Nicole really didn't want to field any questions about this.

"So, you guys are here for some vacation?" Nicole asked, grasping for a new topic.

"Yep. Actually, it's our first vacation together. Jacob is a detective with Austin PD."

"Oh yeah?"

"It's hard for him to get away. I'm sure you can relate."

"I can."

The fact that Bailey was engaged to a cop made Nicole feel guilty for being so distrustful. But Nicole had seen cases blow up because of media leaks, and she had more than enough problems to deal with right now. She'd burned her entire Sunday driving to San Antonio for a face-to-face with one of the investigators up there only to have him cancel their meeting at the last minute when he got a callout.

At least, he had *said* he had a callout. Nicole still wasn't sure whether she believed him.

"It's been so nice being down here, especially before the summer rush," Bailey said. "With the exception of the Beanery, we haven't had too many crowds anywhere."

Nicole glanced at the line again, which only seemed to have gotten longer.

"Whoa."

She looked at Bailey. "What?"

"That's Miguel Vidales."

Nicole glanced at the door.

"Side door. Coming in from the deck."

Nicole turned around. Sure enough, the San Antonio reporter who had provided her with her best lead to date had just stepped into the coffee shop. Coincidence? Or had he seen her come in? There was also the unsettling possibility that he'd followed her over here from the police station.

Bailey leaned closer. "You know who that is, right? If you're avoiding reporters, you may want to slip out."

Nicole turned away before the guy could make eye contact. Of course, if he had come here specifically to talk to her, it was already too late.

"I wonder what he's doing down here," Bailey said with a frown. "He's with the *San Antonio Tribune*."

Nicole pretended to be clueless. "Is that right?"

"Yeah, and he's a heavy hitter. He won an AP award a year ago for a series about official corruption in Mexico. But as far as I know, his paper isn't covering the Albright thing." Bailey's gaze settled on Nicole, and she could see the reporter's wheels turning.

Damn it. Would Miguel be bold enough to waltz up to her in a public place? Probably not, given his obsession with encrypted phone apps. Still, Nicole didn't want to risk being cornered.

"Well." Nicole checked her watch. "The line's getting longer, not shorter. I think I'll come back later."

Bailey nodded.

"Nice meeting you, Bailey. You guys enjoy the rest of your stay."

"We will."

Nicole made her escape, careful not to look at the customers standing in line as she slipped out of the café. She returned to her car and had just popped the locks when she heard someone say her name.

"Damn it," she muttered, turning around.

Miguel stood beside a gray Corolla in the row behind her. He nodded slightly.

Nicole stared back at him. The intense look in his dark eyes told her he really wanted to talk to her. But she didn't want to be seen standing in front of a popular hangout talking to a reporter.

On the other hand, this man had provided her with the single most important lead of this entire case. So, was he here now for payback? The other half of his quid pro quo? Or did he have another tip for her?

He lifted his eyebrows and made another subtle nod toward his vehicle. Then he opened the door and slid behind the wheel.

"Damn it," Nicole muttered again, almost certain she was about to do something she'd regret.

She walked over and got into his car.

* * *

SEAN LEANED AGAINST the kitchen counter, watching Leyla give instructions in that brisk voice that she'd used on him the moment they met.

She shoved a lidded bowl into the fridge, then turned around and motioned for him to follow her out of the kitchen. His pulse picked up as she led him down the narrow hallway and into her tiny office.

"Hey." She closed the door, and his pulse picked up again. "I don't have long. I—"

He kissed her. He had to. She froze for a moment, and he thought he'd crossed some line. But then her fingers went into his hair, and she pressed herself against him.

He turned her, easing her up against the door she'd just closed. He slid his leg between her thighs, and she made a soft moan that sent a pang of lust through him.

"Sean."

"Hmm?"

He kissed her mouth, her chin, the little spot below her ear.

Whatever she'd wanted to say, he'd distracted her, because her fingernails dug into his scalp.

"Sean."

He pulled away.

"I have to get back. My whole staff's going to know what we're doing."

He gazed down at her flushed cheeks and worried expression. He didn't give a damn what her staff thought, but she obviously did.

He eased back and combed a hand through his hair. "Sorry."

"It's okay." She smiled and dropped her hand to his belt buckle. "Did you find out about tonight?"

He stepped back and sat on the edge of her desk, not responding.

Disappointment flickered in her eyes, and he felt a sharp pang of guilt.

"I can't do it tonight," he said.

She gave a shrug. "No problem."

"I wish I could."

She had no idea how much. He'd invited her out on a real date, to a real restaurant, with every intention of giving her his undivided attention. But he'd been kidding himself to think he could pull that off right now.

A little line appeared between her brows. "What's wrong?"

"I'm sorry," he said.

"It's no biggie. We can try later in the week. I've got events Tuesday and Wednesday, but Thursday night could work."

The hope in her voice was like a dart in his chest, and he just looked at her.

"Oh." She took a deep breath and blew it out. "I think I'm getting the picture now."

He didn't say anything. The look in her eyes cooled, and she glanced away.

"I'm going to be tied up tonight," he said. "And after that . . . I don't know. Everything depends."

"On?"

"How my work goes."

She tucked her hands into her apron and watched him. "In other words . . . you're going to be really busy and then you'll probably leave town after that?"

He couldn't confirm or deny that, so he just looked at her.

"You don't need to feel *bad*, Sean. I get it. You're here for work."

"I feel bad because . . ." He rubbed the back of his neck. He couldn't explain it to her. He wasn't even sure he understood it himself.

"Don't." She stepped closer and gave him a forced smile. "It's fine. We'll take a rain check. Maybe next time your work brings you down this way we can grab a drink or something."

Grab a drink. For some reason the words infuriated him. It was exactly what he'd wanted that first night.

But he'd wanted more than that then, and he still did. The time they'd spent together had only made him more desperate to get close to her. And now here he was, just days—or maybe even hours—from wrapping up his job here, and he hadn't spent nearly enough time with her.

She stepped toward him, tipping her head to the side as she watched him. "It's tonight, isn't it?"

Sean's blood went cold.

"What's tonight?"

"Whatever this thing is you came down here to do," she said. "I'm guessing it's some kind of raid or arrest or something?"

"Don't."

She sighed.

He gripped the edge of the desk, trying to keep a grip on his reaction. This was his fault. If it weren't for him, she wouldn't have the slightest inkling of why he was really down here, and she wouldn't be asking questions about it right now.

Her fake smile fell away. She lifted her hand and traced her fingertip over his jaw, just below his cut.

"Is it dangerous?" she asked.

"No."

"Are you lying again?"

"No."

She rolled her eyes. Then she crossed her arms and gave him that pissed-off look that was somehow easier to stomach than the disappointed look she'd had a minute ago.

"Be careful," she said sternly.

"I will."

She gazed up at him with so much intensity, he wanted to wrap his arms around her and kiss her forehead, even though he knew for a fact that would irritate the hell out of her.

She checked her watch. "I have to go." She turned and opened the door. "Thanks for letting me know about dinner."

He stepped into the hallway, then turned and looked back at her.

"Leyla, I'm—"

"*Don't* say it again. I know. Just be careful, okay?"

"I will."

"I mean it."

M IGUEL DROVE PAST the lighthouse and found a space at the end of a long row of cars. He pulled in and parked.

"This okay?" he asked.

Nicole glanced around, still worried about being seen with him. He'd parked facing the beach, but this lot was pretty well patrolled. Someone she knew might see her.

He reached into his back seat and rummaged around. Fast-food bags littered the floor, and the car smelled like cigarettes. He grabbed a foil window screen with suction cups and handed it to her.

"Here," he said. "You can block the view."

Nicole pressed the screen against the side window.

"So." Miguel turned in his seat to face her. "I thought I would have heard from you by now."

"Why?"

"Because you're running into walls."

She frowned. "How would you know?"

He reached into the back again and grabbed a brown ac-
cordion folder. Nicole's curiosity ramped up as he thumbed
through it. He tugged out a paper and passed it to her.

She scanned the page. It was a typed list of names, thir-
teen in all.

"Recognize anyone?" he asked.

"No. Should I?"

"That's a list of known or suspected assassins for a certain
organization you're interested in."

"How would you know what I'm interested in?"

He ignored the comment. "Are any of them on your suspect list?"

She didn't have a suspect list. She was still chasing down
leads and waiting on lab results. But she wasn't about to
admit that to a reporter.

"I can't give you that," he said, "but you can take a picture of it with your phone if you want."

"Where'd you get all this?" she asked.

"Court documents, police reports, news articles. It's all
publicly available." He shrugged. "I've compiled a shit ton
of research about them."

Them being the Saledo cartel.

She glanced at the list again, feeling torn. The name of
Amelia's killer could be sitting right under her nose. But if
she took the list, then she'd owe this guy. Again.

"Nicole, come on. You're in week two here."

She glanced up. With a sigh, she took out her phone and
snapped a shot, then handed the paper back.

"Thank you."

"Sure." He slid the list back into the file.

"Why are you helping me?"

"I told you already."

She studied his face. Miguel Vidales was twenty-nine,

but he seemed older. His eyes had a shadowed, haunted look about them, as though he'd seen some very bad things.

And he had, if his articles were any indication. Nicole had done her homework, too, and this reporter had covered some of the most heinous crimes committed south of the border.

"You're wasting your time with Dumont."

She blinked at him. "How did you know—"

"I saw you at the cop shop in San Antonio yesterday. Now, Detective Romero might be a different story. But Dumont's tight as a tick with info. You won't get anything from him."

"*You* were the one who told me to contact these guys."

"Yeah, to confirm what you already knew. What were they going to do? Deny it? No." He shook his head. "But in terms of handing you new leads, you're probably not going to get anywhere. They want to make the collar themselves."

It was just what Brady had said, too. They were holding out on her.

Nicole shook her head and looked out at the beach, where tourists on lounge chairs baked under the midday sun. She was tired of turf wars and pissing contests. Maybe she should have expected this when she signed up for a male-dominated profession. She'd been dealing with this since her first days at the police academy, and it had only gotten worse since she'd busted her ass and made detective.

"Did they tell you about the tracking?" he asked.

"Who? You mean Dumont and Romero?"

"Yeah."

"No." She paused, trying to read his expression. "You mean tracking a suspect or—"

"Tracking the victims. The hit man—whoever he was—installed a tracking device on the car."

"Which car?"

"Both of them. Massey and Rincon. The devices were discovered at the crime lab when the cars were processed."

"Massey was killed behind the apartment where she lived," Nicole said. "Why would they need to track her car?"

"I don't know, but they did. And Rincon was targeted outside a strip club, but it wasn't a place he frequented. So, him being there was a one-off."

Frustration swelled inside her chest as she thought about what other key details these two detectives might have left out. And all because they were jealously guarding their case.

Nicole's phone beeped with a message. It was Brady. Conference room in 20.

"I have to get back," she told Miguel.

"Sure." He put the car in reverse.

"Did you really drive all the way down here to give me this list?"

"And to talk to you."

"Why?"

He circled the edge of the lot and headed for the exit. "We have a deal, remember? I'm expecting that heads-up before you make an arrest."

An arrest. He sounded so confident. But given all the challenges she was dealing with she had no idea when that was going to happen.

Hot frustration mingled with insecurity in her gut. What if she wasn't up to this case? A woman had been murdered, right here in her backyard. What if her killer went free, and it was all Nicole's fault because she'd overlooked a clue or failed to notice some key detail or trusted the wrong person?

"You download that app I told you about?" he asked.

"No."

"You should do it. You don't want anything getting intercepted."

"Intercepted? By who?"

He shot her a dark look.

"You're seriously worried that a cartel is going to *intercept* one of your phone calls? What, like they're the NSA or something?"

"People's phones can fall into the wrong hands. Especially reporters'," he said grimly. "It happens all the time."

She removed the window screen and tossed it into the back seat.

"You think I'm paranoid?" he asked.

"Yeah. A little."

"It happened just last month. Google 'journalist' and 'Veracruz' if you don't believe me."

She looked at him. "You're serious, aren't you?"

"This reporter was kidnapped, and his cell phone with all his contacts on it fell into the wrong hands."

A knot formed in Nicole's stomach. "What happened to the reporter?"

Miguel's jaw tensed. "Rumor is he took one of those chopper rides."

"Chopper rides?"

"Over the Gulf of Mexico."

CHAPTER

NINETEEN

SEAN HAD COME up with dozens of ways the plan could fail.

And there was really only one way for it to succeed. Everything had to happen perfectly. Given the painstaking planning that had gone into this operation, he gave it about one-in-five odds.

Sean sat in his rented 4Runner, which looked more or less inconspicuous surrounded by pickup trucks and SUVs. The parking lot was shared by a row of commercial fishing docks and the headquarters of an offshore drilling company. Slouched low in his seat, Sean kept his eye on the docks, as he'd been doing for more than an hour.

Specifically, he was watching Pier Eleven, where a shipment of doctored electronic devices was supposed to be delivered at midnight.

Acid roiled in Sean's stomach as he monitored the wooden pier. Midnight had come and gone. It was now 12:36 a.m. and the pier sat empty. A commercial shrimping boat was moored to the dock beside it. The surveillance team had watched the crew unload their catch hours ago, but Pier Eleven continued to be unoccupied.

Sean rubbed the knot at the back of his neck. Tension radiated through him. The heady confidence from last night had become a sour ball in the pit of his stomach. Maybe they had the day wrong. Or the time wrong. Maybe the *M @ midnight Pier 11* that had been scrawled on the notepad on Luc Gagnon's desk referred to a person, not a day. Or maybe the pier he was referencing wasn't even on the island.

Sean glanced around at the shadowy parking lot. Everything was quiet. Near the neighboring dock, a heavyset man in yellow waders smoked a cigarette and hosed off the sidewalk in front of a fish shop. But no one had stepped foot on any of these piers in nearly an hour. Grabbing the binoculars from his passenger seat, Sean hazarded a glance at the corrugated metal shack by Pier Eleven. The building was quiet and dark. No activity except a fat brown pelican on the roof stretching his wings and resettling himself on his perch.

Sean's phone vibrated, and he read the caller ID: Unavailable.

He connected.

"Yeah."

"We're thinking of calling it," Moore said.

Sean peered through the binoculars again. This lead had seemed solid. Sean and Moore had pored over Leyla's photograph, analyzing every scrap of paper on Gagnon's desk. And they'd both concluded that the writing on the yellow sticky pad was the best intel they'd gotten their hands on in days.

"Five minutes more," Sean said.

No response.

His shoulders tightened as he waited. Ultimately, it wasn't Sean's call, but his boss trusted him.

A shadow shifted, and Sean leaned forward. "*Wait.*"

"Hold up," Moore said almost simultaneously. "We have movement."

Sean's heart rate sped up as a shiny black Suburban pulled into the parking lot. It rolled to a stop in front of the pier.

"I've got a black Suburban, tinted windows, just parked in front of Pier Eleven," Sean reported.

"Roger that. Hang on."

Sean heard muffled voices on the other end.

"Okay, there's a boat coming in," Moore said.

"Where?"

But just as Sean asked, he spotted the dark silhouette of a shrimp boat gliding through the water.

"We've got a fifty-foot vessel. No running lights. You seeing it?" Moore asked.

"Affirmative," Sean said as the boat pivoted in the water and then moved toward the pier. A shadowy figure hopped onto the dock. Then someone threw him a line. He crouched down and tethered the line to a cleat and then jumped back onto the boat.

"We're in position," Moore said. "You ready?"

"Affirmative."

"Okay, they cut the engine."

Sean's brain raced as he studied the scene, looking for an opening. This had always been the wild card. He had to figure out how to sneak past the crew of probably two or three men and get aboard. If he waited for the cargo to be off-loaded, he'd miss his best chance.

Another shadowy figure jumped onto the dock, and Sean's heart rate picked up yet again. Everything about this felt suspicious—the deserted pier, the lack of running lights. The black Suburban showing up here right as this boat arrived in the middle of the night.

Sean watched as a pair of men strode from the dock to the parking lot. He caught a glimpse of them as they walked under a bright security light. Dark hair, gray T-shirts, green waders. They disappeared from view as they climbed into the waiting Suburban.

"Are you seeing this?" Moore asked.

"Yep." Sean lifted the binoculars one last time. Then put them on the floor at his feet.

"Looks like the crew is gone. Our spotter says the boat looks empty."

"Not for long," Sean said.

No way was Gagnon going to leave more than a million dollars' worth of merchandise sitting there unguarded.

"I'm going in," Sean said.

"Roger that."

Sean disconnected the call and tucked the phone into his pocket. Lowering the brim of his baseball cap, he slid from his vehicle. The muggy air smelled of diesel fuel. Everything was quiet except for the distant hum of equipment at the drilling company headquarters. Keeping to the shadows of the parked trucks, Sean quickly crossed the lot and strode through a patch of light to the waterfront. He darted around the corner of the corrugated metal building.

Sean pressed his back against the wall and waited a moment for his eyes to adjust to the darkness. He had a flashlight but didn't want to use it if he didn't have to. According to their intel, this boat was carrying eight large ice chests, at least four of which contained product. Sean leaned against the building, mentally going through the plan one last time. The "product" had better not be marijuana, or more than thirty federal agents had wasted thousands of hours on a glorified drug bust.

Sean pulled a pair of work gloves from his pocket and tugged them on. Then he darted around the side of the building, crossed the dock, and stepped right onto the boat. Ducking into a dark shadow, he paused to listen.

Nothing.

Only the lapping of water and the creaking of wood as the boat shifted in the wind.

Sean ducked under a line and crept to the back deck. It was too shadowy to see much, so he switched on his flashlight and glanced around. He spied eight large chests, as expected, four along each side of an empty tank. Clamping the flashlight between his teeth, he stepped to the closest chest. He quietly popped the latches and lifted the lid.

Shrimp. And ice. The smell hit him, and he leaned back for a moment before plunging his hand in. He groped around, getting up to his shoulder in ice and shellfish until his fingers scraped bottom.

Shit.

He re-latched the lid and moved to the next one. By the time he searched through the second chest, his entire arm was frozen. He pivoted to the row of chests behind him. He lifted the lid and plunged his hand in, this time encountering something hard.

Pulse pounding, Sean shoved the ice aside, careful not to spill any as he uncovered a hard-sided suitcase. He fumbled with another set of latches and lifted the lid.

Jackpot.

Sean's breath whooshed from his lungs. Rows and rows of cell phones stared up at him. Until this instant, this whole operation had been based on a theory. Now it was real.

Adrenaline spurred him into action. Technically, he needed only one phone. These devices shared a platform, so infecting one would eventually infect all. But Sean grabbed three, just for good measure, and stuffed them into his front pockets, then quickly closed the suitcase. Glancing around warily, he spread the ice around and lowered the lid. Seconds later, he was out of there, jogging stealthily down the dock and dashing onto the neighboring pier. The door to the corrugated metal building stood ajar. Sean slipped inside and found a man in yellow waders sitting on a stool, watching him from the shadows.

"Anyone see you?" the undercover agent asked.

"Don't think so."

He jerked his head toward the back. "They're ready for you."

Sean strode past a row of empty bins that would be full of ice and fresh-caught seafood by eight a.m. He passed a tank of live bait and opened the door to a walk-in refrigerator.

He stepped inside, blinking at the glare of a mobile spotlight. Two men in waders rushed forward. They wore matching black skull caps and latex gloves.

"You got them?" Hahn asked him.

Sean smirked at the top technician on his team. With his thick glasses and pasty skin, he didn't look much like a commercial fisherman.

Sean pulled the phones from his pockets. "I got three."

"*Three?* Beautiful."

Hahn pulled up his face mask as the other man rolled a cart over. An array of tools had been arranged atop the cart on a blue napkin.

"You guys look like you're ready for surgery," Sean said.

"We are."

They bent over the phones, already taking them apart with tiny tools.

"I'll wait outside."

Hahn grunted.

Sean stepped out of the fridge into the room with the concrete floor. The place smelled of fish and bleach, and someone had recently hosed everything down, from the looks of it. The agent who was on lookout beside the door stepped over, cigarette in hand. He squinted at Sean in the dimness as he took a drag.

"How long?" he asked.

"Three to four minutes," Sean said. It was an estimate based on practice. "Maybe six. I brought them an extra device."

The agent nodded and flicked an ash toward the drain in the middle of the floor. Sean glanced at the door the man was supposed to be guarding.

"Any more vehicles?" Sean asked.

"Not yet. They'll be here soon, though. They're not going to leave that shit sitting around for long."

Sean stepped to the window, which was covered by a thick layer of brine. He could barely see anything.

"There's a crack in the wall," the agent said, walking across the room to a place where the metal siding had come apart. From there, Sean could see the parking lot and the bow of the shrimp boat. Sean scanned the area, his stomach churning as he thought of what he still had left to do.

The door to the fridge opened, and Hahn jerked his head at him. "We're almost done," he said through the mask.

Sean rushed over. "That was fast."

"We've been practicing." Hahn handed him two of the phones. Sean slid them into his pockets as the other technician reassembled the third phone.

"Here." He lunged over and handed it to Sean.

"Thanks, guys."

"Good luck."

Sean glanced at the agent on lookout by the door. The man gave him a nod, and Sean stepped into the dark shadow beside the building. He hurried around the corner, feeling a prick of unease as he detected the sound of a car engine somewhere nearby. He paused for a second by the pier and held his breath, listening.

No voices. No movement. Scanning his surroundings, Sean darted back onto the pier.

Pain reverberated through his skull as he crashed into a wooden beam. He grabbed a post, catching his balance as stars flashed through his vision. In the dimness, he hadn't noticed the wooden **No Trespassing** sign. Biting back a curse, he touched his hand to his forehead. Was he bleeding? The last thing he needed to do was leave a trail of blood everywhere.

Staying in the shadows, Sean silently hopped onto the boat. He ducked under a line again and stepped onto the back deck, switching on his flashlight.

The space was empty. Three of the four chests on this side of the tank were gone.

Someone had been here.

Sean whirled around. The four chests on the other side of the tank were still there, waiting to be off-loaded. But what if none contained a hidden suitcase?

Voices drifted over from the parking lot. Someone was coming. Sean's phone vibrated in his pocket, and he ignored it as he rushed to the nearest chest. He unlatched the lid and flipped it open. He dug his hand in, and his stomach sank as he felt nothing but shrimp and ice.

Fuck.

He shut the lid and moved to the next one. His hand smashed into something hard, and his burst of relief canceled out the pain. Sean opened the hard-sided suitcase and added the three doctored phones to the top layer. Then he closed the lid and spread ice over the case.

"One more," said a gruff voice nearby.

Panicked, Sean darted toward the bow and crouched behind a pile of boat fenders.

A flashlight beam swept over the deck. Sean ducked down, trying to make himself small.

"Here."

The beam swung toward the opposite side.

"You sure?"

"Yeah. See?"

Ice rattled as someone dug through the chest. Then the lid slammed shut.

Sean crouched there, not moving or breathing. Sweat trickled down his back as he listened to the grunts and puffs of two guys hefting the chest and hauling it off the boat. Planks creaked as the men lumbered down the pier.

Sean crab-walked backward out of his spot. Sticking to the shadows, he hurried to the other side of the boat and jumped onto the dock, then darted around the corner of the building.

Pressing his back against the wall, he listened to the low grumble of an idling engine.

Sean crept to the end of the building and peered around the corner. A pickup truck was parked on the grass now, outside the halo of white created by the security light. The men loaded the chest onto the truck bed with three other chests, then closed the tailgate.

One guy went to the driver's side and hitched himself behind the wheel. The other stood at the back, fumbling with his phone for a moment before jogging to the passenger side and sliding into the truck.

The truck moved forward. Its taillights brightened as it slowed to exit the parking lot.

Sean pulled out his phone and shielded the screen with his hand as he read a message from Moore.

Incoming. Get out.

Sean gritted his teeth and shot a furious glare at the window where that dumbass agent should have been on lookout. Sean could have been shot just now. Or captured. He scanned the parking lot for any more surprises, then rushed back to his vehicle.

Thirty seconds later, he was racing down the highway, mentally replaying all that had just happened.

Two seconds. Maybe less.

That was how close everything had come to going sideways.

Sean's hands shook. Gripping the wheel, he realized his palms were slick. And his head was throbbing. He buzzed the window down and sucked in air as wind whipped around him. He glanced at the clock. It was 1:03.

Less than half an hour ago Moore had nearly called it.

And now, just twenty-five minutes later, everything had changed. They'd *done* it. All those days and nights of painstaking work had panned out, and they'd pulled off one of the most daring ops in the history of their unit.

Emotions tornadoed inside him. He felt shocked. Euphoric. Dizzy with disbelief. If the technical side worked, tonight's operation would be paying dividends for months and maybe even years to come. And Sean realized that he'd never completely believed they'd actually pull it off until now.

He glanced out the window at the vast darkness of Laguna Madre. An arc of lights in the distance marked the causeway connecting Lost Beach to the mainland.

The mainland, where soon he'd be catching a flight to return to his normal routine and his normal job and everything he'd been doing before Operation Virgil took over his life.

Everything he'd been doing before he met Leyla.

Regret needled him as he sped down the highway. The last few months had crawled by at a mind-numbingly slow pace, but now everything was happening at warp speed.

His phone vibrated again, and this time he pulled it out. It was Moore with his typical brevity.

Report.

Sean set the phone on his knee and tapped out a text.

Mission complete. I'm out.

CHAPTER

TWENTY

LEYLA LAY IN the dark, staring up at the ceiling. She'd been tossing and turning in bed for hours, gripped by fear as she pictured Sean creeping down some alley with a tactical team, about to kick down a door and arrest some group of thugs who would no doubt be armed to the teeth. Her chest squeezed as she imagined it.

It's tonight, isn't it?

He hadn't said anything, but his eyes had revealed exactly what she needed to know.

Leyla could read him. He couldn't lie to her—at least not successfully—and she knew that whatever top-secret, all-important law enforcement matter had brought him down here was culminating tonight, possibly right this very moment.

She turned onto her side and stared at the window, where the faint combination of moonlight and streetlights seeped through the slats of her mini-blinds.

He'd be leaving soon; of that she was certain. Maybe as soon as tomorrow. Part of her felt frustrated. And disappointed. And *bitter* that the first man she'd taken more than a passing interest in, the first man she'd actually enjoyed being with, in longer than she could remember, lived so impossibly far away.

The smarter, saner, more practical part of her felt grateful that he was leaving soon. Thank God he was leaving before they really got involved.

In the short time she'd known him, Sean had taken over her thoughts, her daydreams, her energy—and they hadn't even slept together.

And thank God she'd been busy last night, or she probably *would have* slept with him. No—she definitely would have. Despite her many reservations, she would have given him exactly what he'd wanted from her since that first night when he approached her on the beach and offered to buy her a drink. Guys were so transparent, Sean especially. He had a certain way of looking at her that made her *know* he was thinking about sex.

Leyla rolled to her other side and checked the glowing red digits. It was 2:16. She groaned. She had to be up in less than two hours. She was bone-tired, and still she couldn't manage to go to sleep.

Just past midnight, after surfing channels for hours and checking her phone for the hundredth time, she'd actually driven to Sean's condo and circled the parking lot, searching for his rental car. And if that weren't pathetic enough, then she'd parked at the beach and walked all the way past his building, looking for a light in his window. But her search had been futile, and she'd come home feeling even more anxious than before she'd gone.

Sean, where are you?

She absolutely hated this. She was a hot mess of worry

and frustration. How did Miranda handle the stress every time Joel went out on some covert assignment? Leyla had never really thought about it before now, but it was agonizing. Every time she closed her eyes, all she could see was Sean in a Kevlar vest, slinking down some dark alley. But those vests didn't cover everything. Head shots, for instance. Kevlar didn't cover those. Leyla squeezed her eyes shut and tried to breathe.

She couldn't do this.

Leyla threw the covers off and swung her legs out of bed. She snagged her running shorts off the floor and pulled them on. Then she grabbed a sweatshirt from the chair and shoved her feet into sandals. Not giving herself even a moment for second thoughts, she strode through her dark apartment and snatched her keys off the counter.

The air outside was thick with humidity. She locked her door, ignoring the bugs swarming around her porch light as well as the loud, urgent voice in her head telling her this was a bad idea. But there was an even louder, more urgent voice telling her to go. She couldn't spend even one more minute lying in bed not knowing if he was okay or . . .

Something else. Something not okay. She didn't know the details of what he was doing tonight, but her vivid imagination had spent the past twelve hours filling in the gaps. She rushed down the stairs and past the window of the bike shop beneath her apartment. She darted her gaze across the street to the sidewalk where a few drunk stragglers made their way home from bars. At the end of the block, a lone man slouched against a building, watching her from beneath the brim of a baseball cap. She looked away and quickened her pace.

"Leyla."

Her heart skipped and she whirled around. Even if she hadn't recognized the low voice, she would have instantly known the broad-shouldered silhouette moving through the shadows.

"What are you doing out here?" Sean stepped into the light of a streetlamp.

"Oh my God." She gaped at the nasty bruise on his forehead. "What happened to you?"

He ignored the question. "Where are you going?"

"I'm . . ." She blinked up at him in the glare of the light, and everything registered at once: his damp hair, the smell of soap, the big purple knot above his eyebrow.

He's not dead, or shot, or bleeding.

Tears burned her eyes as the relief hit her.

"I'm . . ." She swallowed the lump in her throat. ". . . looking for you. I was worried. I didn't want to call your phone in case—"

He kissed her. Emotions flooded her system, and some of her tears leaked out.

Wrapping his arms around her, he lifted her off her feet and pulled her against him. Then he turned and eased her back against the brick and took her mouth with the same pent-up yearning she'd been battling for hours. He tasted hot and masculine and *hungry*, although she'd never before thought that hunger had a taste. And he smelled good, like that bodywash he used. He cradled her head, sliding his hands between her and the hard wall behind her, and she combed her fingers into his damp hair as her brain pieced together what everything meant.

He had showered. He had gone home and cleaned up after whatever sweaty, dirty thing he'd been doing that she wasn't allowed to know about. And then he had come *here*, in the middle of the night. Her one a.m. walk past his condo didn't seem so crazy anymore.

She slid her hands down and pushed against his chest.

He jerked back, panting as he stared down at her with a desperate look. *Don't say no*, his eyes pleaded.

She took his hand and pulled him toward the stairs.

It was the second time she'd led him to her stairs, but this time was different because he followed her up. She dug the key from her pocket, feeling the heat of him behind her as she fumbled with the lock. And then they were inside her dark apartment. She'd barely flipped the bolt when he was kissing her again.

She couldn't think of what to say. But words didn't seem important as he wrapped his arms around her and walked her backward through the dark space. She bumped the back of the armchair, and he stopped, leaning her against it as he held her face between his hands.

"I had to come," he said, kissing her over and over. "But I didn't think you'd be awake."

She pressed against him, grateful for the solid heat of him. He was here now, not off somewhere getting hurt or worse. His warm hands slid over her butt, cupping her through the thin running shorts as he pulled her against his erection. She dragged his head down and kissed him harder. His hands glided under her sweatshirt, then pulled it up, breaking the kiss as he yanked it over her head. It whooshed to the ground, and she rested her palms on his cool leather jacket before pushing it off his shoulders. She slid her hands down his torso, and her fingertips encountered his holster.

She jerked away as reality rushed back—who he was, why he was here.

How he had to get on a plane soon to return to his home more than 1,700 miles away. She knew the distance. That was how obsessed she'd become with this man in the short time she'd known him.

And he could read her, too—even in the dark—because he stopped undressing her and gently stroked her cheek with his thumb, and she knew he was giving her time to put the brakes on.

Instead she kissed him, deeply, like stomping her foot on the gas. She understood the future pain she was signing up for. But she didn't care anymore. Her need to avoid pain wasn't nearly as strong as her need to do this right now. She was too curious. There had been too much buildup between them, starting with that night on the beach when he'd sat down beside her on that piece of driftwood. Really, before that. They'd been on a collision course since outside the wedding reception when she'd first looked up into his green eyes. Every minute she'd spent with him—even the contentious ones—had driven her toward this moment. This was always going to happen, it was just a matter of when.

His hand slid over her breast, cupping it, and the confident way he touched her told her he knew it, too. He was always going to be the man who made her shatter her most important rule, the rule that kept her from getting her emotions trampled on by the parade of cocky guys who showed up here looking for no-strings sex before going home to their real lives.

She eased away, breathing hard, looking up at him in the darkness as he stroked his thumb over her breast, sending ripples of need through her. She took his hand and led him down the hall to the bedroom. Faint bands of light seeped through the blinds and fell across her mussed sheets. She got on her knees on the bed and looked at him.

He paused near the door, probably letting his eyes adjust to the dimness. Then he unbuckled his holster and set it on the dresser. Next came the *thunk* of his phone and wallet, the rattle of keys. Then he bent over, and his boots hit the floor beside her bed with a thud. He pulled his shirt over his head and threw it aside.

He stepped closer, and she looked at him in only his jeans, a perfect sculpture of a man. She scooted to the edge of the bed and leaned forward to press a kiss against his sternum. His skin was hot, and she ran her hands up his arms, absorbing the feel of his muscles under her fingers. His hands slid to her breasts, caressing them through the thin fabric of her tank top as he bent down and took her nipple in his mouth. Her body jolted and she arched her back, savoring the feel of his mouth and his hands as she eased back onto the bed and pulled him with her.

"You are so fucking hot," he murmured, crawling over her.

His weight settled between her legs, and she kissed him, giddy with anticipation. She'd been wanting exactly *this*. Sean alone with her. In the dark. No distractions. She'd been wanting his avid mouth and his skilled hands. He pulled her shirt over her head and tossed it aside. Then his hands moved over her shoulders, grazing her breasts on their way to her naval. In one swift movement, he slid her shorts over her hips and down her legs, and then his mouth was on her.

She gasped, electrified by the hot sweep of his tongue, and he settled his palms on her thighs, anchoring her in place.

"Oh my God. *Sean*."

She slid her fingers into his hair as every nerve in her body came alive, down to the tips of her toes. She dropped her head back, gasping and writhing as sensations flooded her.

She whimpered. "Sean, wait."

"Relax."

"I will. But I want you with me."

He crawled over her again, and she reached inside his jeans, sliding her hand around the hard length of him. She squeezed and stroked him, and he made a low moan in his chest. She pulled her hand away, and together they got rid of the rest of his clothes. She grabbed a condom from the dresser, and he made quick work of getting it on as she scooted back on the sheets.

"Come here," she said, pulling him back where he'd been before, and this time he braced himself with one arm. He pushed inside her, and she squeaked.

He froze. "You okay?"

She bit her lip, squirming under him as she tried to get comfortable.

"Leyla?" He pushed himself up on his palms.

"Yes." She wrapped her legs around him, drawing him closer. "That's good."

He pulled back, then pushed into her again, and the movement made her nerves sing. She slid her hands down his back, marveling at the flex of muscles as he drove into her again and again. It was the hot, perfect fusion she'd been craving since she'd met him, or even before that. They moved faster and faster until her thoughts blurred, and all she could do was cling to him.

Suddenly, he rolled onto his back, hauling her with him, and she found herself straddling his lap. He smiled and adjusted her hips, then gave a little buck beneath her.

She braced her hands against his shoulders and felt a whole new friction as she moved over him. She loved being in control, loved the look on his face as she gripped his shoulders, setting the pace for them, and he held her hips, spurring her on. She slid his hands from her hips to her breasts, right where she needed them as she moved.

"*Sean.*"

He touched her, making her detonate, and the world

came apart. He moved beneath her, drawing out the feeling as she convulsed around him. And then he gave a last powerful push, and she collapsed.

She lay sprawled across him, boneless, unwilling to move except to breathe. Her cheek pressed against his chest, and she felt the pounding of his heart.

Eventually, his hands began to move, skimming up the backs of her thighs, then over her butt, then back down her thighs again.

He heaved a sigh. "Leyla."

She wanted to look at him, wanted to know what he meant. But she couldn't bring herself to move.

His warm hands rested on her hips. Then he gently rolled her onto her side, propping up on his elbow, staring down at her in the dimness. The tender look in his eyes made her heart squeeze.

He kissed her forehead, then untwined their legs and got up.

Leyla flopped onto her back, closing her eyes against the sudden rush of thoughts bombarding her. She didn't want to focus on any of them just now. All she wanted was to lie here, feeling warm and full and sated.

The mattress shifted, and Sean got into bed beside her, dragging the sheet over them. He slid his arm around her shoulders and pulled her close. After a few quiet moments, she tipped her head and looked at him in the dimness. The bands of light fell across his face now. She studied the bruise over his eye, and her stomach tightened.

She reached up and traced her finger over his forehead, stopping just shy of the swelling.

"Can you tell me about it?"

He sighed. "No."

She waited a beat. "Was anyone else hurt?"

"No."

She stroked his forehead again, then trailed her hand down and rested it against his chest.

"Is it over?"

"Yes." He lifted her hand and kissed her knuckles.

"Good," she whispered.

But it was bad, too, because now he had to leave.

Leyla closed her eyes. She didn't want to think about it. He pulled her leg over his stomach, and she sighed quietly.

She felt loose. Her body hummed from exertion, and she knew she would have no trouble sleeping now. But she couldn't. She had to get up in less than an hour. She barely had time to close her eyes.

But she needed to. Only for a minute.

CHAPTER

TWENTY-ONE

SEAN CAME AWAKE with a hammer pounding against his skull. He looked around the still-dark room. The space beside him was empty.

He sat up and swung his legs out of bed, wincing as his head seemed to explode. It was like his worst hangover doubled. He grabbed his jeans off the floor and pulled them on, then followed the smell of coffee to the kitchen.

Leyla stood at the counter, her back to him as she poured coffee into a paper cup. She wore black jeans and a T-shirt, and her hair was damp and loose. He'd missed her shower, apparently. He hadn't even heard it.

He stepped into the kitchen, and she whirled around.

"You're up." She looked surprised. "I thought you'd sleep in."

He walked over and slid his hand around her waist. She had beard burn on her neck, and he felt strangely proud.

She gazed up at him with a wary look. Sean kissed her. Her mouth was soft, but everything else about her seemed tense.

"Your forehead looks terrible." She turned away and opened the freezer. "Do you think you need to get it checked out?"

"No."

She handed him a bag of something frozen. "You might have a concussion."

"I'm fine." He glanced at the bag. Artichokes. He set it on the counter and looked her over. Yep, she was definitely uptight about something. "You going in?"

"Yes, and I'm running late." She nodded at the coffeepot. "That's for you. It'll stay warm for two hours. You can go back to sleep if you want."

Beside the coffeepot was a mug with a pink sticky note tucked under it. That would be for him, too.

He glanced at her. "Gimme a sec."

He went to the bedroom for the rest of his stuff, including the holster he'd taken off barely two hours ago. When he returned to the kitchen, she was standing by the door.

"Mind if I take a to-go cup?" he asked.

"Of course not."

He filled a lidded paper cup like the ones they had at the Beanery. The pink note was gone now, and she'd put the artichokes back in the freezer.

He replaced the coffee carafe and turned around.

"You really don't have to leave yet." She looked guilty, and he knew she wished he had stayed sound asleep so she could have skipped the awkwardness.

"Let's go."

A cool fog had settled over everything, and the streetlights below made hazy white orbs. He waited on the landing as she locked the door and then preceded him down the stairs.

She glanced over her shoulder at him. "Are you parked on the street or—"

"The lot behind the bike shop. I parked beside your car."

The sidewalk was deserted except for a homeless guy stretched out on a bench. Sean peered into doorways as they walked, trying to penetrate the thick shadows. They rounded the corner and walked in silence toward a pothole-filled lot that smelled like piss and garbage. The only other car parked back here besides his and Leyla's was a white hatchback with a crumpled bumper.

She popped her locks with a *chirp*, and Sean reached around her to open her door.

"I'll follow you," he said.

Her eyebrows arched. "You mean to work?"

"Sure. It's on my way."

He wanted to make sure she got there safely. Plus, he wasn't the most romantic guy in the world, but he knew better than to say good-bye to her by a dumpster.

She slid behind the wheel and glanced up at him. "Thanks."

He closed her door and looked around the shadowy lot again as he unlocked his SUV and got inside. He hated that she parked her car here.

Sean followed her out of the lot and checked his phone as he tailed her across downtown. Nothing from Moore yet, which was a small miracle given that he had meetings stacked one on top of the other all morning as everyone scrambled to analyze the implications of last night.

Sean watched Leyla's taillights through the fog as he followed her through town. The streets were empty except for a few stray cars. Sean scrubbed his hand over his bristly chin. He felt like he'd been hit by a truck. And it wasn't just his head. His entire body felt it.

What the fuck now?

In the past twelve hours, he'd achieved every goal he'd been working toward for weeks and months. And that included Leyla.

So, now what?

The coffee shop was dark except for the two new flood-lights shining down on the parking lot. Leyla parked in her usual spot beneath a twisted oak tree. He swung in beside her, and she looked amused as he got out and walked over.

"I do this every day, you know."

"I know." He caught her hand in his and felt her tense as they approached the door.

She was nervous, and he thought he knew why.

She stopped on the sidewalk and looked up at him. "So . . . I'm glad you came over."

He felt like she left the second part unsaid: *Even though I'll probably never see you again.*

"I am, too," he said. "Are you working tonight?"

"I've got an event." She paused. "When are you leaving?"

"I don't know."

She searched his eyes, as if trying to read more into that. "You really don't know, or you don't want to tell me?"

"I don't know yet. I've got meetings this morning, so I'll probably find out the plan. Soon, I'm guessing."

She looked away. "Okay, well—"

"What time does your event end?"

Her eyes looked guarded. "I'm not sure."

"Can I see you after?"

She glanced away, and Sean held his breath as he waited for her response. He didn't know what he'd do if she said no.

"I don't think that's a good idea."

"Leyla." He rested his hands on her waist and waited for her to look at him again. Finally, she did.

"It'll make things harder, don't you think?"

It would. She was right. And Sean wanted to respect her space. This was how she protected herself. She'd told him she didn't date tourists, and he knew this was why. They left. They took what they wanted, and then they were gone. Sean didn't want to do that, but that was exactly what he was doing.

Except he wasn't.

He hadn't gotten nearly what he wanted here. Not even close. No way was she reducing this thing between them to a sticky note.

"I want to see you again."

"Sean—"

He kissed her to keep her from arguing. He pulled her in tight and kissed the hell out of her. It had worked for him before, and it was working now. He could feel it in the loosening of her body, and the pressure of her fingers in his hair, and the play of her tongue. She tasted so fucking good, and he didn't want to let her go.

Lights swept over them, and she jerked back. A black SUV swung into the Take-Out Only spot.

"Rogelio."

Sean looked at her. So, she wasn't completely alone opening her shop this morning. He should feel relieved, but instead he felt a pang of jealousy.

She pulled back and gazed up at him. He could see her brain working, weighing whether to see him again or cut him off now. Meanwhile, Rogelio was just a few feet away, dragging trays out of his car.

"I'll call you later," Sean said before she could tell him no. "We'll make a plan."

"It might be late when I'm finished."

"That's fine."

"Are you sure? You'll probably—"

"I'm sure." He kissed her forehead. "I'll call you."

NICOLE ENTERED THE immaculate garage and scanned the car bays. No sign of a silver Kia.

"Hey, you're early."

She spun around to see Miranda walking over. Last time

Nicole had seen her, she'd been wearing a gorgeous silk wedding gown. Now she wore white coveralls and yellow safety goggles. She slid the goggles onto her forehead.

"I made good time, so I hit the drive-through." Nicole held out one of the two cups she was holding. "Double-shot caramel latte."

"Thanks! That's so sweet." Miranda took the cup. "I've already got some herbal tea going, but I'm sure Ryan will love this. Come on in."

Nicole paused at a shelf beside the door to pull paper covers over her shoes. The county crime lab's garage was clean enough for someone to eat off the floor, and the CSIs who worked in here were vigilant about keeping people from tracking in dirt.

Nicole followed Miranda to a workstation, where she set the latte beside a keyboard.

"So, how was the honeymoon?" Nicole asked. "I've always wanted to go to Costa Rica."

Miranda beamed. "It was amazing. *So* relaxing. And our weather was perfect."

"I'm glad."

"It was wonderful to get away." She smiled again, practically glowing. "The wedding was great, too, but not exactly relaxing. We really needed a break."

She pulled a tea bag from her mug and set it on a napkin. Nicole eyed the bag, then studied Miranda's face as she took a sip.

"Oh my God. You're pregnant."

Miranda choked. "What? Where'd you get that?" She set the mug down.

"You're a coffee addict. Since when do you drink herbal tea at eight in the morning?"

Miranda's cheeks flushed.

"No way. Am I *right*?"

"Shh." She glanced around. "I don't want Ryan to hear you. We haven't told anyone yet."

"Really?" Nicole grinned. "I can't believe I figured it out."

"Well, you *are* a detective. I told Joel that we aren't going to be able to keep this quiet for very much longer. Everyone we know is either an investigator or nosey as hell or both."

"Well, congratulations." Nicole wasn't much of a hugger, but she gave Miranda's shoulders a squeeze.

"Really, you can't say anything. I haven't even told my sisters. We wanted to wait until the dust settles from the wedding. So please don't tell anyone."

"Tell anyone what?"

Miranda smiled. "Thank you." She sighed. "So, how are things back here? Guess we picked a heck of a week to be gone."

Nicole didn't want to lay a guilt trip, but she had definitely missed them. Miranda was the only CSI on staff with Lost Beach PD, and in her absence, they'd had to call someone from the county down for every little thing.

"How's Leyla?" Miranda asked. "I assume you've been talking to her?"

"Some," Nicole said, although she hadn't touched base with Leyla about the case in days.

"Joel's worried about her."

"She seems to be doing all right. I know she wasted no time getting a security system installed at the café."

"Not just that. I hear she's been spending time with that FBI agent. Sean Moran."

Nicole got the distinct impression that Miranda was fishing for information.

"Have you met him?" Miranda asked.

"Yeah."

She had no idea what, if anything, Miranda knew about the Albright case or its connection to the Saledo cartel.

"What do you think of him?" Miranda watched her over the rim of her mug as she took a sip.

It was an easy question. Nicole liked the guy. Despite her initial reservations, he was turning out to be way more helpful than the FBI agents she'd worked with last summer.

But mainly she liked that he treated her as an equal. Nicole could spot sexism a mile away, and she had grown accustomed to men talking down to her. Or worse, not talking to her at all, acting as though she were invisible.

"I like him," Nicole said simply. "But I honestly haven't been around him that much. What does Joel think?"

She sighed. "He's not happy. But he hasn't really explained why, so I can only guess."

"He's probably just being protective."

Miranda smiled. "Who, Joel?"

Obviously, that was part of Joel's reaction, but Nicole thought there was likely more to it. Joel probably knew at least something about Sean's operation down here. As a member of the local task force targeting drug and human traffickers, Joel knew all about the Saledo network.

"So . . ." Nicole glanced around, ready to change the subject. "I don't see the car."

"It's in the far bay, behind that van. Ryan worked on it."

Miranda led Nicole past a row of vehicles in various stages of disrepair. There was a yellow convertible whose driver's side was completely smashed in. Then a pickup with a crumpled back bumper. Next was a white minivan with its two front seats sitting on the concrete floor, foam padding bulging through the slashed upholstery.

"What happened there?" Nicole asked.

"What? Oh, that. Meth smugglers." They walked past the van, and on the other side was Amelia Albright's little silver Kia.

"As you know, the car was locked when police arrived

on the scene," Miranda said. "So we weren't necessarily expecting to find any useful fingerprints inside. And that ended up being the case. Nothing except the victim's."

Nicole had heard this already from the lab supervisor.

"Ditto the exterior of the vehicle," Miranda added.

"Yeah, I wasn't expecting fingerprints in the car. I'm here about a tracking device."

Miranda's eyebrows shot up. "Oh yeah?"

"There's a potentially related homicide in San Antonio, and a tracking device was installed on both victims' cars. That's how he stalked them before they were killed."

"Interesting. So, *two* potentially related homicides, then?"

"Correct," Nicole said. "Any chance we can take a look, see if there's something on this vehicle?"

"Where would it be installed?"

"I don't know. I don't exactly know the details of the other two cases."

"Hmm. Okay." Miranda looked over Nicole's shoulder. "Hey, Ryan. Do you have a minute?"

Nicole turned to see a tall guy with a goatee walking through the garage. He was dressed the same as Miranda in white coveralls.

"What's that?" he asked, taking out his earbuds.

"This is Detective Lawson from Lost Beach. She's here about the silver Kia. You processed it, right?"

The guy looked at Nicole. "I finished it last week. Why?"

"We got a tip that there might be a tracking device on the vehicle somewhere. Any idea where something like that would be installed?"

"Depends." He slid his earbuds into his pocket and walked over, surveying the car. "Is it battery operated or OBD?"

"No idea," Nicole said, wishing now that she'd thought to ask Miguel for specifics. At the time she hadn't wanted to admit how little she knew about her own case, but she should have just swallowed her pride and grilled him about every detail.

"Well, let's have a look." Ryan pulled a pair of latex gloves from a box sitting on a workbench nearby. "Some trackers run on a lithium battery. Some hook up to the vehicle's port." He snapped the gloves on and pulled a mini flashlight from his pocket. Then he went around to open the driver's side door and crouched beside it.

Miranda turned to Nicole. "He's our best vehicle technician. Anything to do with fibers, tire tread, transfer."

"Transfer?"

"Paint transfer. You know, with hit-and-runs? We get quite a few in here, usually involving a drunk driver who hits someone and then takes off. If the police get a suspect and bring the car in, we can typically find some trace paint from the victim's vehicle."

"Nothing near the steering column," Ryan said, closing the door. He sat down by the front tire and shimmied underneath the car. Nicole admired his long body while he rooted around.

"Bingo."

Her pulse jumped. "Bingo?"

"Yep."

He shimmied out from beneath the car and held up his gloved hand. On his palm was a small black box.

Nicole's stomach knotted. There it was, right there. Further proof that the hit man in the San Antonio murders had killed Amelia Albright, too.

"It was just, what, stuck under there?" She looked at Ryan.

He slid his goggles to his forehead. "It's magnetic." He flipped the box over in his palm. "See? Two strong magnets."

"I can examine it for fingerprints," Miranda said.

"Please." Nicole gave Miranda a sharp look. Nothing

against Ryan, but she wanted Miranda to do it. She did the best latent-print work Nicole had ever seen. The woman performed miracles.

"I'm happy to try," Miranda said. "But don't get too excited. There's all that road grime."

"This is just a protective case." Ryan got to his feet and held out the black box. "The actual GPS device is inside this. So, maybe there could be prints on that."

"It's worth a shot," Nicole said.

"Although whoever handled it could have worn gloves," Miranda said.

"True. But if he was careless enough to leave the device on the vehicle, maybe he was careless enough to skip the gloves."

"You never know. You might get lucky with this one."

"So far, I haven't had much luck with anything on this case," Nicole said. "But it's worth a try."

CHAPTER

TWENTY-TWO

I T'S OUT AGAIN."

Leyla looked up from the rose she was piping onto a cupcake as Rogelio slapped down an oven mitt.

"What's out?" she asked.

"The fridge in front. It's the compressor again."

Leyla set down her piping bag and stepped to the door between the Windjammer kitchen and the Java Place. The café was bustling with afternoon customers. Their newest hire had her hands full at the register, and Rachel was busy unloading jugs of milk from the fridge.

Leyla strode over to help her. "How long has it been out?" she asked.

"No idea. I just noticed it."

Leyla grabbed two gallon-size jugs in each hand. They felt cool, thank goodness. But the fridge was definitely warmer than it should have been.

She went into the kitchen and handed the jugs to Rogelio,

who was already rearranging the big reach-in that, technically, was reserved for the hotel's restaurant.

"Leyla."

She whirled around to see her brother standing in the doorway.

"Hey." She rushed over and gave him a hug. Joel looked tanner and more serious than when she'd last seen him. He was dressed in his typical work clothes, right down to the badge and gun. "Back to work already?"

"Yeah. How are you?"

"Busy. You want to give me a hand?"

She went back to the front and grabbed a load of creamers. She passed them off to Joel and then pulled out a bin of walnut chicken salad and a plastic squeeze bottle of chipotle mayo.

She returned to the kitchen and handed everything to Rogelio.

"What is it? The compressor?" Joel asked.

"I think so. I need to call the guy out. *Dang it.*" She was already running late with a giant cupcake order.

Joel was watching her with a look she knew well.

"How was the honeymoon?" she asked brightly.

"Good. You have a minute to talk?"

"Not right now."

"Take a break."

"I have to help Rachel unload the fridge."

Rachel walked in with an armload of milks and creamers. "I can handle it."

Joel took Leyla by the elbow and steered her out of the kitchen into the empty seafood restaurant, where staffers were rolling silver and laying out glassware. He guided her to a crescent-shaped booth.

"Sit."

She sat, thoroughly annoyed, and he slid in behind her.

"Joel, I *really* can't talk right now. I've got—"

He covered her hand with his. "I'm sorry about Amelia."

Tears sprang into her eyes.

"How are you doing with everything?"

She pulled her hand away. "Fine."

He just looked at her.

"Better than last week." She blinked her tears back and looked away. She hadn't expected this conversation right now. They'd been through this already when he called her from Costa Rica last Sunday after he heard the news.

She took a deep breath. "We're doing all right. Everyone's holding it together. Siena's been amazing, as usual." She forced a smile. "What about you? How was Costa Rica?"

"I'm worried about you," he said, swatting away her attempt to change the subject.

"Well, don't be."

"Mom said you're having trouble sleeping."

Leyla sighed. She knew she should have omitted that detail when she stopped by her mother's house the other day. But her mom had asked point-blank how she was sleeping, and Leyla hadn't been able to lie to her.

"I heard about Sean Moran," Joel said.

She kept her face blank. "What about him?"

He gave her a stern look.

"Is *that* why you're really here on your first day back? When you're bound to be up to your eyeballs in work?"

"You need to be careful with him," he said.

"Joel, seriously?"

"Yes."

"Why?"

"You know why."

"What, because he's some big, tough FBI agent and has a dangerous job?"

Joel nodded. "That's part of it."

She tipped her head back against the booth. "I can't believe you. And Owen. This is déjà vu all over again."

"What is?"

"All this macho bullshit. How does Miranda put up with this crap?"

He frowned. "What does she have to do with it?"

"Joel, do you even hear yourself? You're warning me off Sean Moran because you think his *job* is dangerous."

"It is dangerous."

He still didn't get it.

She leaned forward. "Joel, *your* job is dangerous. So is Owen's. You're both cops. Most of your friends are cops. Half the people who attended your wedding are cops. It's ironic—and *patently absurd!*—for you to be sitting here telling me I shouldn't hang around cops."

"Not cops in general. Sean Moran. He's working on something sensitive right now."

Leyla never enjoyed arguing with her oldest brother, but she particularly didn't want to do it now. She hadn't seen him since his wedding, and he should still be floating on a cloud of newlywed bliss.

She scooted around the curve of the booth. "I have to get back."

"Leyla, I'm not joking around with this. You need to steer clear."

"Too late."

"What's that mean?"

"I don't want to steer clear. I like him."

He looked genuinely perplexed. "Why?"

"What do you mean *why*? Because I do."

"That doesn't make sense. He doesn't even live here. He lives in Washington, D.C. You know that, right?"

Irritation needled her. "Yes, I'm aware. What does it

matter? We're just having some fun. And by fun I mean sex. Get over it."

His eyes narrowed.

Leyla slid out of the booth before she said something really bitchy on his first day back.

"I think you're making a mistake, Leyla."

"Well, good thing it's my mistake and it's none of your business."

N ICOLE DROVE THROUGH town, running yellow lights as she glanced at the clock on her dashboard. She was going to be late for the team meeting for the second time in two days. She'd gotten sidetracked with a car theft on the north end of the island, and now she had a ton of paperwork to do on top of everything else.

In an ideal world, she'd be like one of those TV detectives who only worked one case at a time. But in addition to being the lead on a high-profile homicide, she also had to juggle the regular flow of assaults, thefts, and drunken stupidity that happened daily in a busy resort town.

Nicole rolled to a stop at a light and checked the clock again. Her stomach tensed.

She was worried about more than being late. Once again, she was showing up to the meeting with nothing new to share with the team. She was pretty sure Brady had started to regret tapping her for this job. And to make matters worse, Joel was back in town, and even though he wasn't officially working the case, Nicole knew he would find a way to sit in on the meeting and get the scoop about whatever was going on.

But there was no scoop to get. Despite busting her butt and working around the clock for days, Nicole still didn't have a single actual suspect in Amelia Albright's homicide.

The closest she had was a person of interest, who happened to have a rock-solid alibi because he'd been at a tech conference in California at the time of the murder.

She waited impatiently for the light to change and tapped her phone to call Miranda. Again, no answer. She scrolled through her contacts and found the number for the lab technician she'd been working with all week.

"Hi, it's Detective Lawson," she said when he picked up. "I'm checking on the status of an item I submitted for fingerprinting."

"Oh, hi. Just a sec."

She heard muffled voices on the other end and pictured the skinny young man pressing the phone against his lab coat.

The light turned green, and she waited for the car in front of her to wake up.

"Detective, you there?"

"I'm here."

"Are you calling about the GPS device?"

"Yes."

"We haven't run the prints from that yet."

"She got prints?"

"You're talking about the package from Miranda Rhoads? Yes, she lifted prints off the battery—"

"Battery? What battery?"

"It looks like . . . Okay, yes. The notes say she dusted the GPS device for fingerprints, including the battery inside, and she lifted two partials. We'll be running them through the system shortly. She put a rush on this."

"She did?"

"Yeah. It's next in the queue."

Thank goodness for Miranda. And she'd actually gotten prints off the battery *inside* the GPS. Nicole wouldn't even have thought to check that, and this was exactly why she always preferred it when Miranda handled their evidence.

"Okay, and when do you think you'll have that result?"

"Soon. Definitely. I have a note here to call Miranda as soon as it comes through. Did she tell you about the other one?"

"What other one?"

"I have another item here that you submitted. Looks like . . . three days ago? An aluminum can?"

"Yes! It's in?" Nicole had almost forgotten about the beer can, but she felt quite sure Sean wouldn't have.

"We lifted three fingerprints off the can and ran them through the system. The results just came in."

Progress, *finally*, after days and days of nothing. Nicole gripped the wheel, afraid to even let herself hope. "And?" she asked.

"And looks like we got a hit."

CHAPTER

TWENTY-THREE

LEYLA LOADED THE petits fours into the pastry box, careful not to mar the sugar-icing baby booties. Then she added a row of pale pink macarons.

"Oooh, those are pretty." Siena whisked into the kitchen with an empty tray. "What are they for?"

"A baby shower tonight up in Commander's Cove."

"Anyone I know?"

"Annamarie Holmes?"

Siena made a face. "Damn. So sorry I'm not invited to that. Is it a big crowd?"

"Thirty-five women. Her mother's bridge club is hosting it."

Siena leaned against the counter and wiped her hands on a side towel. "I heard about the fridge over at the Java Place."

"Ugh. Don't even get me started." Leyla looked up from the pastries.

"Is it the compressor again?"

"Yeah. And that reminds me. I have to make the salad dressing." Leyla stepped over to the fridge, which was now crammed with catering orders she'd had to move over from the other shop. She grabbed a jar of mayo and tried to recall the other ingredients in her recipe.

"Are they picking up or are we delivering?" Siena asked.

"I'm delivering at five and setting up, if I can get my act together in time."

"What's on the menu? Do you need a hand? I can get Katie to cover things out front."

"I think I've got it. I just have to slice the fruit and cut the finger sandwiches." Leyla checked her watch. "Oh! And brew the tea."

She'd almost forgotten about the beverages. She strode into the hallway, annoyed with herself. She'd been scatter-brained all day. Between lack of sleep and her conversation with Sean this morning, and then her run-in with Joel, she hadn't been able to focus on anything.

She stepped into the stockroom and closed her eyes, grateful to have a few seconds alone. Her real problem to-day wasn't lack of sleep. It was the fact that it was after four and Sean still hadn't called her about his plans. She didn't know if he still wanted to see her tonight, or if he was even on the island anymore. For all she knew, he was already on a plane back to Washington. But he wouldn't leave without calling her.

Would he?

Her chest tightened and she leaned her hand against the wall. *You promised yourself you wouldn't do this.*

She didn't want to be thinking about him, obsessing over whether he'd call or not. She didn't want to be one of those women.

But she couldn't help it. She wanted to see him tonight. She *needed* to see him, if for no other reason than to assure herself that she hadn't imagined how good it had been with him. She thought of the way he'd looked at her and touched her and slept with his arm draped over her waist. They'd had a genuine connection. And the prospect of him leaving without telling her made her physically sick.

Get a grip.

She took a deep breath and massaged her temples. What she needed was a double espresso to wake her up. She was running on fumes.

Scanning the shelf in front of her, she grabbed a box of hibiscus mint tea. She needed peach, too. And cups. The hostess had specifically requested plain white cups with no logo. The woman had ordered pink coffee sleeves with little gold storks printed on them. It seemed a bit over the top, but Leyla was quickly discovering that a lot of her customers' requests were like that. Her job was to smile and take orders and make sure she got paid.

Katie stuck her head into the stockroom. "Oh, good. You're here."

"What's up?" Leyla asked, scanning the shelf for the peach.

"You've got a client waiting in your office."

She glanced up. "Who?"

"I don't know. She said she's worked with you before and she wants to book another event?"

Leyla grabbed the box of peach tea. "Can you put these in the kitchen?" She handed Katie the boxes. "And this." She added a long tube of cups and lids.

"Sure."

"Next time, invite any prospective clients to wait in the dining room. My office is a mess."

"Got it."

Leyla wiped her hands on her apron and hurried into the hallway. She was a mess, too. She was tempted to duck into the bathroom to fix her hair, but she didn't have time, so she settled for smoothing it and making sure she didn't have icing on her hands.

Her office door stood open. A woman was seated in the guest chair, and Leyla recognized the artful blond twist in her hair.

Jillian got to her feet as Leyla stepped into the room.

"Leyla!" She smiled. "I'm so glad I caught you. Do you have a minute?"

"Sure. What can I do for you?"

"Come with me."

"Pardon?"

Fingers clamped around Leyla's arm, and she glanced down at Jillian's hands.

She had a shiny silver pistol pointed at Leyla's chest.

the bathroom and took her time but she didn't have time. There
weren't any windows . . . and nothing was the right shape . . .
figured her . . . . his . . .

CHAPTER

TWENTY-FOUR

SEAN LET HIMSELF into the condo and went straight to his
computer on the bar. He'd been in Brownsville all
morning but decided to work from Lost Beach this afternoon and join the five o'clock team meeting remotely—a
decision that had raised eyebrows when he'd mentioned it to
Moore.

Sean dumped his phone and keys on the counter as he
turned on his laptop. He didn't care about raised eyebrows.
He wanted to be on the island right now. Despite being buried under an avalanche of meetings and paperwork, he was
determined to find a way to see Leyla tonight.

Before he had to get on a flight at seven a.m. Sean's
stomach tightened as he thought about it.

He'd been thinking about Leyla all day and dreading the
conversation he knew he needed to have with her. He was
scheduled to leave in a matter of hours, but he wasn't ready
to say good-bye yet. And he'd started searching for ways to
get out of it. He had some vacation days stacked up, and he

was considering taking them, even though his timing couldn't have been worse. Moore was counting on him to help manage the far-reaching repercussions of their operation.

Sean's phone buzzed, and he checked the screen.

"Hi, Nicole."

"Hey, I don't have much time. I'm on my way to the police station, but I wanted to let you know I got your results back."

"Results?"

"The beer can. The one you begged me to run for you? I called in about three different favors to have them put a rush on it."

"Oh. Yeah, sorry, I've been distracted."

Silence.

"Well, do you still want this or not?"

His pulse picked up. "You got a hit?"

"Yeah, and it's a badge."

"What do you mean?"

"He's one of your guys. A fed. Name's Brian Wentworth. No, wait. *Bentworth*."

"Bentworth with a *B*?"

"Yeah. You know him?"

Sean's head started spinning. He knew the name. He clicked open his email. He entered the name in the search field and clenched his teeth as he waited.

An email popped up, and Sean bit back a curse. Brian Bentworth was DEA. He was copied on a thread with Sean two years ago during a joint operation based in Houston. Sean must have met him at some point, too, which was why he'd looked familiar standing around that pump jack the other night.

"Sean?"

"Yeah?"

"Did you get the name down?"

"Yeah, I'll check it out. Thanks."

"Well, do you want me to—"

"Don't mention this to anyone."

"Okay."

"No one, Nicole. Do you understand?"

"I got it."

Sean ended the call, sweating as he set down his phone. Bentworth was a federal agent. And he was tied in with both that rancher, Tillman, and Luc Gagnon. But Moore had insisted they didn't have any undercover agents working on this.

But clearly someone *was*, which meant one of two things. Either someone was working undercover and Moore was being intentionally kept out of the loop.

Or the operation was compromised.

Sean shut his laptop and got up from the stool. He needed to talk to Moore, ASAP. If someone was keeping Moore in the dark—and by extension, keeping his whole team in the dark—that was a major problem. It meant someone didn't trust him, and Sean found that difficult to believe. He'd worked with Moore for almost eight years. If there were doubts floating around about him, then the Bureau's top brass wouldn't have placed him in charge of one of the most important operations the cyber crimes unit had ever undertaken.

Sean raked his hand through his hair and looked around. He needed to suss out what the hell was going on without tipping Moore off in case *he* was the problem.

He grabbed his keys and phone and walked out the door, his mind racing a million miles an hour as he tried to formulate a plan. Moore was in Brownsville right now. Sean would have to drive down there, then find a way to get him alone and talk to him.

Sean stepped onto the elevator just as his phone buzzed. Leyla.

Shit.

He needed to let it go to voicemail. He should have called her by now, but he still hadn't nailed down his plans.

If he didn't pick up, though, she'd think he was blowing her off. He connected the call.

"Hi," he said.

"Sean?"

The call cut out as the elevator started moving.

"Hello?" He looked at the phone.

"Sean—" The voice cut out again. "—to her?"

"*Hello?*" The door whisked open, and Sean stepped into the lobby.

"Sean, are you there?"

He halted in his tracks. "Who is this?"

"It's Siena at the Beanery. I'm calling on Leyla's phone."

Dread filled his stomach. "Where's Leyla?"

"That's why I'm calling. We can't find her anywhere. I thought maybe she was with you."

THE AIR SMELLED of sunbaked garbage as Nicole stood beside the alley interviewing the young barista.

"Here. Right next to the door." The woman pointed to the concrete step where she said she had found Leyla Breda's cell phone twenty minutes ago.

"So, *outside* the door, just lying here on the sidewalk?" Nicole asked.

"Yes, that's right." She fidgeted with the ties of her black apron. "I came out here to look for her, and I almost walked right past it."

An SUV whipped into the parking lot, and Nicole muttered

a curse as Sean Moran jumped out. He wore street clothes but had his badge and gun in plain view today.

The barista's eyes widened as he charged up to them.

"What happened?" he demanded, whipping off his sunglasses.

"I'm trying to find out," Nicole said.

"Where's her phone?"

"In the office." Nicole turned to the barista. "Could you excuse us, Katie? I'll come find you inside if I have any more questions."

The barista walked inside, and Nicole jerked her head, motioning for Sean to follow her to her unmarked police unit. It was parked almost exactly where Amelia's car had been parked the day her body was discovered in the nearby alley.

"What the fuck happened?" Sean asked, darting his gaze around the tiny parking lot. "Leyla's car is out front."

"I know. That's why Siena called me. Her purse and keys are here, too, but she isn't." Nicole looked Sean over, noting his wild eyes and the beads of sweat on his brow. Every other time she had seen him he'd been calm and in control.

"Siena says Leyla was in the middle of prepping a big catering order in the kitchen," Nicole said, "and then she suddenly disappeared."

"What time was this?"

"About thirty minutes ago." Nicole checked her watch. "It was four twenty when they found the phone out here on the step, just outside the door. About five minutes after that, Siena called me."

Sean whipped around to look at the concrete step just as Siena walked outside.

She looked relieved to see Sean. But her relief quickly turned to worry as she got a look at the distress on the man's face.

She turned to Nicole. "It doesn't make any sense," Siena said. "She was rushing to get this delivery out. She went into her office to meet with someone and—"

"*Who?*" Sean asked.

"A prospective client. Jillian somebody."

The color drained from Sean's face. "Jillian Wendt? Luc Gagnon's assistant?"

"Yeah. We did an event for her Sunday, and she wanted to hire us again—"

"Siena, let me talk to Agent Moran for a second," Nicole said.

Siena bit her lip. Then she turned and walked back inside.

Sean combed both hands into his hair. "*Fuck!*"

"Calm down. Maybe Leyla went somewhere with her willingly."

"No way."

"Well, does Leyla know about Luc Gagnon?" Nicole asked. "And that he's potentially involved in a homicide?"

"She has an idea, yeah."

"How would she—"

"That's why she dropped the phone on the ground. It's a signal." Sean's attention snapped to the security camera above the door. "We need that footage."

Nicole glanced up at the newly installed camera. "If anyone besides Leyla would know how to access the system, it would be Siena. I'll talk to her." Nicole started for the door just as it swung open.

Joel Breda stepped out. His gaze landed on Sean, and he rushed up to him, slamming him back against the police car.

"*Son of a bitch!*"

Nicole lunged forward, grabbing Joel's shirt. "Hey!"

"*You* did this! You fucking sent her to his *house*? What were you thinking?"

"Hey!" Nicole wedged herself between them as Joel

tried to give him another shove. Pain zinged through her shoulder as Joel's palm connected. "Stop it!" She pressed her fists to Joel's chest and pushed him back, which sent another zing of pain through her body.

Joel stepped away, panting and glaring at the man behind her.

"I didn't *send her* anywhere," Sean snapped.

"Bullshit!"

"*Stop.*" She turned to glare at Sean, then back at Joel. "This isn't helping anything! Sean, go inside and track down that camera footage."

He stared over Nicole's shoulder, his face flushed with anger.

"Sean."

He met her gaze and seemed to calm down a fraction. He stepped around her and stormed into the building.

"Jesus." Nicole turned to Joel. "Are you out of your damn mind? You just assaulted a federal agent!"

"He deserved it."

She looked at Joel, dumbstruck. She'd known the man her whole life, and she'd never seen him lose his cool like this.

Her LBPD cap had come off in the struggle and she bent down to scoop it up, sending yet another lightning bolt of pain through her body.

"Damn it." She clutched her bruised ribs and stood up slowly. "Are you trying to end your career?"

But Joel wasn't paying attention. He was frowning down at his phone now, his brow furrowed with worry. "Owen hasn't heard from her either. *Shit!*"

The door opened, and Siena poked her head out. "We pulled up the security camera footage."

Joel strode inside and Nicole followed, holding her hand against her ribs as she walked into the tiny office where

Leyla kept her file cabinets and a workstation. The room was warm from all the bodies crowded inside it.

Sean sat at the desk in front of the computer. Siena must have provided the passcode, and the agent's hands moved quickly over the keyboard as he navigated the security app. Nicole assumed the program was part of the new alarm system.

"Here's today," Sean said, clicking on an icon with to-day's date.

Joel leaned over Sean's shoulder and watched the screen as three squares appeared. They showed black-and-white camera footage of the cash register, the front parking lot, and the lot behind the building.

Sean clicked the mouse and moved a bar on the side of the screen, scrolling through the hours of the day until he got to 3:55 p.m. Then he slowed.

The room went silent as all four of them eased closer to the screen. Nicole kept her gaze on the footage of the back lot. The only car parked there was an old white car belonging to Katie, the barista Nicole had just interviewed.

"There." Joel tapped the screen as a vehicle moved into the frame. It was a black Suburban with tinted windows.

Sean muttered a curse, and Joel looked at him.

"That's Gagnon's," Sean said.

"What, the vehicle?" Joel asked.

"Yeah."

"But Jillian came in the *front*," Siena said. "I saw her walk in."

Nicole didn't bother saying what everyone else surely knew. The woman had probably been dropped off, and this vehicle was waiting for them in back, where no one would witness whatever was about to happen.

Nicole watched the screen as the back door opened and two figures emerged—a blonde and a brunet.

Nicole sucked in a breath. She didn't recognize the blonde, but the other woman was clearly Leyla. She shot a glance directly at the camera over her shoulder. Then the back door of the Suburban swung open, and Leyla climbed inside, followed closely by the blonde.

"Shit!" Joel tapped the screen. "Go back."

Sean moved the mouse and rewound the footage. Again, they watched in tense silence as the two women stepped through the back door.

Sean froze the footage. "There."

Nicole leaned closer. "What?"

"Look at her hand. She's got a gun."

CHAPTER

TWENTY-FIVE

LEYLA LAY ON the floor, desperately trying to breathe through the panic. The bandanna tied around her face tasted like dirt, and every time her tongue touched it a wave of nausea gripped her. She couldn't throw up—she'd choke. She inhaled through her nose and tried to think of what to do. The closed Suburban was a sauna, and stinging sweat seeped into her eyes.

How long had she been back here? Minutes? Hours?

When they'd first pulled in here—wherever *here* was— she'd been sandwiched between Jillian and a giant blond man who looked like a Viking. He'd secured her hands behind her back with zip ties and pointed a gun at her face. *Shut up! And stay the fuck down.* Then everyone had piled out of the SUV, leaving her alone, and the gunshot-like sound of the locks engaging had sent a jolt of terror through her.

Get out get out get out.

The urgent voice in her head was back again, and she

knew she had to escape this place, no matter what, even if she got shot doing it.

Leyla squirmed onto her side and pressed her elbow against the floor mat to prop herself up so she could look out the window. She'd tried to look before, but the Viking guy and another man had been standing just a few feet away. They could have been brothers, or even twins, but one of them was slightly taller. She thought the taller one was the driver, but she'd only gotten a glimpse of the man before the other one shoved her to the floor.

Twisting around, Leyla peered out the tinted window behind her. It was dark, and they were in some kind of windowless garage or warehouse. She sat forward and craned her neck to check out the other side of the room. A narrow band of light came from a door that was slightly ajar.

The taller Viking stood there now, his face lit by the glow of his phone.

Leyla ducked her head down.

He was distracted. Now was her chance. Yes, he was standing only a few feet away, but now might be her only moment. She couldn't just sit here, waiting for whatever they planned to do to her.

She pulled against the zip ties, desperate to get her hands free. The skin on her wrists was already raw and bleeding, and tears filled her eyes as she used all her might to try and snap the plastic.

No use. Her heart hammered, and she felt another wave of panic coming on.

Think! Don't panic.

She had to get out of here. Even with a guard standing there, she had to find a way. She couldn't just sit.

She should have tried to run back at the Beanery, but the sight of that gun had sent her into shock. She'd had the presence of mind to nudge her phone out of her apron pocket and drop it on the ground. Would someone find it? Would they realize it was an SOS? Anyone who knew her knew she never went anywhere without her phone. Siena would figure out that she was missing and call Owen or Joel.

Wouldn't she?

Or maybe Leyla's phone was still baking on the sidewalk, and no one was looking for her at all. And even if they were, how would they ever find her here? She didn't even know where the hell she was.

Leyla's chest squeezed. She tried to breathe, but the air was hot and stifling, and she felt like a fist was clamped around her heart.

Was this how Amelia felt in her final moments? Had she had time to realize what was happening? Leyla somehow knew, with certainty, that Luc Gagnon was the reason Amelia was dead. Had one of these armed thugs killed her?

Get out get out get out.

She sat forward again and craned her neck to look out the window. Tall Viking was still looking at his phone.

Leyla twisted her body around to reach for the door handle behind her with her bound hands. Slowly, quietly, she pressed the button to unlock it.

Nothing.

She pressed the button again. Again, nothing happened.

Fear gripped her. They must have the child safety locks on. She'd have to squirm into the front seat to get out of here.

A door slammed, and Leyla slumped back onto the floor.

Muffled voices. The Viking was talking to someone. She didn't know what language they were speaking, but it wasn't English.

The locks clicked, and she jumped, startled, as the door near her feet swung open.

"Let's go."

Two meaty hands reached in and grabbed her ankles. She kicked him, and he whipped his gun out and pointed it at her.

"Watch it, bitch."

He shoved the gun into the front of his pants. Grabbing her ankles again, he dragged her out. She thought she'd land on the ground, but then another hand clamped around her arm and roughly hauled her up.

"Let's go. Move."

"Where are we—"

"*Move*."

S EAN RACED DOWN the highway, scanning the cars around him for any sign of Gagnon or one of his vehicles.

"Are you coming?" Nicole asked over the phone. "We're about to start."

"I'm almost there."

His phone beeped with an incoming call. Moore. Sean hung up on Nicole to answer it.

"What's the word?" Sean demanded.

"I checked with the surveillance team," Moore said. "Gagnon was at Playa del Rey playing golf all afternoon."

"Where is he now?"

"They don't know."

"*What?* I thought we had eyes on him."

"We did. Two separate teams, but he must have given them the slip. His car is still at the golf club, but no one's seen him in over an hour."

Sean gripped the wheel. "How could *two teams* have lost him?"

"I don't know. Where are you?"

"On my way to the police station." Sean sped through a yellow light, then swerved around a Jeep loaded with teenagers. "The chief called an all-hands meeting to launch a search for Leyla."

"Leyla Breda."

"Yes." Hell, did Moore even know who Leyla was?

"And just to make sure I understand," Moore said, "this woman is the *caterer* who was in Gagnon's house the other night and snapped the photo of Gagnon's desk for us?"

"Correct."

Sean's stomach churned at the reminder. If it weren't for him, Leyla never would have been there in the first place. If it weren't for him, she wouldn't even *know* about the investigation of Luc Gagnon.

All of this was Sean's fault.

"He must have found out she's working with us," Moore said. "Any idea how?"

Sean could think of a lot of ways. Leyla wasn't a trained agent and didn't know how to cover her tracks. This was exactly why Sean hadn't wanted her over there.

"Maybe he saw her in his office," Sean said. "Or maybe he has security cams inside his house. Anyway, *how* isn't as important right now as the fact that *she's been abducted* by someone who works for him, and she's probably with him right now and—"

"You realize this means Operation Virgil is compromised," Moore cut in. "I don't know how, but—"

"I do. I think we have a mole," Sean said. "Someone feeding Gagnon and Saledo information. Remember that unidentified man who was at the oil well with Gagnon and the rancher, Tillman? I got an ID on him. It's Brian Bentworth."

Silence.

Sean swung into the police station parking lot.

"Brian Bentworth, the DEA agent from Houston?" Moore asked.

"Yes. You know him?" Sean shoved his car into park and jumped out.

"Brian Bentworth is dead."

Sean halted. A slimy ball of dread filled his stomach.

"Sean?"

"He's—"

"This just came in. He was found in his pickup truck behind a grocery store in Brownsville this morning. Shot in the back of the head. Looked like he'd gone there to meet someone."

Sean's mind was sprinting. Bentworth was dead. Executed. Gagnon was now somehow involved in the killing of a federal agent, which ramped everything up to a whole new level.

"If Bentworth was working with Saledo, possibly tipping him off in exchange for money—"

"He was," Sean said hoarsely. "That handoff I saw was probably his payment."

"Okay. Fair assumption. But I don't know why he was taken out now."

"I do. I just ran his prints."

"You what? How?" Moore asked. "And how would *they* know you ran his prints?"

"We have a leak somewhere. Someone acting as a trip-wire, giving them a heads-up if their mole's cover is blown."

"Shit."

The ball of dread in Sean's gut expanded as he realized just how far and deep this crime syndicate's connections went. He'd heard Saledo was getting his tentacles into law enforcement agencies in the region, but this was worse than he'd imagined.

And worse for Leyla.

Sean glanced around the parking lot just as Owen Breda whipped into a space right by the door. He hopped out of his pickup with his cell phone pressed to his ear and rushed inside the building.

"Do you understand the implications here? Our entire op is compromised," Moore was saying.

"I know."

"That shipment of phones we managed to get ahold of, that was probably a decoy. Gagnon knew we were coming for it."

"I know." Sean strode for the door. "But we need to focus on Leyla Breda. We can't—"

"The real shipment is likely still out there."

He walked into the building and stopped for a second to finish the call. He didn't give a shit about the shipment right now. He needed to *find Leyla*, and he needed Moore to pull out all the stops in getting the FBI to help with that.

"Sean? Are you listening? I know you're personally involved with this woman, but I need you to keep your eye on the ball. That shipment of hardened electronic devices is probably still in transit. We can salvage this operation."

Sean made eye contact with the receptionist—Denise— and she buzzed him through the secure door leading into the bullpen. The place was filled with frantic-looking cops, and Sean hoped to hell they were searching for Leyla.

"Sean?"

"I understand. But right now—"

"I still believe that Gagnon intends to take possession of that shipment personally and distribute the phones to his VIP clients," Moore went on. "So, if we can locate the shipment, we can locate Gagnon. And if Leyla Breda is *with* Gagnon, we locate her, too. You understand what I'm saying?"

"I do."

"Good. Now, we don't have nearly enough boots on the ground there to look for her, so you need to get their police chief—Brady—to throw everything he's got at this. And I need *you* to keep me informed. I want to know what you know the second you know it."

"Sean."

He turned around to see Nicole striding across the bull-pen toward him. The grim look on her face filled him with terror.

"I'll call you back," Sean said, and hung up.

"Did you hear about dispatch?" Nicole asked.

"No. What?" Sean braced himself.

"We just got a call from some woman who was buying shrimp at Sam's Fish Market. That's down by the docks, right across from the headquarters of DL Offshore Drilling."

Sean pictured Leyla being forced onto one of those shrimp boats.

"This lady claims she saw a dark-haired woman with two men on the landing pad there beside the drilling company."

Sean's stomach dropped. "Landing pad?"

"She said this woman was being forced into a helicopter."

He put one hand on her with a flinch to join Avon, tilting his head. He reached over and she held out her arm so he could take her pulse. He did. Her throat was

CHAPTER

TWENTY-SIX

LEYLA WAS DIZZY. And nauseous. A lack of food and sleep, along with two-plus hours of adrenaline overload was playing hell with her system.

Not to mention, she'd never liked heights.

Swallowing the bile in the back of her throat, she looked across the helicopter at Luc Gagnon. He was texting on his phone and had been for the last five minutes.

The chopper lurched down, and Leyla's stomach lurched, too. She leaned as far forward as the harness would let her.

"I'm going to puke."

Gagnon's head snapped up. "What?" he yelled over the noise.

"I think *I'm going to puke*," she said louder. "I'm dehydrated."

He pulled his fancy leather shoes closer to his seat. Then he tucked his phone into his jeans pocket, grabbed a water bottle from the cup holder, and held it out to her.

She just looked at him.

He took out a key chain with a mini Swiss Army knife attached. He reached over and she turned in her seat so he could use the blade to cut through the zip ties.

Pain pulsed through her shoulders as she pulled her hands in front of her for the first time in hours. She accepted the water bottle from him.

"Thank you." She took a sip.

He stared at her with an irritated look as she took another sip, rinsing the sour taste from her mouth. She wiped her lips with a trembling hand and gave the bottle back.

Leyla's wrists were raw and caked with dried blood. She settled her hands in her lap as she peered through the window at the ocean below. The setting sun reflected off the water, making the waves shimmer with gold. Tears burned her eyes as she thought about how much time had elapsed. With every minute, her hopes of someone coming for her faded.

She cleared her throat. "Where are we going?"

Gagnon ignored her and looked out his window.

Were *they* going anywhere? Or was it just him?

Since the instant she'd seen the helicopter, she'd been fixated on the idea of someone pushing her out of it. She was a strong swimmer, but this far from shore she didn't stand a chance.

No one would ever know.

Leyla's lungs constricted and her heart thudded wildly. Fear and panic coalesced into one big, greasy ball in the center of her stomach.

Another death in Leyla's tight-knit family would decimate her mother. And her brothers.

She closed her eyes, praying they were looking for her. And Sean, too. He would know something was wrong by now, wouldn't he?

But how would they *locate* her? And even if they did, it would probably be too late.

Leyla glanced at the water bottle in Gagnon's cup holder again. She should have had more when she had the chance. She needed to fortify herself. She couldn't count on anyone to find her, and she needed to escape somehow.

She looked at the pilot with that big headset over his ears. He'd watched her through his mirrored aviators as Gagnon's two armed thugs loaded her onto this thing, and he hadn't even flinched. He'd acted like it was perfectly normal, like flying bound captives around was something he'd done before.

The thought made her queasy again.

At least the Vikings had stayed behind. Wherever they were going now, it was just her and Gagnon, plus the pilot.

Leyla didn't know what to make of that.

Gagnon glanced over and caught her watching him. He scowled.

"You have no one to blame but yourself."

Hysterical laughter bubbled up. "How is *that*?"

He shook his head. "If you'd had that drink with me instead of spying"—he reached over and chucked her chin, and Leyla recoiled—"then this wouldn't be happening."

Then *what* wouldn't be happening? She wanted to scream the question at him, but instead she turned away.

Spying.

So he obviously knew about her snooping through his office.

Had Amelia done something similar? Had she eavesdropped on the wrong conversation, or snapped a picture of something illegal, or witnessed something she shouldn't have?

She studied Gagnon's face, seeing him clearly for the very first time. The man was a narcissist. In his warped view, the entire world revolved around him. Everything was all about his image and his business empire and perpetuat-

ing the idea of his boundless wealth. Everything he owned—
the cars, the house, the plane, even the "artwork" lining his
walls—was about showing off his supposed success to the
world. He didn't care whom he hurt or cheated or *murdered*,
as long as he came out ahead.

It was all about him.

The engine noise suddenly changed pitch, and the chopper swooped lower. Leyla clutched her abdomen and struggled not to heave up the contents of her stomach.

"You don't like flying?"

She glanced up, and he was smiling at her.

"Amelia didn't either." He crossed his ankle over his
knee, as though they were having a normal conversation.
"She liked boats, though. Most women do."

Leyla stared at him, not bothering to conceal her con-
tempt.

She glanced at the water again. Were they headed for a
boat way out here? She didn't know how far offshore they
were, but it was well beyond the yachts and catamarans that
cruised around the island.

"Hey."

She looked up, and Gagnon's face was serious now. The
flat look in his eyes filled her with icy terror.

"Ride's almost over," he said. "Enjoy it while you can."

T HE MEN CROWDED around the wall map turned to look
when Nicole entered the conference room.

"Anything?" Joel demanded.

"Not yet," she told him. "They're getting in position."

The Coast Guard had just dispatched a pair of response
boats to go check out DL Offshore Drilling's two platforms,
which were about thirty miles off the coast.

"When they get close enough," she added, "they plan to

send a drone up to see whether a helicopter is on either of the rigs. He'll call me when they know."

Owen and Joel turned back to face the big map taped to the whiteboard. Red dots indicated the known locations of drilling platforms in the region.

Nicole stepped over to Brady and Emmet. "Any news here?"

"Moran just got off the phone with an agent on their surveillance team," Brady said. "He says the chopper hasn't returned to the drilling company's headquarters, which might or might not be a good thing."

Nicole hoped to hell that meant the helo had landed on one of the platforms. DL Offshore Drilling had a business connection to some rancher that Gagnon knew, so they were checking the platforms first. But there was always the depressing possibility the chopper had flown south of the border.

She glanced at Sean, who stood near the window with his back to everyone as he talked on his cell phone.

"Who's he on with?" she asked the chief.

"HRT."

"HRT?"

"The FBI's Hostage Rescue Team is mounting an op."

"Where?" Nicole asked. "We don't even have a location."

Joel turned and glared at her.

"We're optimistic we'll get one," Brady said as Joel turned his attention back to the map. "CBP has been in touch. They haven't had any helos move through the airspace near the border in the last hour. So, it's likely it was bound for one of the rigs."

Nicole wasn't so sure. Just because Customs and Border Patrol hadn't detected something crossing the border didn't mean the helicopter was headed for one of the offshore platforms. It might be meeting up with a boat. Or heading far out to sea.

She thought of Miguel Vidales, and a chill went down her spine as she remembered his words about the kidnapped reporter.

Rumor is he took one of those chopper rides . . . over the Gulf of Mexico.

Sean stepped over. "We've got a team en route from Houston." He checked his watch. "ETA twenty minutes."

"Where are they going?" Joel asked him.

"They plan to stage at the Coast Guard station in Corpus Christi. Hopefully, by the time they get there we'll know where that helicopter landed."

Assuming it landed.

From the grim looks on Joel's and Owen's faces, Nicole could tell they weren't assuming anything.

Nicole's phone buzzed with a text message, and she pulled it out.

Her pulse picked up.

"I've got something from the Coast Guard," she said, skimming the message. "Okay, a drone sighted a yellow helicopter—"

"That's it!" Sean crowded closer to read over her shoulder.

"—and it's on one of the platforms," Nicole said. "I've got GPS coordinates here. And he sent a map."

"Let me see," Owen said.

She handed him the phone.

Sean was already back on his cell. "Hey, we've got a location," he told someone.

Owen typed on Nicole's phone, presumably sending himself the message. He handed the phone back to Nicole and looked at Joel.

"Let's go."

Joel nodded.

"Wait. Go where?" she asked.

"The task force has a boat ready out back," Joel said, already moving for the door.

"But . . . does the FBI want you there?"

Joel shot her a look. "We're going."

Nicole glanced at Brady, who seemed to recognize the futility of telling Leyla's brothers they had to stay back. They rushed out the door, followed by Sean and Emmet.

Brady grabbed his phone off the table and looked at her. "Come or stay here, Lawson. Your call."

"I'm coming."

THE DARKNESS WAS absolute. Not even a sliver of light this time.

Leyla groped along the wall, using her hands to try to get a sense of the space.

They had landed on a white X on one of those giant oil rigs, which was surrounded by water as far as she could see. Her relief at not being thrown from the helicopter had been replaced by fear after they landed as Gagnon grabbed her arm and hauled her into a metal structure that looked like a shipping container. She hadn't struggled, hoping maybe he wouldn't think to bind her hands again. And he hadn't. But now that she was stuck in this pitch-dark vault that smelled like tires, she wondered if she should have tried to make a run for it.

Of course, *where* would she have gone? They were in the middle of freaking nowhere.

Muffled voices seeped through the metal walls, and she heard the steady drone of mechanical equipment nearby. The sound—and everything else—was giving her a pounding headache. But on the good side, no one could hear her as she stumbled around in here, crashing into things.

Her hand bumped into something hard and round. A metal drum? That's what it felt like. She shuffled along and encountered another one. Then her knee connected with something hard, and she let out a yelp. She felt the object. Smooth and metal again, but this object was more like an egg than a cylinder. She slid her hands over it. There was a nozzle on top. She considered turning it, but then realized it could be a propane tank.

She kept shuffling along and encountered another similar tank. And another. And another.

Perfect. They'd locked her in a storage room with combustible chemicals.

Her hands encountered the wall again, then a corner filled with something soft and sticky. Spider webs? A shudder moved through her, but she continued her reconnaissance mission. She had to get her bearings and come up with a plan. Maybe there was another way out of this place. The door she'd come through was locked tight—she'd tried it—but she had to at least check. Now that she was free of the zip ties she needed to use every possible advantage.

"Ouch!"

She jerked her hand back. She'd sliced her finger on something sharp, and she could feel the warm trickle of blood sliding down her hand.

She pressed the cut against her jeans to stop the bleeding. Not that it mattered, really. She'd cut her hands hundreds of times in the kitchen, and she barely noticed anymore.

Shaking her hand out, she kept going. This vault was essentially her death chamber. Gagnon planned to have her executed tonight. Or do it himself. His candid conversation

with her made her *know* that he didn't intend to let her out
of this alive.

Her hand slid over something straight and metal, and her
pulse quickened. Was that . . . ?

Yes. A doorframe.

She moved her fingers over the shape, making out a rectangle that was slightly shorter than she was, probably five
feet tall. She remembered ducking her head coming in here,
so this was likely a door at the opposite end of the small
room.

Her hands encountered a latch, and her pulse picked up
again. It was one of those turn latches. Holding her breath,
she moved it ninety degrees. Then she lifted the metal flap
and pushed. A narrow strip of gray appeared.

Thank God.

The hinges creaked as she eased open the door. Damp
ocean air wafted into the room.

Clang!

She jumped as what sounded like a heavy metal chain
landed on the roof. She closed the door and looked up. Footsteps thudded over her, and she could tell at least one person
was within a few yards of her location. The footsteps shifted
to the other side of the roof and then disappeared altogether.

Leyla eased the door open again, blinking at the dimness. She glanced up. The sky was gray and dusky—but not
dark yet. A bright floodlight nearby cast shadows along the
concrete decking.

Peering out, she checked for people but only heard
voices in the distance, along with the steady hum of mechanical equipment. She slipped through the door and
eased it shut behind her. It had been latched from the inside,
so would it swing open now and attract attention? She didn't
know, and she didn't have time to worry about it. She
needed to find a place to hide.

Slowly, cautiously, she ducked low and stayed near the wall as she crept toward another large metal structure. This one was a shipping container, too, but it had a window, and light spilled out, creating a white rectangle on the concrete.

What now?

She'd escaped the death chamber, but she was still stuck in the middle of nowhere. It was a windy night, too, and she visualized the whitecaps she'd seen on the water as the helicopter had landed.

She had to get her hands on a phone. Or maybe a radio. She had to call for help and then find a good hiding place where she could wait for help to reach her.

Shouts suddenly went up nearby. She ducked behind a stack of wooden platforms. People were yelling back and forth, but she couldn't make out the words. Then she heard a rhythmic noise in the distance.

Another helicopter landing?

She slid along the wall until she reached a corner. Leaning her head around, she caught sight of the front of the yellow helicopter.

No pilot. So, Gagnon wasn't going anywhere yet. Which was good, probably.

Or was it?

The helicopter noise grew louder, and she squinted her eyes as dust whipped up. She still couldn't see it, but the thunder of the rotor blades was unmistakable. Where was it going to land? Gagnon's helicopter was still parked on the X.

Someone stepped into view. A man she didn't recognize from the back. Not Gagnon—this one had a long dark ponytail.

Then Gagnon walked into view.

Leyla's breath caught. He had a pistol tucked in the back of his jeans. It was the first time she'd seen him armed, she realized. Was he planning to come looking for her?

She ducked against the side of the building, squinting her eyes at the dust as the helicopter swooped lower. The side door was open, and a man stood beside a rope, lowering a large crate. Men on deck crowded below as the load came down.

Everyone was distracted. Now was her moment.

Leyla crept around the corner of the metal structure and spied an orange forklift parked beside a corrugated metal building with windows. Beside the building was a tangle of ducts and pipes. It looked shadowy there, lots of places to hide. And maybe she could sneak into that building and find a phone or a radio. But first she had to make it across a wide-open space.

The helicopter noise was deafening now, and the air vibrated all around her. She set her sights on the building and made a sprint for it.

CHAPTER

TWENTY-SEVEN

S EAN GRIPPED THE rail, soaked to the skin as the speedboat sliced through the swells. The oil rig was a glowing behemoth several football fields away. Sean lifted the
binoculars, struggling to hold them steady with one hand
while gripping the rail with the other.

The boat slowed, and Sean whipped around.

Joel pulled the throttle back, bringing the boat to a stop.
The bow pitched forward, and Sean caught himself on the rail.

"What?" Sean yelled over the noise.

"We're stopping."

"Why?"

"Coast Guard's orders."

Sean turned east, where a Coast Guard cutter carrying
the FBI's Hostage Rescue Team lurked in the darkness.
Sean couldn't see them. Like this boat, they were operating
without running lights, attempting a stealth approach. But
Sean knew they were there.

The boat lurched down, then up again, and Sean grabbed

the railing. The swells out here were bigger than this police boat was designed to handle.

Sean peered through the binoculars, scanning the surface of the rig. It was a two-level structure, with pipes and ducts and scaffolding everywhere. The helo pad was on the south side, out of view, but Gagnon's bird was still there, according to the Coast Guard drone. So, they were assuming Gagnon was still there, too.

And Leyla.

Sean's lungs constricted as he scanned the deck under the floodlights, looking for any sign of her.

Owen was on his phone now. He exchanged words with Joel and then the boat was moving again.

"We're positioning closer," Joel yelled.

Good.

Sean trained his binoculars on the massive platform as Joel made a wide arc, coming around to the south side.

Owen walked over, catching himself on the railing as the boat hit a bump. In chop like this, it wouldn't take much to go overboard, and everyone wore red life jackets equipped with lights and whistles.

"They're getting a drop right now," Owen said.

"The rig is?" Sean aimed the binoculars, but it was impossible to focus in the bumpy water. He lowered the binoculars and looked at Owen. "How do you know?"

"Coasties said there's a black helo hovering on the other side."

Sean squinted into the night sky. As they neared the rig, he heard the distant sound of rotor blades.

Was this the "drop" of Gagnon's shipment of devices? The real one, not the decoy?

Maybe.

But Sean didn't care. The only thing that mattered right now was locating Leyla on that giant rig.

The boat arced around, and the yellow helicopter came into view.

Sean's gut tightened. Gagnon was still there. Which meant Leyla was, too.

He hoped.

And prayed.

Sean's stomach clenched as the police boat got closer and closer. He peered through the binoculars, desperate to find her. Men in jeans and hard hats walked around—rig workers, maybe, or people who worked for Gagnon. But no Luc Gagnon.

And no Leyla.

"See anything?" Owen asked beside him.

"No."

Sean could barely see Owen's face in the darkness, but his voice was thick with tension.

"These HRT guys, you know them?" Owen asked.

"No."

"You know if they're any good?"

Sean's gut clenched. "Yeah. Supposedly, the best."

"They'd better be."

LEYLA HID BEHIND the forklift, praying they wouldn't see her. Her heart was thudding so hard, she thought it would pound right out of her body.

Voices neared her, and she tried to melt into the shadows. People were looking for her. She couldn't make out all their words, but she could tell from the urgent tone of their voices. Gagnon knew she was missing, and he had put the word out to search. Now she could hear men rushing around, combing every inch of this place.

More footsteps, and she hunched low, trying to be invisible. She hadn't gotten anywhere near a door yet, or any sort of room where she might find a phone or radio. She needed a weapon, too, preferably a blade. A chef's knife would be beautiful, but she'd settle for anything sharp. Or heavy. She glanced around, looking for a wrench or a crowbar or even a glass bottle. But there was nothing out here. Sure, there was plenty of heavy equipment, but everything was either bolted down or secured with chains. She looked behind a pile of wooden platforms and saw a roll of orange twine. Not helpful. But then she spied a pair of pointed pliers with rubber handles. No match for a gun, but better than nothing. She snatched them up.

Ducking around a pipe, she spotted a metal staircase leading to the lower level. She made a dash for it, trying to keep her footsteps quiet as she hurried down the stairs. The lower level was darker, with more pipes and ducts and places to hide. But she still needed to locate a phone.

Footsteps thudded closer, and a pair of big men rushed by, so close she could smell the sweat on them. She moved deeper into the shadows, closer and closer to the edge of the drilling platform. Wind whipped her hair against her face, and she could smell the saltwater. She was out here *in the middle of the Gulf of Mexico*! And this platform had to be forty feet off the water.

She had to find a better hiding place than this. And she had to get her hands on a phone or a radio. She had to make a call for help and then—

A hand clamped around the back of her neck. She whirled around and found herself face-to-face with Gagnon.

Leyla stabbed him with the pliers and wrestled free.

"THERE! LOOK!"

Sean jerked his head around. Joel was looking through his binoculars and pointing at the rig. Sean rushed to the starboard side and lifted his binoculars.

Leyla.

She was crouched low, running along beside a metal railing.

"She's running from someone," Joel said. "See?"

Sean scanned the area, looking for someone chasing her.

"That team needs to get in there *now*," Owen said. "Sean?"

Sean whipped out his phone and with a trembling hand dialed his contact.

LEYLA DARTED BEHIND a big metal duct and stopped to catch her breath. Her heart was thundering. Where had he gone? Where? He was just behind her.

She kept moving, trying to keep to the shadows as she stumbled forward. She reached a thick yellow pipe and climbed over it, landing hard on her knee. Then she scrambled to her feet.

"Stop."

Her skin went cold, and she whirled around.

Gagnon strode toward her, his black pistol pointed right at her.

Leyla looked to the side. Her stomach lurched. In the glow of the rig lights, she saw whitecaps on the churning water.

"Don't bother," Gagnon said. "It's a long way down."

She glanced at the water again and caught sight of a dark shape just between the light and the shadow. *A boat?*

She looked at Gagnon. He kept his gun pointed at her chest as he climbed over the pipe. Sweat soaked his shirt, and the look in his eyes was cold and irritated, like she was an unpleasant chore he had to take care of.

Gagnon lifted his gun as he neared her. She grabbed the railing and threw her leg over it, and his face crumpled into a confused scowl.

"What the—"

She jumped.

* * *

NICOLE'S HEART LEAPED into her throat.

"Holy *shit*, she jumped!" Owen yelled.

Sean scrambled to the front of the boat.

"Go!" Sean looked back at Joel. "*Go, go, go!*"

The boat surged forward, and Nicole caught her hand on the side as she scanned the swells, looking for Leyla.

"There!" she yelled.

"Where? *Where?*" Owen bellowed.

"There! By the big column!" She pointed at a bobbing dot on the waves.

Sean climbed onto the side and dived in.

THE WATER CRASHED over her, pushing her down with punishing force, then tossing her up again. She broke the surface and gasped for air.

Water filled her lungs, and she plunged down again. Panic set in as she fought for the surface, but the current was pulling her down.

She flailed her arms, straining for the surface, desperate for oxygen. The water was dark and churning, tossing her like a giant washing machine.

Which way?

Terror seized her as she tried to figure out which way was up. Her lungs burned. She needed air. She kicked and pulled, but the water kept sucking her down, down, down.

Leyla!"

Sean pulled through the water, frantically searching for her dark head. Salt burned his eyes as he scanned the surface.

A wave swept him up, and he caught a glimpse of her.

"Leyla! Here!"

He swam through the swells, desperately trying to keep her in view. Her head disappeared beneath the surface, and terror shot through him. He powered through the water, arms and legs and lungs burning as he reached for her.

His fingers caught on something and he dove down, grabbing hold of her hair, her shirt, her arm. He dragged her up, hooking another arm around her body.

"Leyla!"

She coughed and choked, and Sean used his hip to thrust her up.

"Breathe, Leyla!"

He adjusted her weight, pushing her chest and head above the surface as the swells rose and sank around them. Then her fingers dug into his arm, and he felt a blinding rush of relief.

"Hold on! I got you."

He scanned the water, searching for the boat. Something splashed behind them, and suddenly a rescue diver was next to him, wrestling Leyla out of his grip.

"Let go!" the diver yelled. "I have her."

"She's choking. We gotta get her *out!*"

Then he saw the bow of a boat and arms reaching down. A yellow sling appeared, and Sean helped the diver position it around Leyla's body. An instant later, she was being lifted aboard the boat.

Someone hooked a ladder over the side, and Sean grabbed hold of it and started climbing as the vessel pitched and lurched in the waves. Joel and Owen helped pull him into the boat.

Leyla was on her side on the floor, coughing and sputtering.

Sean scrambled to her and scraped the wet hair away from her face. "Cough it out!"

She looked up, her face pale and splotchy.

"Sean," she gasped, reaching for him.

He pulled her up and dragged her against him. "Can you breathe? Leyla?"

She gripped his arm.

"Say something! Can you breathe?"

She gripped harder. "Yes."

CHAPTER

TWENTY-EIGHT

Nicole scooped up her keys and took a last look around the bullpen before heading out. The mountain of paperwork she had to deal with would still be here tomorrow, and she desperately needed some food and a shower. She walked past the reception desk as Sean Moran strode into the police station.

"Hey," she said. "I thought you were in Brownsville?"

"I was." He glanced past her at the sea of cubicles, which were empty except for one lone patrol officer tapping away at a computer. "Is Brady still around?"

"He left at midnight."

Sean mumbled a curse and ran a hand through his hair, mussing it even more. He looked better than he had earlier—but not by much. He'd gotten hold of some dry clothes, at least, but his eyes were bloodshot and he looked to be in dire need of some sleep. Or failing that, a stiff drink.

"How's it going in B-ville?" she asked him.

"It's a zoo there."

"Yeah, I figured."

After the Coast Guard had boarded the drilling platform, Luc Gagnon and his pilot had been taken into custody. Gagnon had been handed over to the FBI, who had transported him to the Brownsville field office for questioning.

The last time Nicole had seen Sean, he'd been helping Leyla into a police SUV so her brothers could take her to the hospital on the mainland to get checked out.

"What's that?" Nicole asked, nodding at the file folder in Sean's hand.

He glanced at the empty bullpen again and then looked at her. He seemed to be debating something.

"You still the lead on the Albright case?" he asked.

"Yeah."

He handed her the folder, which was presumably intended for Brady.

Nicole stepped over to the reception desk and set down her car keys. Then she opened the folder and found a stack of printouts. Each page contained a color photograph.

"What are these?" she asked.

"Amelia's pictures."

She stared down at a photo of Amelia wearing a white bikini aboard a boat. She and another woman were mugging for the camera with a pair of pink umbrella drinks in their hands.

"We recovered these from her iPad," Sean said. "She took them with her phone, then emailed them to herself."

"Why would she—" Nicole stopped as she came to a photo of Luc Gagnon. He sat on the deck of what appeared to be a luxury yacht, smoking cigars with a couple of men in sunglasses. Nicole held up the photo. "Who are they?"

"The one on the left is one of Saledo's top lieutenants. This one here"—he tapped the man beside Gagnon—"is Ricardo Ariza. He's wanted by the FBI for narcotics trafficking and racketeering. Keep going."

Nicole flipped to the next picture. It was a close-up shot of a black duffel. The unzipped bag was stuffed with stacks of cash.

"Holy crap." She looked at Sean. "Amelia took these with her phone?"

"We think so, yeah. She emailed these shots to herself about three weeks ago."

"Why?"

"We don't know. But it seems clear she'd figured out her boyfriend and his associates were into something illegal. Could be she was planning to ask him for hush money, or maybe report him to the feds. We may never know."

Nicole flipped to another picture showing a close-up of the cash. "This is our motive right here," she said. "This is why he killed her."

"*He* didn't kill her. He was in San Jose at the time."

"Yeah, but he hired someone to do it. And now we can prove motive," she said. "Sean, this is *great*. This is practically a smoking gun!"

He just looked at her.

Nicole's stomach sank. "Shit, don't tell me. You guys cut him a deal, didn't you?"

The look on his face answered her question.

"*Shit!*" She slapped the folder shut.

"*I* didn't cut a deal with him."

Nicole's chest tightened with anger. "But your boss did? And you're okay with this?"

"No, I'm not. But people higher up the chain have decided he's more useful working *for* us, not against us."

"So . . . let me guess. You guys seized his phones, and now you're going to eavesdrop on his whole damn network. That's what this is about, isn't it?" She glared at him, but he didn't respond. "Oh, right, I forgot. You can't tell me because I don't have a federal badge. So, what, now Gagnon's just going to *walk* after hiring a hit on an innocent young woman? And what about what he did to Leyla? He was obviously planning to kill her, too!"

Sean's jaw tightened, and she could feel the tension coming off him in waves.

Nicole shook her head. "This is crap, Sean."

"I agree."

She watched him, noting the slight twitch of his eye. He was obviously stressed to the limit. And no doubt completely drained after tonight's water rescue thirty miles offshore.

Nicole sighed. "How is Leyla doing?"

"All right." He combed his hand through his hair again, and she felt a twinge of sympathy for him. "She's at the hospital. No concussion, evidently, but she's bruised up and needed some stitches in her hand. Joel's supposed to text me when they leave."

"He's at home."

Sean frowned. "Who?"

"Joel. I talked to Miranda an hour ago, and he was there at their house."

Anger flared in Sean's eyes. He looked at his watch again.

"I need to go," he said. "Make sure Brady gets those pictures."

"I will."

He turned to leave.

"Hey, tell Leyla I hope she feels better," Nicole called after him. "She had us all scared to death."

* * *

LEYLA AWOKE TO a soft tapping.

She blinked at the dimness. Where was she? She jolted up with a start. The room pulsated with a bluish glow, and she glanced around, panicked.

She was in her living room. Her shirt was damp, and she looked down at the empty water bottle on the cushion beside her. She'd fallen asleep curled up in her armchair watching *Planet Earth* on her TV.

Tap tap tap.

Shaking off the daze, she got to her feet and padded barefoot across the room, and her nerves jumped as she recognized the silhouette on the other side of the window shade. She checked the peephole to be sure, then flipped the bolt and opened the door.

Sean stood in the yellow glow of her porch light. He stepped inside without speaking. After she closed and locked the door, he wrapped his arms around her and eased her against him.

"Hi," she whispered.

"Hi."

She rested her head against his chest, absorbing the solid heat of him. Sliding her arms around his waist, she inhaled the scent of his warm skin. They stood there without moving for a few long moments.

He kissed the top of her head. "I didn't know you were back," he said.

"Yeah." She cleared her throat. "I told Joel not to call you."

His body tensed. "Why?"

"I figured you probably had your hands full."

He frowned down at her in the dimness, and she pulled out of his arms.

"Want some tea?" she asked, turning away.

She smoothed her hair and stepped into the kitchen, where a dim light glowed above the sink. She probably looked terrible. After a shower, she'd fallen asleep in her oldest T-shirt and softest sweatpants, and her hair was a tangled mess.

She looked at Sean over her shoulder as she grabbed the kettle and turned on the faucet. He leaned back against the counter, watching her.

"Lemon chamomile?" she asked.

He shook his head.

She switched on the stove. She'd made tea earlier, in an attempt to calm her nerves. The car ride back from the hospital with Joel had been fraught with tension as he'd forced her to repeat every detail of the account she'd given to an FBI agent at the hospital. She'd never been so rattled in her life. Joel and Owen and their mom had all implored her to stay with one of them for the night instead of being by herself. But she'd known she was headed for a crash—both physically and emotionally—and she'd wanted to be alone.

She turned around, and Sean was watching her closely. His gaze went to the bandages on her wrists, and he stepped over.

"What did the doctor say?" he asked, tracing his finger up her arm.

"I'm fine. No concussion."

He took her right hand and gently turned it over. Her index finger was wrapped, too.

"And this?" he asked.

"Four stitches." She tugged her hand away and rested it on his hip. "They'll dissolve, so I don't have to go back, which is good."

"What did you cut it on?"

"I don't know. I couldn't see. Something inside the shipping container."

He stared down at her, and his hands settled on her hips. The worried look on his face made her chest ache.

"Sorry I'm late getting here," he said.

His eyes were tired and bloodshot. He hadn't had the benefit of a nap, like she had, and she saw the events of the last twenty-four hours—plus everything else—weighing on him.

It felt so *good* just standing here in her kitchen with him. She felt grateful and amazingly lucky to be safe at home with Sean's hands resting solidly on her hips.

Lying on the floor of that Suburban in the suffocating heat, she'd had a chance to think, and second-guess, and *regret* so many things in her life. Her sharpest regret was about her mother—how she'd avoided so many conversations with her ever since her dad died, as though talking about him would somehow make the grief worse. Leyla had had a burst of clarity while she lay on that floor. Now, she knew that she shouldn't have held back. She should have told her mom everything in her heart, especially how much she loved her.

Her other regret was about Sean. It had been with her in that Suburban, and it was like a sharp thorn in her heart now as she stared up at him. The moment stretched out as he held her loosely, taking care not to squeeze her.

She lifted her good hand and traced her finger over his stubbly jaw. "When do you leave?" she asked.

"That depends."

"On?"

A whistle emanated from the teakettle. As the whistle became a shriek, she stepped over to switch the stove off and move the kettle to the back burner.

Sean took her hand and tugged her over to the chair beside her drop-leaf table. He sat down and pulled her onto his lap.

"Leyla," he sighed, wrapping his arms around her. He rested his forehead on her chest, and she smoothed her hands over his shoulders.

He looked up at her, and the raw emotion in his eyes made her throat feel tight.

"It depends?" she asked again.

"On you." He reached up and brushed a strand of hair out of her eyes. "I'm taking some time off."

"Good. You probably need it after . . . well, after everything. How long are you taking?"

"Four days. That's as much as I can get for now. Even that's a stretch, given everything going on." He paused. "I just want to be with you right now."

Nervous butterflies filled her stomach.

"What's that look?" he asked.

"I'm worried."

"Why?"

She gazed down at him. "I'm worried—" A hot lump clogged her throat.

He reached up and stroked her lower lip with his thumb. "What? You can tell me."

"If we spend more time together, I'm worried we'll get too attached."

He kissed her softly. "Too late." He kissed her again. "I'm already attached."

"Really?"

He nodded. "Completely."

Her chest filled with joy and fear and confusion. Why did this have to be happening? Why was she letting herself fall for a man who lived almost two thousand miles away?

He kissed her, and the questions evaporated as she focused on the hot, urgent feel of his mouth. His fingers tangled in her hair, and he kissed her with all that fierce need she'd been feeling—and trying *not* to feel—for days now. His tongue tangled with hers, and his hand slid under her shirt and his warm palm surrounded her breast. She squirmed on his lap, pressing against him as his thumb rasped over her nipple.

"Sean."

She kissed his mouth, his jaw, his neck, breathing in the wonderful heat of him.

"I was so damn scared today," he said.

She pulled back to look at him. She'd been scared, too. Not just scared—utterly terrified. And she still hadn't gotten her head around the thought that it was over. Really. And she was home now, with Sean, after she'd thought she might never see him again.

She snuggled as close as she could as his arms locked around her. He kissed her, hard, and she kissed him just as hard right back. It was forceful and demanding and possessive, and it felt *right*. And then her stomach clenched as she thought about how she was going to feel when he had to leave. It was going to be excruciating.

"Sean," she whispered. "What are we doing?"

"I honestly don't know." He rested his forehead against hers. "But I know that I need you."

She wrapped her arms around his shoulders. "Same."

SEAN STEPPED OUT of the police station into the blazing sun. He started for his car, but then spied Nicole pulling into a space in the front row. She was in an unmarked police unit, which told him she was on duty. Sean hadn't seen her since the night of the rescue operation five days before.

"Hi," Nicole said, walking over. "I thought you went back to D.C.?"

"Not yet."

She removed her sunglasses as she stopped in front of him. "What's wrong?" She frowned. "You look stressed."

Sean had a long list of things making him stressed at the moment, at the top of which was saying good-bye to Leyla less than an hour ago.

"I just had a meeting with Brady," Sean said.

Nicole's frown deepened. "Bad news?"

"Unfortunately, yes."

"Damn. I'm melting. Tell me in the shade." She led him to the side of the building and folded her arms over her chest, like she was bracing herself. "Okay, what is it?"

"Your department submitted a GPS tracking device for processing."

"I know. *I* submitted it. What about it?"

"The county crime lab lifted some latent prints," he said. "They came back to Brian Bentworth."

Her eyebrows shot up. "Brian Bentworth. *Your* Brian Bentworth?"

"Well, he's not ours."

"You're talking about the DEA agent from Houston? The guy whose prints were on that beer can you asked me to run?"

She'd been doing her homework, apparently. Sean wasn't surprised.

"That's him," Sean said, and he could see her absorbing the implications.

"You're telling me a *federal agent* put that tracking device on Amelia Albright's car." She leaned closer. "In other words, he killed her."

"We believe so, yeah."

She shook her head and looked away. For the first time since he'd known her, she seemed at a loss for words.

"That's . . . I can't believe it."

Sean could. But he'd been doing this longer than she had.

"You told Brady all this?" she asked.

"Yeah, just now." Sean paused, hating the next part even more. "The other thing I told him is that Bentworth is dead."

Her mouth dropped open. "He's—"

"Someone shot him in the back of the head in an alley in Brownsville."

"He was executed."

Sean nodded.

"By Saledo's people?"

"We don't know," Sean said. "But that would be my guess."

Nicole closed her eyes and pinched the bridge of her nose. "*Damn it to hell.*"

"I know."

"I can't believe this," she said. "So . . . you think he was, what, on Saledo's payroll?"

"It looks like he was working for him in some capacity. We're looking into it now."

She shook her head again. Then she put her hand on her stomach and bent over.

"You okay?" Sean asked.

"No." She straightened. "I'm . . . I don't know what I am. Disgusted. Disappointed. *Disillusioned*, I guess you could say."

Sean felt the same way. The feeling wasn't new to him, but Nicole had less experience than he did. Plus, it was her first big investigation to lead, and she had no doubt been striving to get an arrest and see the case go to trial. Now she was going to have to live with an outcome that wasn't at all what she'd hoped for. Sean knew that feeling, too.

He checked his watch. "I need to go. I've got a plane to catch."

"Back to D.C.?"

"Yeah."

She held out her hand. "Well, if I don't see you again, thanks."

Sean shook her hand. "For what?"

"For keeping me in the loop."

"I wish I had better news," Sean said. "And I'm sorry that after all your work on this thing, your perp will never see the inside of a prison cell."

"Well . . . if he was a *cop* working for Saledo, then in my book he got what he deserved."

CHAPTER

TWENTY-NINE

Three weeks later

As hard as she'd expected it to be after Sean left, it was worse.

Leyla threw herself into work, partly to keep from dwelling on the shock of what had happened. And partly to distract herself from the bleak emptiness she felt now that Sean was back to his job and his life in D.C.

Working helped—at least as far as being a distraction. She immersed herself in the chaos of her busy kitchen. But nothing would dull the pain she felt every time she thought about him. Each night, as the minutes crawled by and she found herself tossing and turning and unable to sleep, her thoughts would inevitably slide backward, and she would relive every hour they'd spent together, every touch and every conversation, in vivid detail. She'd even relived their arguments—that was how much she missed him. And morning after morning, she'd drag herself out of bed feeling tired and emotionally depleted. And then she'd face another day of work, wondering—*obsessing*—over whether tonight would be a night they would exchange text messages or maybe even a phone call.

The past three weeks had been miserable. But Leyla was dealing.

Except for days like today, when nothing went right, and she hadn't had so much as a text from Sean in more than forty-eight hours.

Leyla pulled a baking sheet from the oven and dropped it on the counter.

"Crap!"

Rogelio stepped into the kitchen. Setting a tray of focaccia bread on the counter, he looked at her failed macarons and lifted an eyebrow. "It's raining, *chiquita*. What'd you expect?"

She surveyed the cracked pink shells as he walked out of the room. Tears burned her eyes. Which was *so stupid*! Since when did she cry over pastries? But it had been one thing after another today. First, she'd overslept and been late to work. Then she'd somehow lost an order for a kid's birthday and had to scramble to substitute two dozen dino-themed cupcakes with two dozen mix-and-match. And then, just when she'd finished comping the order and apologizing to the huffy mom, *her own* mom had walked into the store. Ostensibly, her mother was there for a panini, but her real mission was to encourage Leyla to make an appointment with a therapist to deal with the PTSD that Leyla was supposedly in denial about.

Leyla had made the appointment, mostly to placate her mother. But now she had a therapy session looming on her calendar, and just the thought of talking about everything she was feeling right now made her stomach hurt.

She opened the oven and yanked out another tray of cracked macaron shells.

"Fuck!"

"Leyla?"

She glanced up to see Miranda standing in the doorway. Her sister-in-law's hair was damp, and she wore a wet blue windbreaker.

"Oh, damn. We were supposed to meet, weren't we?"

Miranda smiled. "It's three-ten, so I figured you forgot." She held up a lemonade. "I got a drink already."

"I'm *so* sorry." Leyla set the baking sheet on the counter. "It's been one of those insane days."

"No problem." Miranda leaned back against the counter and glanced at the two trays of pink shells. "Wow, those are . . ." She seemed to be struggling for something nice to say.

"Hideous. I know. Fucking weatherman."

Miranda looked at her. "What does the weatherman have to do with it?"

"This storm front was supposed to come tomorrow, not today." She tossed her oven mitt onto the counter and sighed. "The moisture in the air makes them crack."

"Oh." Miranda frowned at the trays. "It there any way to salvage them?"

"No." Leyla glanced at the oven timer. "Maybe my lemon ones will turn out. Who knows? It all depends on the fickle pastry gods." She looked at Miranda and forced a smile. "So. How have you been?"

"Great." Miranda sipped her drink, watching Leyla over the top of her cup. "How about you?"

"Busy."

"Oh yeah?"

"Two wedding cakes this week." Leyla wiped her forehead with the back of her arm. "Plus, I've got four events booked."

"Sounds like a lot. Are you getting any rest?"

Leyla sighed. "Did my mom tell you to ask me that?"

"No." She looked sheepish. "Joel did."

Leyla rolled her eyes.

"He's worried about you. I take it your mom is, too?"

"She thinks I have post-traumatic stress disorder and that I'm having trouble sleeping."

"Are you?"

She shrugged. "Yeah."

But it wasn't PTSD keeping her awake at night. It was Sean. She missed him so much it was a constant ache in the center of her chest.

Miranda set her cup down, and her attention caught on the laptop computer sitting open on the counter. Her eyebrows arched as she read the screen. While the macarons had been baking, Leyla had been researching commercial kitchen regulations in the state of Maryland.

Miranda looked at her. "Are you thinking of moving your business?"

"No." Leyla sighed. "Not really. It's just research at this point."

"Big decision."

"I know."

And it was *way* early to be making a decision like that. Or even thinking about it.

"Don't tell Joel," Leyla said.

"I won't."

"That's the last thing I need."

"I understand." Miranda tipped her head to the side. "So, how are things going with Sean?"

"Terrible."

Miranda's instant look of sympathy brought tears to Leyla's eyes. Telling her sister-in-law somehow made it more real.

"Sorry." Leyla lifted her apron and dabbed her cheeks. "I don't know what's wrong with me today. My emotions are all over the place."

"It's okay." Miranda reached over and squeezed her hand, and the tears welled again.

"Sorry."

"It's fine." Miranda glanced at the computer. "So . . . things must be serious if you're thinking of moving up there."

"They are. At least from my perspective."

Miranda frowned. "What does Sean think?"

"I don't know." She blew out a sigh. "We haven't talked about it."

"No?"

"I've hardly talked to him at all in three days. He's been slammed with work, and so have I."

"Does he know how you feel?"

She lifted a shoulder.

"If you're in love with him, maybe you should tell him."

Tears burned Leyla's eyes. That was the whole problem. She was terrified. Not only of her feelings, but of telling him and finding out he wasn't on the same page.

Leyla shook her head. "Part of me thinks it's crazy to even be thinking about moving. Especially because I feel like we're drifting apart."

"You do?"

She nodded. "I felt so close to him when he was here." Leyla had never experienced anything like it. It was like he could anticipate everything she wanted. And read her thoughts. "But now I'm worried. I mean, it was great in person, but what if that doesn't translate to a long-distance relationship? What if he doesn't want that level of commitment?"

Miranda tipped her head to the side. "Well, I don't know him that well. But he doesn't seem like someone to run from a challenge. Besides that, Joel respects him, and he's a good judge of character."

"Joel hates him."

Miranda smiled. "No, he doesn't."

"Doesn't he? I thought everything that happened caused a rift between them."

Miranda shook her head. "I don't think so. Or if it did, they've worked it out. The fact that Sean saved your life probably helped."

Leyla sighed. Hearing that was good, but it didn't lessen her stress. She wiped her eyes, annoyed with herself for getting weepy yet again today.

"I hate all this emotional drama," she told Miranda. "It's so not *me*. This is why I never wanted a long-distance relationship. It's a lot harder than I thought it would be, and I thought it would suck."

"Do you guys talk on the phone a lot?" Miranda asked.

"Not regularly, no. I didn't want to get into that, where he feels obligated to call me every night, you know? I didn't want to put that kind of pressure on everything. So we agreed to keep it to a few times a week."

Miranda pursed her lips.

"Anyway, he's been really busy. And I've been totally in the weeds. I'm *buried* with catering jobs right now. I've been staying late every night and working weekends."

"Is that by design?" Miranda asked.

"Probably. I mean, yeah, it is," Leyla admitted. "I refuse to let myself sit around moping. But he's swamped, too. Especially this week. He's been supporting a tactical team and working round the clock."

The timer beeped. Leyla grabbed her mitt and turned to check the oven.

"It'll get better, I'm sure," Miranda said. "Joel says things should settle down after the raid tonight."

Leyla got a cramp in her stomach as she pulled the baking sheet from the oven. She looked at Miranda.

"Joel is with Sean?"

Miranda's eyebrows arched. "Oh . . . I'm not sure. Maybe?"

Leyla struggled to keep her face blank as she set the sheet on the counter.

"I'm sorry," Miranda said. "I thought you knew."

"No. He didn't mention what exactly he was working on right now."

Or that he was in Texas.

She tossed the oven mitt on the counter and surveyed the lemon macarons. "*Shit.* These, too. I'm going to have to start all over."

Miranda looked pained.

"Leyla, I'm—"

"It's fine. Really." She held up her hand. "You don't need to apologize."

DEEP TIDE

THIRTY

Nicole parked beside the lighthouse and watched the morning light glimmer off the highest windows. It had been raining all week, but now the sun was out, which meant she was fresh out of excuses for not squeezing in a jog after work.

A familiar hatchback pulled up beside her, and Nicole got out of her car.

Miguel Vidales slid from his car and eyed her over the top of his roof.

"I'm surprised you wanted to meet in public," he said as he joined her on the sidewalk.

Nicole led him to a picnic table beside a sno-cone truck. She sat on the weathered wooden bench, and he took a seat across from her.

"All the cameras have left town," she told him. "With no new headlines here, they're off covering other stories."

Miguel lifted an eyebrow as he twisted the top off a water bottle.

"What's up?" Nicole took off her sunglasses and checked her watch. "I've only got a few minutes before I have to go back for a staff meeting."

He took a sip of water and placed the bottle in front of him on the graffiti-covered table. "So, I never got your phone call."

"I never made any promises about that."

He nodded. "Still. I gave you *a lot* of help. The Saledo connection. The tracking devices. The list of contractors working for him."

Which hadn't included Brian Bentworth.

Nicole still couldn't believe *a cop* had done it.

Or maybe she could. An FBI Evidence Response Team had searched an apartment rented by Bentworth in nearby Brownsville and discovered a box hidden in the AC vent. The box contained a six-inch hunting knife, blue twine, and a box of latex gloves.

A murder kit. Right there in the guy's apartment. Nicole's lingering doubts about the case—as well as her blind faith in her fellow cops—had disappeared the instant she saw those crime scene photos.

"That's a lot of help, wouldn't you say?"

Nicole nodded.

"Now, I need a favor from you," Miguel told her. "I need you to answer a question for me."

She watched him, waiting for what he'd say next. She'd known this was coming the second she got his message this morning.

"You haven't arrested anyone in Amelia Albright's murder," he stated, "and we both know you're not going to."

Her shoulders tensed.

"I have a source that tells me a certain DEA agent who was recently murdered down here in Brownsville is linked to two unsolved murders in San Antonio."

She tried to keep her face neutral.

"Massey and Rincon," he added.

"Is there a question in there?"

"Another source tells me the FBI is investigating this guy in connection with a *third* murder. Amelia Albright." He waited a beat. "Can you confirm that?"

"No."

"No, you can't confirm? Or no, the FBI is not looking at him for that?"

"No, I can't confirm or deny any information for you."

Miguel's brown-black eyes bored into hers. "How about on deep background?"

"Can't do it."

He darted an exasperated glance at the bright blue sky. "Look." He met her gaze. "This source is solid gold, as far as reliability. I know Brian Bentworth was doing hits for Saledo."

Just hearing his name put a sour taste in her mouth.

"The feds have *proof.*"

"What kind of proof?" she asked, disturbed by the idea that someone was leaking details of that search warrant to someone in the media.

Miguel's mouth curved into a sly smile. "Pick up a copy of my paper on Sunday and read about it for yourself. What I need is confirmation of whether he's being investigated in connection with Amelia, too."

Nicole stared at the reporter. He was tenacious as hell, she'd give him that.

She watched him, battling the urge to give him Luc Gagnon's name. It was *so* damn tempting. The wealthy young tech mogul was skating almost scot-free, as far as Nicole could tell. Both Joel and Brady had told her not to get hung up on that and to see it as a valuable trade. Gagnon's cooperation, evidently, was netting big new leads for a long list of law enforcement agencies. Just last weekend, some tip gleaned from an intercepted message from one of Gagnon's doctored phones had led police to bust a sex trafficking ring operating in Corpus Christi. So, that was good, obviously.

But Nicole still felt bitter about it. Whatever reduced punishment Gagnon's lawyers had negotiated for him would never be nearly enough.

And then there was Gagnon's company, which seemed to be humming along just fine. Nicole hadn't seen a single headline about GhostSend in the past few weeks, and she'd been looking.

Encrypted phone apps were a double-edged sword. They allowed thugs like Saledo to operate secretly as they trafficked drugs and guns and people, all the while keeping their criminal activities hidden from law enforcement. But those same encryption apps were used by journalists and dissidents all over the world.

Miguel leaned closer and lowered his voice. "Come on, Nicole. Totally off the record."

She stared at him, realizing just how brave it was that he was here, talking to her about an investigation into one of the most dangerous criminals in the Western Hemisphere. He risked his life sniffing out information and bringing corruption to light. Some people hated reporters, but Nicole was grateful for them. At least for this one.

"I'm not confirming or denying anything," she told him. "But if you were to write a story like you're describing, I wouldn't have a problem with it."

Something flared in his eyes. Pride? Gloating? She couldn't tell.

"And that, too, is off the record."

He nodded. "What I can't figure out is motive," he went on. "Why would Saledo want to take out this young woman who worked at a coffee shop?"

"Can't help you there." She glanced at her watch. "And looks like my time is up."

He smirked. Then they both stood up from the table.

"Good luck with your story for Sunday." She put her sunglasses back on. "I better not see my name in it."

I T'S NO PROBLEM," Leyla lied.

"Are you sure?"

"Absolutely," she told Siena over the phone. "Take the whole day if you need it."

Leyla grabbed her purse and took one last look around the kitchen. Then she switched off the light.

"I only need the morning," Siena said. "I should be done by ten."

Leyla lifted the cardboard box off the counter and balanced it on her hip as she snagged her keys. "Really, it's fine."

Someone knocked on the door, and Leyla shot an annoyed look across the dining room. It was after nine, and they were clearly closed.

"I'll call you when I leave the dentist," Siena said.

Another knock, and Leyla froze in her tracks.

Sean stood on the other side of the glass, shielding his eyes from the glare of the floodlight as he peered through the window.

She walked over and hesitated a moment before flipping the bolt and opening the door.

"Leyla?"

"Yeah. Sounds good. I'll see you tomorrow." She hung up and dropped the phone into her purse.

Sean wore a navy suit and a white dress shirt with the collar open at the neck. He didn't move to come inside, and the intense look in his eyes put a knot in her stomach.

"What are you doing here?" she asked him.

"I got your text."

The knot in her stomach tightened.

"Need a hand?" He nodded at the box in her arms, and she handed it over without thinking.

She started out the door, then remembered the alarm. She stepped back inside to set the code, then stepped out again and locked the door.

Sean watched her, holding the box in his arms. She couldn't believe he was here. *Here.* After nearly four long weeks.

Leyla's SUV was in its usual place under the tree, but it was the only car in the lot. Had Sean gotten a ride here?

She glanced at him as they walked toward her car. She popped the back hatch open and watched as he loaded in the box. It contained cups and lids for the other store—which she was going to have to find time to deliver herself because now Siena needed the morning off.

"Thank you," Leyla said, glancing up. Sean was watching her with a look of silent desperation, and her heart jumped into her throat.

"I can't believe you're here," she said.

"I can't believe you're breaking up with me."

She looked away and bit her lip.

"What's going on, Leyla?"

Her chest squeezed and she shook her head.

"Look at me."

She turned to face him. Her heart was thudding now as she looked up into those eyes that she hadn't seen up close in nearly a month.

"This is much harder than I thought it would be," she said.

"This what? This relationship? Or this conversation?" His brow furrowed, and she felt a sharp jolt of attraction— which absolutely was *not* helping her right now.

"This whole long-distance thing. It's not working." She

looked at his chest because she didn't want to look at his eyes anymore. "It's making me a wreck, Sean. I'm distracted all the time. And insecure. And I'm being a bitch to everyone." She shook her head. "And then I heard how you were here, and you didn't even call me."

He tipped his head back and cursed, and Leyla's heart sank. She realized she'd been holding out hope that maybe she'd been wrong, or somehow misunderstood.

He looked at her and sighed. "Joel told you?"

"Miranda."

She looked away. A tear leaked out, and she swiped at her cheek, angry at herself for letting him see her get emotional.

"I don't want to do this anymore, Sean."

"Leyla." He took her hand, and she pulled it away.

He huffed out a sigh.

"Let's walk on the beach and talk through this."

She looked him over. "You're in a *suit*."

"I don't care."

She swallowed the lump in her throat.

"Please?"

She made the mistake of looking up at his eyes. He was pleading with her, and she couldn't tell him no.

"Fine." She opened the car again and took off her apron. She wedged her purse in beside the box and spread her apron over it to hide it from view, then slammed the hatch shut. "Let's go."

They walked in silence onto the deck beside the coffee shop. When they reached the wooden bridge spanning the sand dunes, he caught her hand.

Her heart lurched as his big, warm hand enveloped hers. She'd been longing for the solid, secure feel of him for weeks now, and his hand was a reminder of everything she'd been yearning for while he'd been away.

They reached the beach, and she kicked off her sandals. He didn't move to take off his black leather shoes, so she guessed he didn't care if they filled up with grit.

"Which way?" she asked.

"South."

He looked at her as they started down the beach. "How is everything else going?"

"Okay."

"Are you sleeping all right?"

She shrugged.

"I'm not."

She cast a sidelong glance at him. She hadn't seen him wearing a suit since Joel's wedding, and once again it looked really good on him. She noted the tip of a pale blue tie sticking out of his side pocket.

"How long have you been here?" she asked.

He glanced at his watch. "About an hour. I came straight from the airport."

"You were in D.C.?"

"I had meetings all morning. I got the first flight I could."

Leyla's stomach clenched. He'd gotten a flight because of her? Because of the text she'd sent him at six o'clock this morning?

This isn't working. I think we need a break.

She'd sent it just before she'd opened, so she wouldn't have a chance to stare at her phone all morning and obsess over his reaction.

Of course, she'd obsessed over it anyway. And when he hadn't responded by noon, she'd convinced herself that she'd made the right decision.

They reached a firm stretch of sand close to the shore,

and Sean stopped to look at the surf. Then he turned to face her.

"You have no idea how much I've missed you," he said.

"You're right. I don't."

He rested his free hand on her shoulder. "I'm sorry I didn't call you earlier this week. I couldn't."

She looked away.

"I wanted to. I was *dying* to call you. And to come see you. But I couldn't." He paused. "Leyla?"

She looked at him.

"You know I can't tell you about my work. But please believe me when I say it wasn't possible."

She nodded. "I believe you. That's not really the problem, though. I just—"

"Listen. Will you just hear me out for a minute?"

She waited.

He took a deep breath. "The thing I was working on before—that operation—it's resulted in a lot more work here. Me and my team, we've been really busy and we're about to get busier." He took a deep breath. "They offered me a position leading a team here."

"Where?"

"Here. The Brownsville field office."

She stared up at him. "*Who* offered you this?"

"My boss in Washington."

The Brownsville field office. Brownsville was only an hour away from Lost Beach. Leyla held her breath as she tried to read his expression.

"Are you going to take it?"

"I was." He squeezed her hand. "Until this morning."

"Why didn't you tell me about this?"

"I'm trying to right now." He raked a hand through his hair. "Just—hear me out." He took off his jacket and dropped it on the sand. "Sit down and let's talk."

She sat, no longer worried about getting his nice clothes dirty. Her mind was spinning as he lowered himself onto the ground beside her.

She looked at him, noting the dark stubble along his jaw. And his eyes looked red and tired. Clearly, he'd been working a lot and probably not getting much rest.

"So, what do you think?" he asked her.

"I don't know." Her pulse was thrumming now. "I had no idea you were thinking of moving down here. I thought you liked working in D.C."

"I did. I do." He took her hand and squeezed it. "But then I met you."

Emotions swirled inside her, making her dizzy. She looked out at the water. The surf was up, and moonlight glistened off the frothy waves.

"I wish you'd talked to me about this. I've been feeling so confused about everything."

"I'm sorry." He lifted her hand and kissed it. "I guess I'm not the best at communicating. I haven't been in a relationship in a long time."

She looked at him. "Me either."

The breeze whipped a strand of hair against her face, and he gently moved it away. Her heart was racing. But not in the scared, panicked way it had been doing so much for the past month. This was a good sort of racing. A buzzy excitement filled her as she thought about a possible future together.

He leaned over and kissed her. It was warm and sweet, but then she opened her mouth and everything changed. She pulled his head down, savoring the taste of him and combing her fingers into that thick, soft hair she'd been missing.

It felt good. Sure. *Right*, in a way it had never felt with anyone else, and she couldn't believe she'd sent him that damn text message. And that he'd gotten on a *plane* over it.

He eased her back, and then his weight was on her, pressing her into the sand. She loved the way he felt, the way he kissed, the way he touched her with so much confidence it set her skin on fire. This was what she'd been dying for, every day and every night since they'd been apart.

He pulled back. "Come home with me," he said gruffly.

She blinked up at him. "Where is that?"

"I've got a room at Sea Isle." He nodded down the beach toward the condominium where he'd stayed before. "It's a second-floor studio. That's all they had left."

"You didn't want to stay with me?"

"Of course I did. But I wasn't sure." He kissed her forehead. "You broke up with me."

He stood up and held his hand out for her.

She smiled up at him and took it.

L EYLA LEANED AGAINST the balcony railing and stared at the water under the full moon. A light winked on the distant horizon. It was an oil rig. Maybe even the same rig she'd been trapped on weeks ago. A shudder moved through her, and she clasped her arms to her body, still unable to believe everything that had happened in such a short time.

And all of it had started with her brother's wedding.

The glass door behind her slid open, and she glanced back as Sean stepped out in only his black boxer briefs. He eased up behind her and slid his arms around her waist.

"I recognize this shirt," he said, kissing the side of her neck.

She liked the shirt because it smelled like him. She nestled deeper into it and pulled the cuffs over her wrists.

"The surf's down," he said. "When did that happen?"

"The clouds moved through. Now it's calm as glass."

She turned to face him, leaning her hip against the railing.

"I like this room," she said.

"View's not as good as last time."

"Still better than mine. We should spend the weekend here."

He smiled and kissed her. "I won't be looking at the view."

She turned and faced the water again.

"You okay?"

She looked at him. "Yeah. Why?"

His look was serious as he brushed a lock of hair from her eyes. "I know you've been going through a lot. I'm sorry I haven't been here to help you."

She reached up and ran her fingertip over his jaw.

"What is it? I can tell something's wrong," he said.

"Not wrong. I'm just worried."

"Why?"

She took a deep breath and thought of the fear that had been lurking in her heart for weeks, ever since she'd started gaming out all the possible ways they could be together, including uprooting her business and moving to the other side of the country.

"Leyla, tell me."

She let out a sigh. "What if you move all the way here and you don't like the job? Or the people?"

He gazed down at her.

"It could happen," she said.

"Then I'll make the best of it." He brushed the backs of his fingers over her cheek.

"It's a big risk," she pointed out.

"I'm good with it. As long as you are." He held her gaze. "Are you having second thoughts?"

"No."

"Are you sure?"

"I love you. I'm sure about that. The rest is just logistics."

He smiled, and she felt it deep in the pit of her stomach.

"You don't look surprised," she said.

"I'm not." He wrapped his arms around her and pressed her head against his chest. "I think I knew that already. That's why I was so stunned that you dumped me in a text message."

She pulled back. "I'm not sorry."

"No?"

"Not if it got you down here."

He smiled at her in the dimness. He hadn't said it back. But she wasn't going to freak out. She could be patient. Patience had never been one of her strengths, but she could learn.

"I love you, Leyla."

A smile spread across her face. He'd somehow read her mind again, and she pulled his head down to kiss him. It was sweet and perfect, and she felt that warm, bone-deep *rightness* that she'd never felt with anyone else.

She eased back. "It's late," she whispered. "I have to be up in two hours."

"I know." He tugged her toward the door. "Let's go back to bed."

EVIE WAITED UNTIL the third ring to pick up.

"Are you bailing?" Hannah asked.

"Sorry."

"Evie, you *promised*."

"I'm not up for it tonight." Evie stripped off the sexy black tank top that she'd ridiculously put on earlier—because Drew liked it—and grabbed her terry cloth robe off the chair.

"What happened?" Hannah asked over the din of conversation, and Evie pictured her sister in the crowded sports bar where they had planned to meet.

"Nothing."

"Not *nothing*. Spill it."

Evie tied the belt of her robe and sighed. "I saw him tonight."

"Who?"

"Drew. He came by to get Bella after work."

Or at least he'd claimed he had come from work. Given

the beer on his breath, he had probably been to a happy hour with "the team" first.

"Oh, Eves. I'm sorry."

Evie padded barefoot across the hardwood floors that she and Drew had carefully picked out together. After checking the lock on the patio door, she peered out at the dim yard. Her daughter's swing swayed in the breeze, and her Big Wheel sat abandoned on a carpet of crunchy brown leaves.

"I know that sucks," Hannah said. "Why don't you come out with us? You'll feel better."

"I'm already in bed."

"You are not. It's barely nine o'clock."

Evie returned to the bottle of merlot by the fridge and topped off her glass.

"Come on," Hannah persisted. "We're playing darts. Blake says he'll even let you win."

Evie smiled. Her sister's boyfriend was a gem, a genuine *nice guy*. But she didn't want to be a third wheel again.

"Really, I'm not up for it."

"Well." She heard the resignation in Hannah's voice. "You're still coming Thursday, right?"

"Absolutely." She took a hearty swig at the thought of her sister's Thanksgiving potluck, which was sure to be an awkward mix of friends and coworkers. Evie had offered to bring a pie, but Hannah had assigned her mashed potatoes in a transparent attempt to make sure she didn't cancel.

"What time are we eating again?" Evie asked.

"Um . . . I don't know. Four, probably?"

So eight, then. Which was fine. Evie would be there all evening, which would cut into the ice cream binge that would inevitably accompany her first holiday in six years without Drew.

And Bella's first holiday ever without her mother.

Tears burned Evie's eyes, and she took another gulp.

"So get this," she told Hannah. "He took my silver locket." Fury tightened her chest as soon as the words were out. "You know the one he gave me for Mother's Day? He stole it right out of my jewelry box."

"Oh, come on," Hannah said. "You probably misplaced it."

"No. I did not."

"Evie, the man drives a Porsche. What would he want with a silver locket?"

"He knew it would needle me." She headed down the hall and paused at Bella's room to switch off the light, ignoring the lingering scent of baby shampoo as she closed the door.

"Do you want me to come over?"

"No, I'm fine. I'm just being, I don't know, *emotional*."

"Hey, you're allowed to be emotional. Your ex is a prick. How about we walk the lake tomorrow? We can catch up."

Evie stepped into the bathroom and confronted her reflection in the mirror above the sink. Messy hair, sallow skin, dingy bathrobe. She opened the medicine cabinet and eyed the contents. The prescription sleeping pills called out to her. But she had more willpower than that. She closed the cabinet.

"What time?" she asked Hannah.

"Let's do nine. I'll meet you at the bridge."

"Are you sure? Nine sounds early."

Evie was fine with it, but Hannah's body clock didn't work that way. She hadn't had kids.

"All right, let's make it ten," Hannah said.

"Ten at the bridge."

"It's a date. Love you, Eves."

"You, too."

She set the phone down and stared at her reflection as she took another sip. A four-mile loop around the lake would do her good. Maybe she'd stop at the store afterward and get some fresh produce. She could make soup. Or maybe a pie for next week. She stepped into the bedroom.

A man in a ski mask stood in the doorway.

Her wineglass crashed to the floor as she registered everything at once—the wide shoulders, the black clothes, the heavy boots.

His hands were empty, but the latex gloves he wore turned her throat to dust.

"Don't scream, Evelyn."

Her heart seized. He knew her *name*.

She thought of her cell phone in the bathroom only a few feet away. She could lock herself inside and then—

He stepped into the bedroom and pulled the door shut with a terrifying *click*.

Evie's mind raced even as time slowed to a crawl. She had to survive this. Whatever happened, she had to survive for Bella.

What did he *want*? Her heart thundered as her eyes returned to those gloved hands.

God help me.

She inched toward the bathroom, stalling for time.

"How—" She cleared her throat. "How did you get in here?"

The hole in the mask shifted—a flash of white teeth as his mouth formed a smile.

"I've been here."

THE LUCKY DUCK was half-empty, which was just how Rowan liked it.

Johnny Cash drifted from the speakers. A young couple occupied a high-top table in the corner, and several regulars sat at the bar, chatting up Lila as she pulled a pint.

Rowan's favorite booth was taken, so she grabbed one

near the window beneath a neon **Shiner Bock** sign. Lila darted her a questioning glance, and Rowan gave her a nod as she slid into the torn vinyl seat.

She grabbed the plastic menu behind the condiment bottles and looked for something decadent. She was starving, she suddenly realized. For the past five days, she had subsisted on cereal and microwave popcorn.

As she skimmed the choices, Rowan tugged out her scrunchie and combed her hand through her hair. She probably should have showered or at least put on a clean sweatshirt before coming here. Oh well. Too late now.

"You finally came up for air."

Rowan looked up as Lila slid a Tanqueray and tonic in front of her.

"*Thank* you," Rowan said. "You read my mind."

Lila sipped a ginger ale—her hydration beverage of choice when she was working.

"Busy night?" Rowan asked.

"Not really." She shrugged. "Good tips, though."

"Has Dara been by?"

"*Yes*." Lila's eyes sparkled. "She was here earlier. With a date."

"Oh yeah?"

"They left after an hour, so you'll have to get the scoop. Are you eating?"

"Yes, but I can't decide."

"Try the nachos," Lila said. "We've got fresh guac today."

"That sounds good."

A couple walked into the bar and claimed a pair of stools on the corner. Lila eyed them as she nursed her drink. "I have to get back. I'll give Sasha your order."

"Thanks."

Lila returned to her post, and Rowan scanned the faces around the room, trying to guess people's stories. It was a game she played whenever she came here alone. All the singles tonight were regulars. Ditto for the two guys shooting pool in the back. Her attention settled on the couple at the high-top table. Based on their age, they might be students at the University of Texas, maybe seeking a night away from the crowds on Sixth Street. But they had a seasoned look about them. The woman's makeup was perfect. And they both exuded the stiff body language that screamed *first date*.

Rowan watched them subtly from her booth. Head tilts. Intense eye contact. The woman arched her brows as she sipped her margarita through a straw, displaying just the right amount of interest in whatever the guy was saying. He rested a hand on his knee and looked confident—but slightly nervous—as he expounded on whichever first-date topic he'd selected for the evening.

A chime emanated from Rowan's purse. She pulled out her phone and read a text from the Austin lawyer whose client Rowan had been working for all week.

Got your email. Omg TY!!

The words were followed by three halo emojis, and Rowan felt a swell of pride.

Anytime, she texted back. So glad I could help.

This attorney had sent her four referrals over the past six months, and now there would likely be more on the way. Rowan's anemic bank account was finally getting a boost. It couldn't come soon enough.

"Rowan Healy?"

She jerked her head up as a man stepped over. Tall, broad-shouldered, dark hair. He wore a black leather jacket with droplets of rain clinging to it. Rowan darted a glance at Lila. Her friend didn't look up, but she lifted an eyebrow in a way that told Rowan she'd sent this guy over here.

"Who's asking?" Rowan responded, even though she had a sneaking suspicion she knew based on his deep voice. Not to mention the super-direct look in his brown eyes.

"Jack Bruner, Austin PD." He smiled slightly. "Mind if I sit?"

She sighed and nodded at the empty seat across from her.

He slid into the booth and rested his elbows on the table. He looked her over, and she managed not to squirm.

"You're a hard woman to reach."

Ha. He had no idea how true that was.

"How'd you know to find me here?" she asked.

"Ric Santos told me you hang out here."

She couldn't hide her surprise at the mention of Ric. She hadn't known they were friends. But she probably should have guessed. Law enforcement was a tight-knit group.

She gave him what she hoped was a confident smile. "Look, Detective, I appreciate you coming all the way out here, but I'm afraid you've wasted your time."

"Just listen."

Two words.

A command, but not. When combined with that slight smile, it was more like a statement. Something that she was *going* to do, even if she didn't realize it yet.

Rowan felt a surge of annoyance. But again, she gave him a nod.

Sasha appeared at the table and rested her cocktail tray on her hip. "Can I get you something to drink?" she asked the detective.

"A Coke, please."

She nodded. "Rowan?"

"I'm good, thanks."

She walked off, her cascade of blond hair swinging behind her.

Rowan settled her attention on the detective.

"I'm with APD's violent crimes unit, as I mentioned on the phone," he said.

With every call, he'd politely identified himself and given a callback number. Rowan had called the number once and—equally politely—left a message with her response. But he'd stubbornly ignored it.

"I'm working on a case," he said, "and I could use your help."

Rowan nodded. "Like I told you before—"

He held up his hand and gave her a sharp look. *Listen.*

"It's a serial offender," he continued. "Eight sexual assaults." His dark brows furrowed. "This guy's careful. We've only recovered one DNA profile, from the second attack in the series."

"If you've only got one profile, how do you know it's the same guy?"

"Because—"

Sasha was back already with a flirty smile. She placed the detective's soft drink in front of him, and he nodded his thanks.

"Because we know," he said after she left.

Rowan looked the man over. He had an athletic build but not the steroid-infused look she was used to seeing with young cops. Then again, he wasn't that young. The touch of gray at his temples told her he was maybe ten years older than she was, probably late-thirties. Or maybe it was the wise look in his eyes that told her that.

She sipped her drink and waited for more.

"A while ago we had the sample analyzed by a genetic genealogist," he said. "Spent a lot of money and time on that. The results were inconclusive, they said."

"What's 'a while'?"

"Come again?"

"How long ago did you have it analyzed?"

He hesitated a beat.

"Four years."

Rowan's breath caught. In terms of DNA technology, four years was like four decades. A lot had changed in that time—new techniques, new tools, new profiles in the databases.

But she tried to keep her face impassive as she folded her hands in front of her.

"I appreciate your effort to track me down," she said. It told her a lot about what kind of detective he was—precisely the kind that had prompted her to shift careers. "But unfortunately, I don't do police work anymore. You could say I'm retired."

"That's not what Ric told me."

She gritted her teeth. Damn it, she'd *known* doing him a favor would come back to bite her.

"Ric said you're selective, not retired." He paused, watching her. "He told me you gave him an assist recently and that your help was invaluable."

"I know what you're doing," Rowan said. She was immune to flattery, even from smooth-talking detectives who liked to play head games. "And I can appreciate the pressure you guys must be under with a serial case. But I'm not in that line of work anymore."

He leaned forward, and she eased back slightly.

"Let me be straight, Rowan." His eyes bored into hers. "I need your help right *now*. Not next month or next year. Not whenever you get bored with what you're doing and decide to come out of retirement. I don't care if I sound desperate. I'm on a ticking clock here."

Her stomach tightened at his words. And his prediction that she would backtrack on her decision irked her.

But he held her gaze across the table, and she felt that inexorable *pull* that had turned her life upside down too many times to count.

She took in the detective's sharp eyes and the determined set to his jaw. She admired that determination—she had it, too—but she had to resist this time.

At this very moment, she had an inbox full of requests from prospective clients who were willing to pay top dollar for her work. *Positive* work. *Rewarding* work. The kind of work that made her get out of bed in the morning with a sense of purpose. She'd spent three years building her reputation as one of the best in her field, and the last thing she needed to do was put all those clients on hold and get sucked back into the vortex of police work.

A buzz emanated from beneath the table, and Jack Bruner took out his phone. His expression remained blank, but she caught the slight tensing of his shoulders.

A callout. Someone was dead or bleeding or in some emergency room somewhere.

He pulled out his wallet and tucked a twenty under his untouched Coke. Then he took out a business card and slid it across the table.

"My cell's on the back. Call me if you change your mind."

He scooted from the booth, and she felt small as he towered over her. He held out his hand.

Against her better judgment, she shook it.

Ready to find
your next great read?

Let us help.

Visit prh.com/nextread

Penguin
Random
House